Praise
Kind of, Sort of, Maybe,
But Probably Not

'Imbi Neeme writes the big and small moments of life with huge heart and boundless empathy. I finished this book in one great delicious gulp, laughing out loud, and I felt GOOD. And HAPPY. More books like this in the world, please.'

– Kate Mildenhall

'Warm, wacky and wonderful. The mystery at the heart of this story cuts a path through the mysteries of all hearts, illuminating new, old and rekindled relationships with the sparkle, hope and melancholy of a '90s share-house party.'

– Paul Dalgarno

'I'm jealous of people who haven't read this book yet, because they get to read it for the first time. *Kind of, Sort of, Maybe, But Probably Not* is spectacular, an absolute delight to read. Heartwarming, insightful and funny, I give it eleven thumbs up.'

– Katherine Collette

Kind of Sort of Maybe ...

but probably not

ALSO BY IMBI NEEME

The Spill
(Winner of the 2019 Penguin Literary Prize)

Kind of Sort of Maybe ...
but probably not

Imbi Neeme

VIKING
an imprint of
PENGUIN BOOKS

VIKING

UK | USA | Canada | Ireland | Australia
India | New Zealand | South Africa | China

Viking is part of the Penguin Random House group of companies whose addresses can be found at global.penguinrandomhouse.com

Penguin
Random House
Australia

First published by Viking in 2024

Copyright © Imbi Neeme 2024

The moral right of the author has been asserted.

Cover photography by Kiwihug on Unsplash (background texture) and mikroman6/ Getty Images (illustrated hydrangea)
Cover design by Alex Ross Creative © Penguin Random House Australia Pty Ltd
Typeset in 12.75/17 pt Bembo MT Pro by Post Pre-press Group, Australia

Printed and bound in Australia by Griffin Press, an accredited ISO AS/NZS 14001 Environmental Management Systems printer

A catalogue record for this book is available from the National Library of Australia

ISBN 978 1 76134 106 9

penguin.com.au

MIX
Paper | Supporting
responsible forestry
FSC® C018684

We at Penguin Random House Australia acknowledge that Aboriginal and Torres Strait Islander peoples are the Traditional Custodians and the first storytellers of the lands on which we live and work. We honour Aboriginal and Torres Strait Islander peoples' continuous connection to Country, waters, skies and communities. We celebrate Aboriginal and Torres Strait Islander stories, traditions and living cultures; and we pay our respects to Elders past and present.

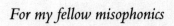

For my fellow misophonics

Chapter 1

Thursday 4 May 1995, West Footscray

IT WAS FAIR to say that Phoebe Cotton's brain was like a mixing desk where some of the controls were a little bit broken. Some sounds, once she heard them, she couldn't fade out. In fact, if anything, once she'd picked up on a certain noise, it was like that track became instantly isolated and the volume on everything else dropped away.

Jasmine eating an apple with her mouth open in the library staffroom was a good example. Even though the handyman was using his drill on an industrially loud setting in the next room, the wet crunch of the apple cut through, making Phoebe's fists clench and her toes curl.

She looked longingly out the rain-streaked window. Usually, she would be eating her lunch outside on her own, but the weather was so bad that she'd had no option but to eat in the library's small staffroom alongside Jasmine.

And her apple.

'Have you seen *Outbreak* yet?' Jasmine asked her, in between enthusiastic bites. Phoebe could see white bits of apple in her mouth, swilling around like a shirt in a tumble dryer.

Phoebe did her best to push past the red mist that was threatening to consume her and shook her head.

'No, I haven't,' she said.

'Cameron and I saw it last night in the city.'

Phoebe nodded. She didn't know who Cameron was, but then she had only been in the job – her third maternity leave replacement position in a row – for a few months and she didn't know much of anything. The only thing she *did* know was that she needed to start talking so Jasmine could finish her apple and put Phoebe out of her misery, but she had no idea what to say.

She was therefore relieved when Des Rollerson walked into the staffroom. Des Rollerson always had plenty of things to say.

'Have *you* seen *Outbreak* yet?' Jasmine asked him.

'No, but I'll tell you why.' As he started to list his issues with the American blockbuster format and Jasmine made some real progress towards finishing her apple, Phoebe silently gave thanks. Des had saved the day. But then she realised that, as he was banging on about the 'cult of mediocrity', he was heading towards the urn to make himself a cup of tea. The situation was going from bad to worse. Des always drank his tea like he was trying to suck it up without his lips ever touching the liquid. Some days, when it was quiet in the library, Phoebe could hear him slurping his tea in the staffroom all the way from the front desk.

Before she knew it, Des was standing in front of Phoebe and Jasmine, with one leg resting on a chair and his groin on display like an open book, bringing a mug of hot tea to his lips. Meanwhile, Jasmine had finished her apple and produced a carrot from thin air.

'You look pale,' Jasmine remarked, her carrot lifted to her mouth like a microphone.

'Yeah, everything alright?' Des repeated with a creepy wink. He brought his mug up to his mouth and Phoebe felt the urge to shout. At him. At Jasmine. At a too-loud world.

'Everything's fine,' Phoebe said, her voice small and tight as she packed up her untouched cheese sandwich. 'I think I'm going to go back to the desk.'

'But you haven't eaten your lunch,' Des lowered his mug and raised one of his eyebrows instead.

'I'm not hungry.'

Actually, she was starving but she'd have to wait.

AFTER WORK, PHOEBE decided to walk home from Footscray rather than risk the 216 bus. In the morning, there'd been someone on the seat behind her snapping their gum, and even though she'd turned the volume on her Walkman right up, the sound had still seeped through the music and poked at her brain, like a thousand tiny needles.

It wasn't a long walk and thankfully the rain had stopped. As she walked, she ate her cheese sandwich and listened to the soundtrack from *The Piano* through her headphones. The music, combined with the grey clouds swirling overhead, filled her with an unnamed melancholy that sat heavily in her chest the entire walk. By the time she got to Salmon Street, she'd decided two things: to change the disk to something more upbeat for the next day; and to immediately cheer herself up with a nice cup of tea and a few chapters of *The Convenient Marriage*.

She stopped at the front gate of Number 6 and pushed the overgrown hydrangea back to get the mail out of the letterbox. Today's haul was so large it came with a complimentary elastic band. Phoebe knew that the majority of it would be for her grandmother Dorothy – mostly bills – with a sizeable chance of another letter from *Reader's Digest* telling her grandfather Edward that he might have won a million dollars. Many times, she'd thought of writing to them to let them know Edward had passed away, but she kind of liked getting the letters.

She wondered if Edward had enjoyed getting them too. It had been fifteen years since his heart had quietly stopped beating while he slept in the front room of this house. While everyone had mourned him, nobody had been particularly surprised, considering the amount he drank and smoked. Phoebe and her parents had thought Dorothy, too, would eventually die in that same front room, but not in her sleep. They imagined her sitting upright in bed with her gardening log, closing her eyes after carefully making her daily notes and never opening them again. But then a year ago, at the ripe young age of sixty-eight, she had surprised them all with an announcement. She'd told them she no longer had the lower-back strength to maintain her beloved garden and that she was moving to a retirement village called the Western Retreat.

This left Phoebe's parents, Phil and Ellen, with the dilemma of what to do with the property. At the time, Phoebe had been living miserably in a share house in Kensington. At any given moment, it had seemed, there was at least one person eating a big bowl of cornflakes in the kitchen. Cereal, with the opportunities it presented its eater for crunching *and* slurping, was at the top of Phoebe's 'Avoid at All Costs' list. But along with two-minute noodles (no crunch, but all slurp), it seemed to be the only thing that her housemates ever ate.

So, when Phil had suggested she look after the Salmon Street house while they decided what to do with it, she'd jumped at the chance.

Of course, she hadn't factored in how much work the garden required, nor her complete lack of aptitude or appetite for gardening. Nor had she known how drafty the old weatherboard bungalow was, particularly now that winter was approaching, nor how easily dust gathered on every single surface, making it impossible to keep clean, nor how often she would need to vacuum the floral Axminster carpet. She also hadn't realised that living by herself would drive her even further into her shell. These days, her life consisted of her latest library job, a weekly dinner with her parents, and bad TV choices. Also, the large collection of Georgette Heyer Regency romance novels that her grandmother had left behind in the spare bedroom.

As Phoebe stepped into the house, the first thing she saw was the light blinking on the answering machine. Her mother had bought the machine for her last Christmas because she didn't want Phoebe to miss any important job offers or invitations to social events. So far, she'd received neither, and the answering machine sat on the art deco telephone table in the hallway as a constant reminder of her failings.

She pushed the button.

'Hi, Phoebe,' a voice said, surprising Phoebe even further. The only messages she ever received were for Dorothy, mostly from the secretary at the Williamstown RSL who a) never managed to update her records with Dorothy's new number and b) always started the message thinking that she was speaking to an actual person. The voice continued. 'It's Sandy. Long time, no talk! Your mum gave me your new number. She said you're living in your grandmother's house – I can't believe it. Are you following all her rules? Listen, I'm coming to Melbourne for a few days at the end of this month and it would be great to catch up.'

For the briefest of moments, Phoebe thought about ringing her back but then she remembered the last time they'd spoken and how it had effectively resulted in a four-year pause in the middle of a sentence.

Unfinished sentences: Phoebe's life was full of them.

She deleted the message and headed to the small kitchen at the back of the house to make herself that cup of tea.

While she waited for the kettle to boil, she sat down at the square formica table to sift through the mail. There, wedged between a Coles catalogue and the gas bill, she found a postcard of Big Ben in London. She couldn't imagine any of Dorothy's RSL friends ever leaving the western suburbs, let alone enduring a twenty-eight-hour flight to England. Perhaps she had underestimated them. But when she turned the postcard over, she found it wasn't for Dorothy at all. Instead, it was addressed in the most glorious copperplate handwriting – all loops and flourishes – to an Elizabeth Winsome at 6 Salmon Street.

My dear Elizabeth,

We've just arrived in London. It's dirty and grey and crowded. The plane trip lasted forever and ever. I think it will take most of my time in Europe for me to recover. I'm walking around in a dream, seeing faces like yours in the crowd.

Yours, always yours,

T

She flipped the card back over to the picture side and stared at Big Ben and the Palace of Westminster, looking just like the Thames TV logo from the shows she had watched when she was a kid. It even had the same faded colour she always associated with the 1970s, that made it look like the world had been dipped in vinegar. Whoever this Elizabeth Winsome was, she was lucky to have someone like 'T' longing for her.

Phoebe sighed as her gaze drifted out the kitchen window towards the mulberry tree in the backyard, stripped of all its fruit and the last of its yellowing leaves clinging to stick-like branches. She hadn't pruned the tree at the end of its fruiting season like she'd promised Dorothy.

Looking at it now, it was hard not to feel like the tree had somehow become a metaphor for her life.

Chapter 2

Phoebe had been rostered on for a half-day at the library, so she'd rushed home, hoping to catch the beginning of *Donahue* on Channel 10. That day's topic was 'Nudist Families'. Phoebe liked to hear about other people's lives, even if they didn't have any clothes on. At least they were living.

But the arrival of another postcard – this time from Stratford-upon-Avon – made her forget about the naked families and Phoebe found herself reading it before she'd even got to the front door.

My Elizabeth,

Here I am, in the birthplace of Shakespeare. Last night we saw A Comedy of Errors. *I kept thinking of that time we went down to Williamstown beach and read each other sonnets. It feels like another lifetime ago, especially now that I'm on the other side of the world without you by my side.*

Yours, sans you, sans meaning, sans everything,

T

Phoebe closed her eyes and felt the autumn air against her cheeks and breathed in the scent of the damp earth and fallen leaves.

Sans you, sans meaning, sans everything.

If she were a heroine in one of Dorothy's Regency romance books, she might have swooned. In any case, she reminded herself that the postcard wasn't intended for her. She didn't want to be one of those characters that thwarted true love, even just through inaction. She needed to get the two postcards to Elizabeth Winsome.

She considered the address. Maybe Elizabeth lived at 16 Salmon Street or 9 Salmon Street. Mrs Papathanasiou across the road would know. Phoebe looked at her watch. If she gave up on *Donahue*, there was just over an hour before *Oprah* started, giving her enough time to drop by Mrs Pap's house. Nobody was ever able to 'drop by' Mrs Pap's house for less than forty-five minutes, although legend had it that Phoebe's father, Phil, once managed to leave after fifteen minutes – but that was only because a neighbour's car was on fire.

The front yard of Mrs Pap's two-storey brick house was bursting with carefully tended life. With vines climbing up trellises, baskets of herbs hanging off the walls and raised garden beds creating complex mazes in the front and back yard, not a single inch of land was wasted. Phoebe had long been expecting Mrs Pap to start growing things on her roof.

Mrs Pap must have seen Phoebe coming, because she'd opened the door and was greeting her before Phoebe had even stepped through the front gate.

'Pheeee-beeee,' she said, drawing the name out like taffy. 'You not working? You lost your job?'

Mrs Pap always assumed that anybody seen on the street between the hours of nine and five must be unemployed.

'Yes, I'm working,' Phoebe replied, as she followed Mrs Pap inside. 'I just have the afternoon off.'

'Afternoon off is not proper job.'

'I work for the library, which means I work for the council, Mrs Pap. It is a proper job.'

'Council isn't proper job. They just send letters about chickens.'

Mrs Pap had been forced to get rid of her chickens when someone had complained to the council about the rooster. It must have been a resident from the next block because, even though the rooster woke half the suburb up before dawn, nobody on Salmon Street would have ever been brave enough to dob Mrs Pap in.

'How is your yiayia?' Mrs Pap asked, gesturing to a place on the white leather sofa for Phoebe to sit. Phoebe could still remember a time she'd been considered too young to sit on the white leather sofa. She had really come up in the world.

'Dorothy's fine,' she replied as she sat down.

In truth, it had been a while since she had last visited her grandmother. Her grandmother wasn't the easiest person to visit. She'd never been a 'Nanna' or 'Granny' who baked cookies, knitted you scarves and sent you ten dollars in the mail for your birthday. Instead, she was simply 'Dorothy', who corrected Phoebe's posture and endlessly criticised the length of her fingernails and/or her life choices.

Mrs Pap was more the former kind of grandmother. Whenever she saw Phoebe, she fussed over her, plying her with food and insisting that she have a glass of her homemade tsipouro, known privately as 'liquorice rocket fuel' by Phoebe and her parents. Today was no exception. Before Phoebe knew it, Mrs Pap was bringing out the usual ancient bottle that had an olive branch and the word 'Molivo' embossed on its thick glass. Apparently, Molivo was a brand of olive oil back in Greece and *not* the Greek word for 'rat-arsed drunk' (as Phoebe's father Phil had once claimed).

Mrs Pap had also laid out a plate of crescent-shaped kourabiedes. Normally someone bringing out a plate of biscuits would make Phoebe very anxious, but because Mrs Pap didn't touch anything (other than the tsipouro), Phoebe never had to worry about having to listen to her eat them, what with all the 'Puthhhh!' noises she would make and the icing sugar going everywhere in little clouds.

Now settled in her favourite chair, Mrs Pap started to dole out her usual advice about the garden at Salmon Street ('You need to spray those roses with baking soda, soap and olive oil'), the apparently deficient weight of Phoebe's coat ('You'll catch a cold in your kidney!'), Phoebe's love life ('If a boy breaks your heart, you tell him to go jump to the lake') and complaining about her son Garry's wife, Candy ('She loves money more than family. He should have married a Greek girl'). Eventually, she paused long enough for Phoebe to interject with the whole point of her visit.

'Um, Mrs Pap,' Phoebe said, brushing some icing sugar off her top. 'I've been getting postcards from Europe addressed to an Elizabeth Winsome at Dorothy's house. Is there anyone on the street by that name?'

'Elizabeth?' Mrs Pap tilted her head. 'There's Sari, Phuong, Janet, Selina, Mrs Chan, Felicity, Susan and Alma on this side. And then there's Daphne, Brenda, Mrs Fleet, Pha, Fiona and Therese on your side. Frank at number 17 has lady friends but they're not there long enough to get letters.'

She thought some more, before finally declaring, 'No Elizabeth.'

'No Elizabeth,' Phoebe echoed, picking up her little glass of tsipouro and taking a small sip.

'Your yiayia is good, yes?'

Phoebe felt they had covered this ground already. 'Yes, yes. She's fine.'

'She's a sad lady. I was always telling her, "Dorothy, you need to get yourself some more happy."'

Phoebe had heard Mrs Pap say that a few times about Dorothy, but she'd never quite understood it. The word 'more' suggested that there was already a baseline level of happiness, or even a period of her life where Dorothy had actually been happy. As far as Phoebe could remember, her grandmother had always been cranky, stern and grim, but never sad, not even after her husband died. Phoebe, who'd been nine at the time and far more interested in collecting Smurfs than getting to know her grandfather, had cried more than her grandmother at the funeral. 'Happy' was far too soft a word for such a formidable human being.

'She was a great beauty, your yiayia. You look more like your mother.'

. . . who was a great beauty too, right? Phoebe wanted to joke, knowing full well that neither she nor her mother were ever going to win any beauty contests, except maybe in a game of Monopoly. With their brown hair and brown eyes and complete lack of distinctive features, they easily faded into any background, which suited Phoebe just fine.

Phoebe made a point of looking at her watch. It was almost Oprah o'clock. 'I have to go, Mrs Pap.'

'But Pheee-beee, you only ate one kourabiedes. You must take some home.'

She produced foil out of thin air, like a magician pulling scarves from their fist, and covered the plate of biscuits.

'That's too many for one person,' Phoebe protested.

'You can give some to your mama and papa.' Mrs Pap thrust the plate into her hands. 'Candy won't let Garry eat my biscuits anymore because of his die-beets. They're only little biscuits, I tell her, but she doesn't listen.'

Phoebe was fairly certain that medical science was also saying Garry shouldn't have the biscuits, not just Candy, but she kept that to herself.

'Thank you.' Phoebe accepted the plate on behalf of her parents.

'Would you like some spanakopita for your dinner? I have some in the fridge.'

'No, no, it's okay. I have some dinner already,' Phoebe replied, even though she knew Mrs Pap's spanakopita would be far more delicious than the spaghetti with Dolmio sauce she had planned. However, she'd learned the hard way that accepting the spanakopita only led to more food. The last time she'd said yes, she ended up returning home with three tins of octopus, a bag of Pizzeti crisps and a whole pumpkin, as well as enough spanakopita to feed a Spartan army.

'Pheee-beeee! You can make your yiayia happy by cutting back those hydrangeas,' Mrs Pap sang out after her, as Phoebe crossed the street.

Phoebe turned back to smile and nod, while secretly wondering what she would have to do to buy Mrs Pap's silence.

Chapter 3

THE POSTCARDS KEPT coming. On Friday, there was one from St Peter's Basilica in Rome, and on Monday another arrived from the Louvre in Paris. Reading them was starting to feel voyeuristic, like that Other Baldwin in the movie *Sliver*, but at the same time, keeping them felt just as wrong. Somehow she needed to find Elizabeth Winsome and hand the postcards over to her. But for now, Phoebe just filed them away, out of her sight, behind the flour canister.

ON TUESDAY, PHOEBE went straight from work to her parents' house for their weekly dinner.

'You're just in time,' her mother, Ellen, shouted out from the kitchen as Phoebe hung her bag on the coat rack.

As she walked into the dining room, Phil was already teeing up the stereo in the corner. Soon, the familiar strains of Handel's 'Hallelujah Chorus' were filling the room. They always ate dinner with this piece playing, dating back to when Phoebe was eight and it had become clear that she couldn't possibly eat a meal with other people in a silent room. It was around the same time that Ellen took Phoebe to their GP, who'd dubbed her sound sensitivities a 'quirk of personality' and advised Phoebe to simply move to another room whenever a noise was bothering her. Phoebe, of course, would have been perfectly happy to eat alone in a separate room, but Ellen had insisted that 'the family who eats together stays together', and the 'Hallelujah Chorus Method' was born. For a while, Phil dubbed himself 'DJ Dad' and experimented with some other music, but they'd always come back to the 'Hallelujah Chorus'. Sometimes Phoebe even listened to it when she was eating dinner in the house on Salmon Street, but only to make herself feel less alone. To compound the Not-Quite-Rightness of her Not Quite Right brain, the sound of her own eating didn't actually bother her, but, then again, she was always careful to make as little noise as possible. She felt an obligation to show the world it really was possible to eat almost anything noiselessly.

Even cereal.

'Dinner is served!' Ellen exclaimed. She carried in the casserole dish and Phoebe knew it was her old favourite: apricot chicken, cooked so long in the slow cooker that its very cellular structure had broken down entirely.

They all smiled at each other over the music and then began eating. Phoebe sat at one end of the table, her parents at the other, as they'd always done. Phoebe had been coming to dinner on Tuesday nights ever since she'd moved out of home, back in her second year of university. Mostly, her mother made her favourite meals: lasagne, beef stroganoff, sausages and mash – all food with little crunch and not too much slurp, not that either of her parents would ever dare to slurp in her presence. Once she'd walked into the kitchen at the precise moment that her father was slurping his cup of tea, and her sense of betrayal had only been surpassed by his expression of guilt.

When their plates were clear, Phil gave Ellen and Phoebe a questioning look and they both nodded. It was the signal he needed to turn the stereo off and clear the table.

'So how's your week been?' Ellen asked, once the room was silent.

'Fine,' Phoebe replied. 'The library's been very quiet this week.'

'But aren't libraries supposed to be quiet?' Phil piped up from the kitchen. Ellen and Phoebe both rolled their eyes.

'Sandy rang here looking for you, by the way. I gave her the Salmon Street number,' Ellen said. 'Has she rung you yet?'

'No,' Phoebe lied.

'It's been so long since we last saw her. She's such a lovely girl. Is she still living in Canberra?'

'Yes.'

'What a pity. You two were always as thick as thieves, but at least I knew you were in good hands.'

Phoebe felt the usual pang of shame. She wasn't sure that the reverse was true, that Sandy had been in such good hands with her.

'Have you made any friends in your new job?'

'Not yet,' Phoebe replied.

'It's only been a month.' Phil popped his head around the doorframe. 'Give the girl some time.'

'It's been three months,' Ellen said somewhat curtly as she watched Phil disappear into the kitchen.

Phoebe should have known that her mother had been counting. She often thought of Ellen as a stage parent, but where life was the stage and Ellen was always trying to push her onto it. When she was in primary school and Ellen had found out she'd been spending all her lunchtimes in the library, she'd come to the school and led Phoebe around the playground, trying to matchmake her with the other kids. The only clear memory Phoebe had of that excruciating experience was her mother approaching some younger kid who had a Muppets lunchbox and saying, 'Phoebe likes *The Muppet Movie*, don't you, Phoebe!'

Phoebe had never been able to watch *The Muppet Movie* since then, which was a pity, because she really had liked *The Muppet Movie*.

'Any chance that this one might turn into something permanent?' Ellen asked.

'It's a maternity leave position, Mum. Minglu can only be pregnant for so long.'

'Maternity leave isn't just for the pregnancy, Phoebe. Babies are a lot of work. You cried day and night for months.'

'It was probably because you were eating too loud,' Phoebe quipped in an attempt to lighten her mother's mood. She knew that joking about her hatred of eating noises was risky because it might lead to further lecturing, but this time, it thankfully paid off.

'Good point,' Ellen said with a laugh. 'So . . . are there any cute guys at this library?'

'Don't be gross, Mum. The only male librarian is, like, fifty. He has more hair coming out his ears and nose than he has on his head.'

'There's nothing wrong with that,' said Phil as he re-entered the dining room.

Phoebe never thought of her father as bald, but she felt bad. As he sat back down at the table, she tried to read his face to see if she'd hurt his feelings, but he was smiling in his usual sunny way.

'When you're as bald as me, any hair you can grow is a source of pride,' he said. Ellen reached over and placed her hand on top of his.

Phoebe quickly steered the conversation in a different direction. 'Here's something strange: I've been receiving post-cards from Europe,' she said. 'Well, not me personally. They're for someone called Elizabeth Winsome. The sender got the address wrong and I'm not sure what to do with them.'

'Ask Mrs Pap if she knows an Elizabeth on Salmon Street,' Ellen advised.

'Yeah, I've already done that. "No Elizabeth."' Phoebe did her best Mrs Pap impression. She'd never been good at impressions and this one was no exception.

'Just throw them away,' Ellen suggested.

'Um, I think it might be a federal offence to destroy someone else's mail,' Phil ventured.

'How ever do you know this stuff?' Ellen looked impressed.

'I'm just very, very wise.'

'Then what am I supposed to do?' Phoebe was aware that she was whining.

'You should try to find the intended recipient,' Ellen said. 'Have you looked up Elizabeth Winsome in the phone book? There might be one living at another Salmon Street somewhere else in Melbourne.'

She was right, of course. As Phoebe watched Ellen go to the hallway to grab the White Pages, she felt like she was twelve and not twenty-five and that her mother was the complete boss of her again.

'Here you go.' Ellen dropped the phone book on the table in front of Phoebe with a loud thud and then sat down next to Phil, forming Phoebe's regular audience of two.

Phoebe managed to repress the urge to sigh loudly and instead opened the book up to the W's and started scanning: *Watson, Wilson, Wilton, Winston, Winter, Winton.*

'There's not a single Winsome listed,' she concluded, shutting the White Pages. *Case closed.*

'I can get the Melways from the car,' Phil suggested. 'We can see how many other Salmon Streets there are in Melbourne and then you could visit Number 6 at each one to see if there's an Elizabeth living there.'

While Phil seemed cheery at the prospect, Phoebe could only imagine the awkwardness of knocking on a whole list of 6 Salmon Streets.

'That feels a bit extreme,' she said. 'They're only postcards.'

'Or you can continue to do nothing,' Ellen said in a tone that alluded to all the other ways in which Phoebe did nothing.

I do plenty, she wanted to tell her mother. It was just that none of the things she did were the things her mother wanted her to do or things that she used to want to do, like getting a boyfriend, or landing a permanent position at work, or ringing back her best friend from high school. Maybe those things were no longer that important to her. Maybe she was happy with her loveless, friendless, impermanent life.

But instead of saying all of that, she said through gritted teeth, 'I'll go ask at the post office during the week.'

'Did you know that the name Melways originated from the "Mel" in Melbourne and all the different "ways" you can get around?' Phil piped up. Whenever he sensed conflict between Phoebe and Ellen, he would try and divert their attention. *Look over here, shiny shiny.*

This time it worked.

'Now I've heard everything,' Phoebe replied, her standard response to Phil's 'Did you know . . .' facts. She felt the tension leave her jaw.

'Will you be at home on the weekend?' Phil asked, as if there was anywhere else that Phoebe had to go other than work, Salmon Street and this house.

Phoebe nodded.

'I'll drop by on Saturday. Dorothy wants me to fix that side gate that keeps banging.'

'How does she even know about that?'

'Daphne next door told Mrs Pap, who told Dorothy about it when Garry took her to visit,' Ellen replied.

Phoebe sighed. Dorothy's network of spies had struck again. For the briefest of moments, Phoebe yearned for the anonymity of living in a student share house alongside a whole heap of other student share houses. Nobody was ever up in anyone's business. But then she remembered the cereal and her toes instantly curled.

'When are you going to visit her?' Ellen asked.

'I'll try to go this weekend,' Phoebe said, with a vague wave of her hand.

'I can drive you after I fix the gate,' Phil offered.

'Of course, you could drive yourself if you had bothered to get your driver's licence,' Ellen jumped in, touching on an age-old argument about Phoebe refusing to finish her lessons because the instructor always ate gum.

Phoebe decided not to take her mother's bait and turned to her father instead.

'There's no rush with the gate. I've done a temporary fix.' She had tied it shut with some rope she'd found in the back shed and had thought herself quite resourceful.

'Dorothy thinks the rope isn't going to last long, not with the way Mrs Pap says you've tied it,' Ellen came at her again.

'It's fine, Mum.' Phoebe felt her jaw clench again. 'It's not like the knot needs to restrain a dangerous animal.'

'If I had to restrain a dangerous animal, I'd use a constrictor knot,' Phil interjected. 'The more you pull against it, the tighter it gets. Anyone for dessert?'

'Not tonight, thanks,' Phoebe said, faking a yawn. 'I'm pretty tired. I've got to run Story Time first thing in the morning.'

'So, you really don't think this job will become permanent?' Ellen asked.

Boy is she on a roll tonight, Phoebe thought.

'I don't think so,' she replied, as she stood up to leave. 'Glenda says Minglu definitely wants to come back.'

'Well, maybe you've got enough experience to go for a permanent role next time.'

'Maybe.'

'Or maybe you could try and move sideways into another permanent role at this library.'

'Yeah, maybe that,' Phoebe replied, kissing her mother's forehead like she was a child. But as she turned to go and hug her father, Ellen grabbed her arm.

'You've got to stop living with these maybes and do something, Phoebe Cotton.'

As tempting as it was to reply with another 'Maybe', Phoebe nodded as if she agreed. The truth was, she was happy living in her fog of maybes.

And when the fifth postcard arrived a couple of days later, Phoebe filed it away with all the others behind the flour canister, without even reading it.

Chapter 4

PHOEBE'S GENTLE PROCRASTINATION might have continued forever if she never had to face her mother again. But with another Tuesday dinner just around the corner, she finally forced herself to take action.

During her lunch break, she walked up to the post office and handed the small stack of postcards to the tall guy behind the counter. He was in his mid-twenties and his hair was sticking up like he'd just got out of bed.

'These have been sent to the wrong address,' Phoebe told him. 'I don't know what to do with them.'

'Huh?' the guy replied, like he was surprised she was talking to him. He looked familiar, but also completely out of his depth.

'They've been sent to my house, but the person they're addressed to doesn't live there.'

'Hmmm,' the guy said, as he thoughtfully worked through the stack, taking the time to look at both sides of each postcard. 'Have you asked around your street?'

'Yes.'

'Have you looked in the—'

'—Melways for another 6 Salmon Street? Yes, I have.'

'And the White—'

'—Pages? Yes. There's nobody in Melbourne with the surname of Winsome.'

Phoebe felt pretty proud of her detective work in that moment, even if it had largely been directed by her parents. She was starting to feel like the Nancy Drew of West Footscray, or a member of the Famous Five but without a dog. Or any friends.

'You could look through the White Pages for the other states,' he said, indicating a nearby shelf with the kind of arm gesture generally used by spokesmodels on *Sale of the Century*. Phoebe groaned inwardly at the sheer number of phone books.

'Or . . .' The guy paused and looked slightly sheepish.

'Or what?'

'You could also look up the right surname? I mean, it only says Winsome on one of the postcards,' the guy explained. 'The rest say Winston. Winsome must have been a nickname or an in-joke.'

Phoebe grabbed the postcards back and immediately started flipping through them.

He was right. Phoebe felt embarrassed that she had missed this detail, but thankfully the guy wasn't being smug about it. He was just looking at her earnestly, his eyes big and wide and dark, like chocolate drops.

She then looked over at the phone books and thought of how many Winstons there must be in the whole of Australia. Getting these postcards to Elizabeth Winston was starting to feel like it would become her Life's Work and she just didn't have the energy for it.

'I was going to throw them out but my, um, friend said it's a federal offence to destroy or dispose of someone else's mail.' Phoebe didn't want this guy to know that her main advisors in life were still her parents. 'Is that true?'

'Yeah, that sounds about right.' He didn't sound very certain.

'So do I just give them to you?'

'I don't think so. There's probably a form or something that you're, uh, supposed to fill in,' he replied, looking around in a way that suggested he wanted to appear like he knew what he was looking for, but he really had no idea. If it wasn't for the big Australia Post sign behind his head, Phoebe would have wondered if she'd stepped into the wrong shop altogether. 'But I'd need to check with my, uh, colleague. I'm just watching the store while she gets my grandmother's – I mean her mother's – medication from the chemist.'

We're both pretending to be grown-ups, Phoebe thought.

'She'll be back in ten minutes,' he said, and then he smiled at her. A wide, warm smile that felt like it was shining a bright light on her face.

Phoebe blinked, a rabbit caught in his headlights, and then broke the spell by looking down at her watch. 'I have to get back to work,' she said, not daring to look at him again. 'I'll come back another day.'

'You're a librarian, aren't you?' the guy blurted out, as she went to leave. 'I've brought my niece in to Story Time a couple of times.'

That's when Phoebe realised why he looked familiar. He'd come to the library with a small girl and had looked as much out of his depth as he did now. But she remembered one time when one of the little girl's plaits had fallen out and he'd carefully re-braided it. It had been such a beautiful, careful gesture from such a tall, hapless male.

'Oh, yeah,' Phoebe replied. 'I thought I recognised you.'

Now things had taken an awkward turn. They looked at each other, both unsure of how to end the conversation.

'Well, thanks,' she eventually said and started to leave again.

'Also,' the guy blurted out again. 'You know those postcards weren't posted in Europe, right?'

'What?' She looked back down at the cards in her hands.

'Look at the stamps.'

On the top of the stack was the first one she'd received, the one from London. Phoebe examined the stamp – a picture of the Queen, which her brain must have immediately dismissed as being British. But now she realised it was a commemorative stamp for the Queen's birthday and the word 'Australia' was written quite clearly under it, albeit in small letters.

'Hmmm,' she said, feeling even more foolish as she examined the others, one of which had a stamp with a kangaroo. A kangaroo! 'Why would someone post them saying they are in Europe, when they're not actually in Europe?'

She was talking more to herself than to the guy, but he answered her question anyway.

'Maybe they forgot to post them while they were there?' he suggested.

'Maybe . . .' she said, putting the postcards back into her bag. 'Thanks for your help!'

'Any time,' he replied. 'Well, not any time, because I don't really work here but, um, I'm glad to have helped.'

He gave a little bow, with an awkward sweep of one of his arms, and managed to knock over a box of paperclips. Phoebe did her best not to laugh.

★

WHEN SHE GOT home from work that evening, there was a sixth postcard, quite clearly addressed to Elizabeth *Winston,* and another phone message from Sandy waiting for her. The postcard was from Scarborough Beach in England and featured an image of a donkey wearing a hat. The telephone message, however, was less playful.

'Seriously, Phoebe. Don't be a dickhead. Ring me!'

Sandy was right. Phoebe was being a dickhead, but she'd done enough difficult things that day. The thought of phoning Sandy and finally hearing her out felt like a bridge too far. Instead, she focused on the postcard. The stamp had a ringtail possum on it, clearly not a native animal of North Yorkshire.

'Oh, Elizabeth Winston,' she said out loud. 'How on earth can I get you your postcards?'

But the ensuing silence held no answers.

Chapter 5

Even though Glenda, the head librarian, was formidable and only ever seemed to eat celery sticks for lunch, Phoebe liked to watch her working the front desk. She had the ability to matchmake readers and books without even a glance at the copy of *Who Else Writes Like?* that was kept behind the counter.

Today, she'd paired a man with Coke bottle glasses looking for 'Something like Sherlock Holmes but with more guns' with P. D. James's *Original Sin*.

'It's got even less guns than Conan Doyle,' Glenda confided to Phoebe as he walked away. 'But he'll like it anyway. I can guarantee it.'

Phoebe nodded, secretly wishing she had some of Glenda's confidence. Just half an hour earlier, Phoebe had recommended to another customer the sequel of a book that they had really liked, and she'd still been filled with uncertainty. Maybe this book wasn't as good as the first one. Maybe the thing the reader liked about the first one wasn't in the sequel. Another case of the maybes.

The phone on the counter buzzed and Glenda swooped on it.

'Information-desk-this-is-Glenda-speaking,' she said as if it were one word. Her face tightened.

'It's for you,' she said, handing the phone to Phoebe like it was a dead bird. Glenda didn't like it when the librarians received personal calls at work.

'Information-desk-this-is-Phoebe-speaking,' Phoebe said, hoping her homage to Glenda's telephone manner might appease her.

'Hey there, stranger. It's Sandy.'

'Oh, hello.' Phoebe was conscious that her voice was tight, like an elastic band was wrapped around her larynx.

'Sorry to ring you at work, but you didn't leave me much choice. I'm going to be in Melbourne next week. And I needed to make sure you were still alive and not dead in your grandmother's house being eaten by her German Shepherd. Why don't you ever answer the phone or return my calls?'

'My grandmother doesn't have a dog,' Phoebe replied, and her sentence was punctuated by a cough behind her.

Phoebe gave Glenda a very quick glance and immediately put on her best professional voice. 'So how can I assist you?'

'Is that your grown-up librarian voice? Should I pretend to be reserving a book?'

At that moment, a lady wearing a Mickey Mouse T-shirt approached the counter and started talking at Phoebe, even though she was clearly on the phone. 'I'm looking for a book with the word "lost" in the title, by Harriet or Charlotte Something. I think it's a double-barrelled name. Or maybe there's an initial like J or D. Or R. The cover is blue. Or maybe green.'

'Um,' said Phoebe. She could hear Sandy still talking through the receiver.

Glenda thankfully stepped in. 'American or British writer?'

'I don't know,' the woman replied. 'Probably both.'

Now that Glenda's attention was elsewhere and the Mouseketeer had someone else to talk at, Phoebe returned to the phone call. 'Sorry about that. It's very busy here,' she said in a low voice. 'And look, I'm sorry I haven't rung you back. I've been busy with work and the house and the garden and Mum and Dad. But I really can't talk now. Can I ring you tonight?'

'As long as you pinky promise.'

'I pinky promise.'

Suddenly aware of the silence behind her, she turned around and saw that the Mouseketeer had disappeared, and Glenda was now glowering at Phoebe.

'So, all you need to do is to bring some form of ID and proof of your current address. Have a nice day,' Phoebe said in a loud, confident voice, before placing the receiver back in its cradle.

'Are you aware of the library's policy about receiving personal calls during work hours?' Each of Glenda's words was like a slap on the wrist.

Phoebe started to apologise but was saved by the reappearance of the Mouseketeer.

'I think there was a photo of a lady on the cover,' she told them both. 'Or maybe it was an apple.'

Phoebe could have kissed her.

★

THAT NIGHT, PHOEBE didn't ring Sandy. She knew she was breaking her pinky promise, but the days when that had truly meant something were far behind them. And anyway, maybe it was best for Sandy that she didn't ring. Phoebe hadn't exactly been good medicine for her in high school.

As she washed the pile of dishes that had accumulated during the week, Phoebe found herself thinking about the last time she would have made – and honoured – a pinky promise. It had possibly been around Year 10, when she and Sandy used to take shelter in the library during lunchtimes. Phoebe had been avoiding having to listen to people eating, and Sandy (back then) had been avoiding eating, *full stop*. For most of high school, Sandy had been following some diet from *Dolly* or *Cosmo*, and then she seemed to stop eating altogether. And Phoebe never noticed. Or at least, she hadn't wanted to notice. Sandy's illness had remained in a convenient blindspot for Phoebe, who never had to worry about her friend crunching chips or popping gum or slurping soup.

It wasn't until later, when Sandy had become so sick that her whole family had upped and moved to Canberra, that Phoebe had realised she should have been encouraging Sandy to eat chips, gum and soup. To eat anything.

At first, she'd written to Sandy every day, spending all her pocket money on stamps and strawberry-scented stationery from Granny May's. Sandy didn't write back as often, and her letters were very short when she did, but Phoebe knew she wasn't well. But slowly, writing every day turned into writing every other day, then once a week, until finally, in about her second year of university, she stopped writing to Sandy altogether.

And that's where it might have ended, except one day near the end of Phoebe's third year, Sandy had called Phoebe's parents' house when Phoebe had been there for dinner. She remembered standing in the hallway, twisting the cord of the phone around her hand, conscious that her mother was probably listening in from the next room. Sandy had been full of news about her own uni studies and her new boyfriend, but then she came to the real reason she'd called: she'd had a breakthrough with her therapist, something that she really needed to share with Phoebe, something that she really needed Phoebe to hear.

The problem was that Phoebe hadn't been ready to hear it. She'd literally used the 'I think I hear my mother calling' excuse to end the conversation. And she'd been avoiding having that conversation ever since. Living in the Share House of Cereal had helped because there'd been no phone, and the few times Sandy had been able to catch Phoebe at her parents' house, Phoebe had always been 'just about to eat', or 'just about to get a lift home'. And then Sandy had stopped trying altogether.

Until now.

Sometimes she wished she'd been brave enough to have just heard Sandy out during that first call. The not-quite-knowing-but-guessing-what-it-probably-was had ended up being a different, more drawn-out kind of agony than facing the truth. In any case, she knew what she'd done and hadn't done. She didn't need Sandy to tell her, even if Sandy felt she needed to be told.

The dishes now done, Phoebe dried her hands and pulled the postcards out of her workbag. She needed something to distract her. Even though she had told herself that she wouldn't read any more of them, she picked up the postcard that had arrived yesterday: an aerial shot of a castle on an island surrounded by deep blue water.

Dearest Elizabeth,

I am still writing these cards, even though I haven't posted a single one. I'm worried I'll arrive home before they do, but maybe I should put more trust in the international postal system. I've been thinking I might give you the whole lot at once, tied up in a red ribbon. Today we visited the Château d'If – the prison island in which Dumas set The Count of Monte Cristo. *As I looked out through one of the cell windows, I thought of the prisoners looking at that same patch of sky and longing for freedom.*

You are my patch of blue sky.

Yours,

T

Phoebe looked out the kitchen window, at the darkening sky. There had been a librarian at the last place she had worked who'd said there was a German word for a yearning that couldn't be explained. Phoebe wished she had written the word down. Having a label to pin on a feeling might make it less overwhelming.

Chapter 6

PHOEBE WAS PACKING up the morning's craft activity when the guy from the post office walked in. She'd just read *The Rainbow Fish* out loud to a writhing pit of four-year-olds and then tried to lead them through an activity where they made their own rainbow fish by sticking large sequins onto paper. But it had all gone terribly wrong. Most of the sequins and Clag glue had ended up on the table, floor and walls. Thankfully, it was coming off easily enough. Phoebe didn't fancy telling Glenda she had accidentally bedazzled the children's area.

'You've missed the activity,' she told the post office guy, as she peeled a sequin from the windowpane.

'That's okay, I've actually come to talk to you,' he said in the same sheepish manner he'd used when he'd pointed out her mistake with Elizabeth Winston's last name.

'Well, I'm not supposed to talk on the job, unless it's about books. So if my boss comes along, we'll have to pretend you're asking when we'll have the latest John Grisham in. Okay?'

'Okay,' he said. He had spotted another sequin stuck high on the wall and had reached up to get it. How the hell had that got up there?

'Thanks,' Phoebe said, as he placed the sequin on the growing pile on the table. 'Shouldn't you be at the post office?'

'Nah. I was just filling in.' He continued to hunt for sequins.

'Oh yeah, that's right,' Phoebe said, remembering how he'd pretended his mother was his work colleague.

'Anyway, I wanted to talk to you about those postcards,' he told her.

'So you've solved the mystery of why they were posted in Australia?'

The guy shrugged. 'You don't happen to have them with you, do you?'

'Actually, I do.'

They were still in Phoebe's workbag. She'd had vague plans of going back to the post office when there was an actual grown-up in charge to get the right form, but she didn't tell him that. She went to the corner of the room where she'd stashed her bag.

'Here you go, Dr Watson.' Phoebe handed him the postcards and he handed her the sequins he'd collected.

'I'm clearly the Sherlock Holmes in this situation,' he said, flipping through the cards. He finally stopped on the postcard from Paris. 'Here.'

He showed Phoebe the picture. It was a photo of the Louvre, the large courtyard outside filled with people. Phoebe stared at it, unsure of what she was supposed to be seeing.

'There's no pyramid,' the guy eventually said. 'The pyramid was built in 1989 and this postcard is from before that.'

'So?' Phoebe said. 'It might just be old stock.' She imagined a tourist shop on some Place de Something with a bargain bin full of outdated souvenir stationery.

The guy went back to the stack of postcards and pulled out one from Berlin.

'Yep,' he said, after he'd quickly read the card. 'As I suspected.' He handed it to her.

'It's the Brandenburg Gate,' Phoebe replied. 'So?'

'You need to read it.'

Phoebe took a quick look around to see if Glenda was on the prowl, and then read the message.

Dear Elizabeth,

This is the Brandenburg Gate, part of the awful wall that separates the city. You can see the East through the arches, in all its sober drabness. I stood there and stared for much longer than I should have. I kept thinking that my heart is divided like Berlin, and I'm stuck in the grey part of my normal life, watching you dance in full technicolour on the other side.

T

'It was clearly written before the Wall came down,' the guy said. 'Which happened on the ninth of November, also in 1989.'

'You know your dates.'

'I did a minor in Modern History,' he said, looking bashful. 'My parents actually don't know that I studied Commerce–Arts and not pure Commerce. And now that I'm doing a Master's in Business, they'll never know. It's like the perfect crime.'

At that moment, Phoebe saw Glenda heading over to the

returns chute. It would be only a matter of seconds before she looked their way and saw Phoebe fraternising with a customer.

'Here, come with me,' she said. 'And pretend I'm showing you some books.'

'Uh, okay.'

Phoebe stopped in front of a shelf. Over the guy's shoulder, she could see Glenda turning her laser-beam gaze their way. She quickly pulled out a Goosebumps book called *Welcome to Camp Nightmare.*

'This one is pretty good, actually,' she said. 'It has a surprising ending.'

The guy took the book and pretended to thumb through it.

'You've read this?'

'I've read all the books in the children's section. They don't take long.'

'That's impressive.'

Phoebe could see that Glenda was now walking to the back of the library, and she breathed a sigh of relief. After that long personal call, she wasn't quite ready for another infraction.

'I'm Phoebe Cotton, by the way,' Phoebe said.

'Montgomery Smith, at your service.' He gave a little bow. 'But you can call me Monty.'

'Montgomery Smith?' Phoebe repeated. She didn't say it out loud, but he did not look like a Montgomery Smith.

Montgomery gave a small sigh. He'd clearly had this conversation many times before. 'My mum is from just north of Hanoi in Vietnam and my dad was her English tutor. For some reason, Mum wanted to give me the most English name she could think of.'

'She did pretty well,' Phoebe observed.

'The kids at school used to call me Montgomery *Smythe* and

my mates at uni call me Uncle Monty from, you know, *Withnail and I*. But you can just call me Monty.'

'So, *Monty*,' Phoebe leaned into the name gently. 'What you're telling me is that the postcards were posted at least seven years after they were written.'

'Actually, they were posted here in Melbourne,' Monty said. 'Look here. This postmark clearly says Clifton Hill.'

'Steady on, Sherlock. This is too many developments in the case for me to take in at once.'

'See, I told you I was Sherlock Holmes,' he said with a grin.

Phoebe looked at her watch. She had half an hour left to finish planning tomorrow's after-school activity.

'Thanks for your help,' she said, returning to her basket of craft materials and her bag. 'My people will be in contact with your people.'

'You're welcome,' Monty gave another little bow. 'I hope you get to the bottom of it.'

'So do I,' she replied. 'Um, do you mind putting the book back on the shelf?'

Monty looked down at the Goosebumps book still in his hands. 'I reckon I'll borrow this one. I've heard it has a surprise ending.'

ON THE BUS home that evening, with the Smashing Pumpkins turned up to eleven on her Walkman, she looked at the postcards with fresh eyes. The faded colour that she had assumed to be a result of poor printing standards in Europe was actually an indicator of its age.

She thought about Monty and how weird it was that he'd come in to see her in the library. Weird but nice. He had a goofy, Keanu Reeves in *Parenthood* kind of vibe. For the briefest of moments, she imagined them both shaving each other's head in her grandmother's bathroom.

She then imagined finding Elizabeth Winston and returning the postcards and finding out once and for all why they'd been posted to her so late and so close to home, and she imagined going to the post office to tell Monty about it. He might invite her out for a drink so they could talk about it some more. That would be nice. Maybe she could start tonight by ringing all the people in Melbourne listed under *Winston, E* in the White Pages.

It was with this renewed resolve that Phoebe alighted from the bus and walked the short distance to Number 6, a slight spring in her step. It didn't take her very long to notice a girl dressed head to toe in black – black leggings, Doc Marten boots and an oversized man's jacket – standing at the front gate of her house. She had a short pixie cut, Cleopatra eye make-up and bright red lipstick. Phoebe was fairly certain that this was the first time someone like her had ever crossed the Maribyrnong, let alone cast their shadow on Salmon Street.

'Can I help you?' Phoebe asked her, once she'd reached the house. She was surprised by how calm her voice sounded, considering how hard her heart was beating. There was something about the girl in black that portended doom, like a banshee or one of those goth kids at school that bullied her and Sandy.

'Hi, I'm Suze,' the girl said. 'I'm here about the postcards.'

Phoebe's mouth dropped open, and the postcards, which she had still been holding in her hand, fell to the ground.

Chapter 7

One month earlier
Saturday 29 April 1995, Fitzroy

THE PAINT ON the kitchen ceiling of the Moor Street
house was peeling and big chunks of it occasionally fell
into Suze's hair, but Sacha said they shouldn't say anything to
the landlords in case they put up the rent. Ditto with the broken
power point in the kitchen that meant they had to keep the fridge
in the lounge room and run the extension cord for the electric
oven out to the laundry. Suze tripped over it at least once a day.

She watched J trip over it now as he made his way out
the back door to the garden, where Suze was sitting on the
small patch of grass that grew despite the wall of abandoned
whitegoods around it. Close behind him was Groovy Joe, the
house cat, who ignored all visitors except J, mostly because J
completely ignored him.

J was wearing his black velvet trousers and a long gold chain and nothing else. He'd discovered some beer in the fridge and was cracking one open.

'Breakfast of the gods,' he said now, all teeth and charm, holding up the can of VB. 'Want some?'

Suze shook her head. It was midday, so officially the sun was over the yardarm (as the saying went) but she'd only just woken up. Also, she didn't really know what a yardarm was. Nor where the beer had come from. Sacha and Charlie weren't exactly beer drinkers.

J and Groovy Joe were now stretched out beside her in the autumn sun. She still couldn't believe that J had actually stayed over instead of getting on his bike and riding off into the distance, like he normally did. Suze had lain awake half the night worrying that he'd fallen asleep by mistake and that he'd be annoyed at her for not waking him up.

Even now, she didn't want to ask him why he'd stayed over in case he never did it again.

He lifted his head and took a big gulp of his VB, belched and then lay back down.

'What do you want to do today?' he asked.

Suze just shrugged nonchalantly, acutely aware that this, too, never happened. He always had somewhere else that he needed to be, although he never said where and she never asked either. *At this rate, we'll be living together by the end of the weekend*, she thought.

'You don't have other plans?' She reached over to take a sip of his beer. She knew she should be studying today, but she was suddenly feeling giddy and careless.

'Hey! You had your chance,' he laughed, grabbing the can back. 'Get your own.'

Suze lay back on the grass. 'Let's go op-shopping on Smith Street,' she suggested.

'Nice one,' J replied. 'I'm on the hunt for a new performance project – something where I don't have to clean offal off the walls.'

Of course, it was Suze who cleaned the offal from the walls, as recently as last night at the abandoned cannery where they'd performed their latest 'surgical happening'. J had nailed a cow's heart to the wall and his friend Stig had gone at it with an angle grinder, while Suze had rocked back and forth in a corner singing Roxette's 'Listen to Your Heart' through a megaphone.

Even though her hands still stank from the ammonia she'd used to clean up, Suze felt a small flutter of panic. The surgical happenings were the only thing that joined her to J, and him to her. Without them, she was worried that she'd never see him.

'Don't we have another operation scheduled for next weekend?' she asked, doing her very best to sound unconcerned. J was always telling her to be 'chill', and while it made her feel like some kind of dairy product that would go off if not appropriately refrigerated, it had become her personal mantra.

'Yeah, but I'm thinking of cancelling. Ky says performance is *gauche*.'

'Oh, okay.' The mention of Ky's name (which was actually Kylie) was like a punch to her gut. Ky had just returned from Paris, where she had studied mime with Jacques Lecoq and had somehow lost the second syllable of her name. J had not stopped talking about her since they'd met up at some median strip party on Rathdowne Street that Suze hadn't been invited to. 'What kind of thing are you thinking of doing instead?'

'Dunno. Ky's been telling me more about the (un)art movement, although I shouldn't actually describe it as a movement. The whole concept of (un)art precludes movements. And even talking about it as a concept is against (un)art.'

'Sounds interesting,' Suze lied. It wasn't the first time he'd talked about (un)art, but the only thing Suze could really remember about it was the spelling, which was apparently very important, even for something as allegedly anarchic as (un)art.

She rolled onto her side to face him. She wanted to reach over and touch the scar on his forehead, but she knew he didn't really like that kind of thing. Also, displays of affection were probably too 'performative' for him now.

'Yeah, she's really turned my mind around about a few things.'

As he continued to talk with great excitement about Ky and her mind-turning ways, Suze couldn't help but remember how excited J had been when he'd first met *her* in their second year of uni. She and Charlie had gatecrashed a party in order to get out of a rainstorm and Charlie had put his wet shoes in the clothes dryer. Suze had been drunk enough or high enough to start dancing to the arrhythmic clunk coming from inside the dryer's cylinder, and then J had walked in and had been drunk enough or high enough to find Suze's dancing the most enchanting thing he had ever seen. 'The most enchanting thing' had been his actual words. She had been *enchanting* to him.

And now Ky was his new enchantress.

'Well, I'll keep Saturday night free in case you decide to go ahead with it,' Suze said. 'Maybe we can go out for dinner instead?'

Like a normal couple.

'Coolio.' J lowered his sunglasses and stretched out in the sun. Suze didn't know if that meant 'Yes, we can go for dinner' or not.

'I can ring you later in the week to see how you're feeling.'

'Whatever.' He lifted his hand to make a tiny 'shoo' gesture and Suze immediately backed off. She knew that J didn't like to make plans. He didn't even like to make plans about making plans.

Charlie stuck his head out the back door.

'There you are. Your mum's on the phone,' Charlie said to Suze. When he saw that J was there too, he screwed up his nose. J was an affront to all of Charlie's delicate senses.

'It's cool if you want to talk with your mum,' J said, sitting up again. 'I should probably get going.'

Suze felt the usual panic rise in her chest at the thought of him disappearing into a future where there were no fixed plans to meet up.

'Tell her I'll talk to her later,' Suze told Charlie, who rolled his eyes before retreating into the house.

Suze lay back down and looked up at the clear blue sky. 'She's always ringing me,' she said, her stomach tight with the guilt of not taking the call.

Fifteen months after her stepfather, Greg, had died of bowel cancer, her mother was still neck-deep in grief in her small Bondi apartment. She often said that her weekly conversations with Suze were the one thing she looked forward to. Suze resolved to return her call as soon as possible.

'Yeah, I reckon op-shopping is a good idea,' J said, even though Suze hadn't mentioned it again. 'I've been looking for a fur coat. Fake, of course. I think I'd look good in one.'

Suze nodded and moved her legs so that her foot was pressing lightly against his. He didn't move away, and Suze felt glad.

J GAVE SUZE a dink on his bike to the Salvos on Smith Street. The store was full of treasure-hunting students, and J worked his way through the aisles quickly. His arms were quickly filled with treasures: a 1960s Tupperware jelly mould, a cherry destoner, a hammer with a picture of a naked girl on its grip, and a homemade ceramic bust of Elvis.

'I'm thinking I can give Elvis a jelly crown and then destroy him with the hammer,' he told her.

'How does the cherry destoner fit in?'

'It doesn't. I'm hoping it does olives too. I hate pips in olives.'

Suze nodded, imagining him in a tuxedo at a fancy party, drinking a martini, his face like a balled-up tissue because there was a stone in his olive.

'I'll need to buy a bag or something to fit all this shit, but.'

Suze held up the suitcase she'd been considering: an olive-green case with rounded edges and a silvery quilted lining that had small compartments along the sides. She'd been thinking she could store scarves and satin gloves in it, should she ever become the kind of person who wore scarves and satin gloves. 'Would this be big enough?'

The price tag said five dollars, a little more than she should probably pay to accessorise a largely improbable future version of herself. But the case was so beautiful. Perhaps she could use it for the weekend trips away in the countryside that she'd never taken, nor was ever likely to take.

J appraised it. 'Probably,' he concluded. 'But I'll never be able to take that on the bike, Einstein.'

'I'm buying it anyway, so I can take your stuff back to my house and you can get it later,' Suze said, pleased to have another tendril tying her life to his, and yet fully aware that she was also tying herself to the five-dollar purchase.

She was less pleased when J jumped on his bicycle the minute they left the op shop and she found herself standing on the footpath.

As she set off for Moor Street, lugging the suitcase, she mentally kicked herself. If she hadn't bought the case, he might have given her a dink home too and then she could have invited him in and maybe he would have stayed the night again.

By the time she got to the corner of Johnson and Brunswick Streets, her arm was aching. She stopped and sat down on the case, hoping she looked forlorn-yet-charming and not like she'd just been kicked out of home.

'Nice case,' a guy waiting to cross the road remarked. He was wearing a bowtie and a tuxedo jacket on top of jeans and a pair of bright red Converses. Suze just smiled, unsure of how to respond to such an outfit. Also, he was very good-looking. While he waited for the lights to change, she imagined a different interaction, one where she managed to strike up a proper conversation with the guy and they ended up grabbing a drink at the Black Cat at the table in the front window and J cycled past and saw them and got so jealous that he finally realised he wanted to call her his girlfriend.

She watched Mr Bowtie as he crossed the road to take the hand of another good-looking and well-dressed man waiting for him.

Charlie was always telling her that her gaydar was faulty.

She sighed and stood up.

'We can do this,' she said to the suitcase, psyching herself up for the rest of the walk home.

Chapter 8

'HONEY, I'M HOME!' Suze shouted as she hauled the suitcase into the narrow hall. She paused and waited for Charlie's usual reply of 'Honey, I'm homo!' but was met with silence. She guessed he was out somewhere, wielding his fully operational gaydar. Suze put the suitcase in the lounge room on top of one of the milk crates that served as a chair. Groovy Joe, who had been lying in his usual spot under the window, immediately jumped up onto the case and made himself comfortable.

Much to Suze's surprise, she found Sacha in the kitchen cooking something with a guy. Sacha had never had a proper boyfriend in all the years Suze had known her, just a long string of love-struck guys who she held at arm's length. For a hippy chick who worked at the Friends of the Earth Food Co-op on

Smith Street and frequently wove flowers into her long blonde hair, Sacha was surprisingly aloof.

'This is Matt,' Sacha said nonchalantly, like this wasn't an unprecedented event.

'Hi,' Matt said.

'Hi,' Suze replied, temporarily dazed. At least this explained the beer in the fridge.

'Sash tells me you're doing Honours in English,' Matt said. 'That's cool.'

Suze knew it wasn't cool at all, but she nodded. 'What do you do, Matt?'

'I'm a website designer.'

'What's a website?'

'See?' Sacha slapped Matt playfully on the arm. 'Nobody knows what they are.'

'To be honest, I don't think I do either,' Matt confessed.

'Did Jonathan sleep over last night?' Sacha wanted to know.

Sometimes Suze swore that Sacha could see right into her soul. 'How did you know?'

'One of Matt's beers was missing.'

'Who's Jonathan?' Matt asked.

'Suze's kind-of-sort-of-maybe-but-probably-not boyfriend. I have a theory that he has a secret life in Mordialloc as an insurance underwriter with a darling wife and 2.4 adorable children.'

Matt reached for a handful of nuts from a jar and shoved them in his mouth. 'If that was true, you think he'd pay for his own beer.'

'Don't talk with your mouth full, Matthew,' Sacha scolded him, with a laugh.

'Why not?' Matt said, deliberately spluttering nut crumbs everywhere.

Suze left them to their domestic bliss and went back to the suitcase. Even Groovy Joe had decided it was a bad purchase because he had abandoned it for his usual spot under the window. As Suze lugged the suitcase up the stairs, she tried to imagine J working in an office or wrangling small children. Sacha and her theories. *Seriously.* She had always been deeply suspicious of J for reasons Suze could never quite understand. Suze preferred to think of him as a cat, like Groovy Joe, beyond ownership. ('He comes, he goes, he licks his own arse,' Charlie had once said.)

'By the way, your mum called,' Sacha shouted up the stairs.

Suze felt the usual pang of guilt. That guilt was the chorus in the song of her life right now.

'Thanks,' she shouted back. She'd definitely ring her mum back after she'd had a nap.

ON WEDNESDAY AFTERNOON, Suze was making her fourth cup of International Roast for the day – one of the tried-and-true methods for avoiding her Honours thesis – when Sacha came home from her shift at the Co-op.

'I just saw Jonathan in the front bar of the Standard,' she said as she passed by Suze, on her way to the bathroom.

'Oh, really?' Suze tried to play it cool. J hadn't come to collect Elvis and the rest of his belongings yet, so maybe he would drop by. She immediately abandoned her coffee and went up to her room to change her trackie daks for some flared cords she'd bought half-price at Dangerfield and pulled on her tweed jacket with the fake fur collar (Charlie always said she looked cute in that). She also grabbed a pre-loved Georgette Heyer paperback and her cat's eye sunglasses (even though it was practically winter) before marching back down the stairs.

Sacha was waiting at the bottom, eating muesli from a Snoopy mug, like some kind of sentry (that eats muesli from a Snoopy mug).

'What are you doing?' she asked suspiciously, her spoon suspended midway between the mug and her lips.

'I'm going to read a book,' Suze replied, trying to sound as nonchalant as possible, as she pushed past Sacha and made her way out to the small concrete lawn in the front yard. There, she settled onto the orange deckchair she and Charlie had found on hard-rubbish day and opened *Frederica*. Sitting in the afternoon sun with a book was a perfectly acceptable way to pass a Wednesday afternoon, she told herself.

'Seriously. What are you *really* doing?' Sacha was leaning out of Charlie's bedroom window to scrutinise her more closely.

'I said I'm reading a book!' Suze replied, not daring to lift her eyes from the page in case she exposed her real intentions. She could feel the heat of Sacha's gaze on the back of her neck.

'Don't give yourself away so easily,' Sacha said after a long pause and then shut the window.

Suze tried to shake Sacha's words off, but she knew deep down how ridiculous she was being, sitting there all dressed up and pretending to read, when really she was just hoping J would suddenly realise how great she was and rush to her, his half-finished pint in his hand, and a confession of true love on his lips – just like Lord Alverstoke did to Frederica in her book, except without the half-finished pint.

Eventually she stopped pretending to read and started to actually read. She had become fully immersed in the spring of 1818 when J showed up forty-five minutes later. Suze feigned vague surprise.

'Oh,' she said. 'It's you.'

'I've come to get my stuff,' he said, holding up an empty backpack. 'Oh, and to see you.'

He leaned forward and kissed her, his breath all beer and cigarettes. So much for the confession of true love.

'Sure,' Suze said, leading him into the house and up to her room. She was glad that Sacha was nowhere to be seen.

J immediately dived onto her bed and stretched out on the Indian cotton bedspread to watch her as she pulled the case down from the top of her wardrobe.

'I was starting to worry about you and all those pesky olive pips,' she said as she retrieved his purchases.

'What?' J had evidently forgotten about his plans for the cherry destoner. Suze gave a little shrug in the hope she would appear mysterious, rather than embarrassed.

'Elvis is even better than I remembered,' J said, getting up to appraise the sculpture before shoving him in the backpack. Suze felt a slight flutter of panic that he would just take his stuff and go.

'So, are we going ahead with the surgery this weekend?'

'I'm not sure I'm into that vibe anymore. Ky called us "the Lunts".'

'Who are the Lunts?'

J shrugged. 'Does it matter? It didn't sound like a compliment.'

Suze felt that it did matter and made a mental note to look up the Lunts the next time she was in a library.

'I saw that *A Room with a View* is playing at the Astor on Saturday.'

'I hate that film.'

'You what?' *A Room with a View* was one of her favourite films and she was pretty certain J had told her it was one of his favourites, too.

'It pretends to attack the British class system, while appealing to the very people that it's attacking.'

Suze started to argue with him, but J sprang up and off the bed to look at the suitcase. 'You know what? This lining is perfect for the space-hero costume I'm making for Doggie's party,' he said. It was a party Suze hadn't been invited to, of course. J talked about Doggie all the time, but she'd never met the guy.

'I'm going to use that case,' Suze told him.

'You'll still be able to use it. Anyway, the lining's all torn here.'

He pointed at a corner where a small part of the lining had come away. Suze stepped in closer to examine it while J grabbed a pair of scissors from the desk and started to cut the fabric.

Suze wanted to shout at him to stop, but she knew that was probably the least 'chilled' and '(un)art' that she could be, so she stepped back. *It's just a suitcase*, she tried to tell herself, and she did her very best to surrender to the lining's destruction.

But J had stopped cutting.

'I think there's something in here,' he said.

Suze stepped closer to see what he'd found.

From within the lining, he pulled out a pile of postcards wrapped with a red ribbon.

'Damn it. I thought it was cash,' J muttered, palming the pile off to Suze and returning to his cutting.

Suze sat down on the bed and carefully unwrapped the postcards. There were about twenty or maybe even thirty of them, all from Europe, and the images had that glamorous faded colour of the 1960s. She selected one from Berlin, showing the Brandenburg Gate, and flipped it over. It was covered with beautiful loopy handwriting and addressed to a house in West Footscray, but there was no stamp. She quickly turned over the others to see that none of them had stamps either.

'They were never sent,' Suze said, more to herself than to J.

'Cool,' J said, now beside her, grabbing one of the postcards. 'I can't wait to show these to Ky.'

'What?' Suze tried to grab them back. 'They were in my suitcase, so they're mine. Well, they're not mine *or* yours. They're somebody else's.'

'That somebody else is probably dead. How else do you think this suitcase ended up in the op shop? Estate sale remnants, baby,' J said as they wrestled on the bed. Suze was really hoping this was a prelude to kissing, but J really wanted those postcards. He got clear of her and tucked the pile into his backpack next to Elvis. 'Anyway, you know the rules: finders keepers.'

Suze felt disappointed that he'd stood up.

'Are you hungry? I'm about to make dinner.' The offer of a free meal was usually enough to make him stay a little longer. She really didn't want him to disappear yet, not before he'd even kissed her properly.

'Nah, I had the pot-and-parma special at the Standard,' J replied.

'I heard there's a bar on Smith Street that has a frozen margarita machine.' She didn't know why she suggested it when she knew for a fact that she couldn't afford even half a frozen margarita.

'On a Wednesday night? You're hardcore, Suze,' J said, slapping her arm lightly. 'I was thinking of dropping by the Rainbow. Ky's doing a poetry reading.'

'That doesn't sound very "(un)art".'

'You haven't seen Ky do a poetry reading,' he said, swinging his backpack onto one shoulder.

'Well, maybe I should.'

'Sure,' J shrugged. 'I'll meet you there. Things kick off at nine.'

Suze looked at her watch. It was only six-thirty. She was disappointed that he didn't want to spend the next two-and-a-half hours with her, but at least she'd be meeting up with him later. Also, it gave her some time to do some uni work. Or not.

Chapter 9

IN THE CROWDED upstairs room at the Rainbow Hotel, a man in a leather jacket was screaming into the microphone like he was possessed.

'I'll have what he's having,' Suze said to the guy behind the bar, with a nod towards the stage.

'What? A midlife crisis?' he replied. The leather jacket man was now wiping down the microphone with baby wipes.

'Maybe not. Um, I'll have a pot of Matilda Bay instead.'

'Make that two,' J said appearing beside her. 'But I'll have a pint.'

Suze tried not to think about how the twenty-two dollars in her wallet had to last her until her next Austudy payment came through.

'Sure. But the next round is on you.'

'Of course, of course,' J said, his focus on the stage where Ky was now standing.

Ky was wearing a black dress that touched the floor. Her long dark hair was parted dead in the centre and her face was painted white, like a Japanese Noh dancer. Or Marcel Marceau.

She glared at the audience for a long, uncomfortable moment and then turned her back to the room. The audience waited for a very long time, long enough for J to finish his pint. Suze focused on her arm touching J's and wished he'd put his arm around her. Her pot of beer sweated in her hands.

Slowly, the room started to grow restless. The murmur of voices turned into a dull roar, and when it finally seemed that nobody (except J and Suze) was paying any attention to her any longer, Ky stepped to the side of the stage and vomited in a bucket.

J handed Suze his empty pint glass and began to applaud, but Ky gave him the most severe of looks, the kind that made Suze surprised that J wasn't instantly turned to stone, and he fell silent.

Ky kicked the bucket over and jumped down from the stage. She pushed through the crowd and out the door, leaving behind nothing but the sound of someone dry-retching in the front row.

'Wow,' J said. 'Just wow.'

He set off after Ky.

Suze stood for a moment, the two glasses in her hands, unsure what to do. But just as J was drawn to Ky, she was drawn to J. She put the glasses down and went outside.

She found them across the road from the venue, deep in conversation. Although conversation was probably a generous word to describe what mostly appeared to be a lecture from Ky.

'. . . you have to surrender the whole concept of performance, all its patriarchal trappings. The act of striking one hand
against the other is a symbol of repression by way of violence.'
Noticing Suze standing there, Ky paused and stared at her
severely. 'Can I help you?'

'I'm, um, a friend of J's. That was a very interesting
performance you just gave.'

'It wasn't performance,' J jumped in.

'Sorry, that was, um, interesting,' Suze repeated, this time
avoiding all labels.

'Let's go drink gin at the Perse,' Ky suddenly announced
to nobody in particular, and Suze and J both nodded. She
continued to deliver her lecture to J while he followed at her
heels, an obedient puppy. Suze lagged behind, unsure whether
she was really invited, and worried about who was going to
clean up the vomit back in the pub – and also who was going
to pay for the gin. Judging by her bare feet and too-long dress,
and her distinct lack of any kind of bag or purse, Suze concluded
that Ky was as anti-money as she was anti-art.

Still, Suze followed them, pretending to herself that it was
on her way home anyway. And when Ky stopped at the door
of the Perseverance and gestured for her to enter, Suze found
herself going inside.

Thankfully, J paid for three gin and tonics and the three of
them sat in a corner of the front bar, as far away from a group
of guys drinking flaming sambuca shots as they could manage.

Suze watched J's face as he listened to Ky talk and she felt an
intense panic, deep inside her chest. He had never looked at her
in that kind of enraptured way, not even when they'd first met.

Eventually, Suze excused herself and went to the bathroom,
where she looked at her reflection in the mirror and wondered
what she should do next.

You're embarrassing yourself, Susan, she told her reflection. *You should just go home.*

But even as she told herself that, she knew she wasn't going home. Not yet at least.

When she returned to the table, she saw that J had pulled the postcards out and laid them before Ky, like some kind of offering. She'd hoped he would leave them at home with Elvis and the jelly mould and the cherry destoner and that they would somehow remain something that belonged only to *them*, to J and Suze.

'They're unsent postcards,' Ky was saying, picking up one but not really looking at it.

Suze felt like saying 'Der, Freddy', but there was something rarefied about the situation, like J was a priest lying prostrate before the Pope. She sat down instead.

'I've been thinking about what to do with them . . .' J started.

Ky shut him down. 'Thinking is your first mistake. You need to feel your way through this.'

'I was *feeling* like I should post them. One at a time.'

Ky nodded sagely, as if giving her blessing.

Something new stirred inside Suze. 'But what about the person who's going to receive them. Won't they be confused? Shouldn't you warn them?'

'No, no, it's perfect,' Ky replied. 'An act which is not an act and an audience of one who is an unknowing receiver of the objects of (un)art.'

'It *is* perfect,' J echoed.

'But they're *my* postcards. They were in *my* suitcase,' Suze said, wanting to stop the nonsense.

'Everything belongs to everybody. Nothing belongs to nobody,' Ky replied mysteriously. J nodded, a man hypnotised. 'Do you have a stamp?' Ky asked them both.

57

No, I don't have a stamp. Who the hell has a stamp? Suze wanted to reply, but instead she shook her head and bit her lip.

J fumbled around in his wallet and pulled out a stamp. Suze almost did a double take. She had never pegged him as someone who would have a stamp. She wondered what else might be in that magic wallet of his: a licorice-flavoured condom, a membership card for the Melbourne Club, the blueprints for a bank vault?

'Post one of the cards right now,' Ky commanded. 'There's a PO box across the road.'

'But which card?' he asked.

'If it mattered, it wouldn't be (un)art.'

J pulled out one of the cards at random and Suze saw a flash of Big Ben before he flipped it over and slapped the stamp on it.

He stood up. 'I'll—'

'Hush now,' Ky said, closing her eyes. Suze supposed she was deliberately avoiding watching J, so it wouldn't accidentally turn into performance.

Suze did watch J push his way through the dance floor and out onto the street, postcard held aloft, like he was saving it from drowning. She imagined he'd continue to carry it like that all the way to the postbox across the road.

She looked back at Ky, who was sitting silent, her eyes still closed.

Suze slumped into her chair. The floor beneath her feet felt sticky. She didn't really understand what was happening or what Ky was on about, but it was pretty clear that J wouldn't be coming home with her tonight.

WHEN SUZE GOT home (alone), she decided to ring her mother. The lateness of the hour was a gamble, but not a very risky one. Since her husband's passing, Barbara had been keeping unusual hours, often staying awake watching videos until dawn.

Her mum answered after just two rings.

'Hello, love,' she said, her usual telephone greeting. ('You're the only one who ever calls, except the telemarketers, and the "Hello, love" puts them on the back foot,' she'd once explained.) 'What's up?'

'Nothing. And everything. I don't know.'

'Sounds about right.'

'How are you?'

'The same as always.' As Barbara went on to describe her empty day and her empty life, Suze couldn't help but remember how full her mother's life used to be, when Greg was still alive.

Not for the first time, nor the last, Suze felt guilty for leaving Sydney. When she'd lived with her mum after Greg died, she'd tried everything to get Barbara back out into the world – signing her up for anything from cooking lessons to dolphin-watching experiences, and even going as far as offering to join her at bootscooting classes – but nothing had worked. Finally, Suze had become worried that her mum's lack of a life would gobble up her own life, like the Nothing in *The Neverending Story*. But still she'd stayed. In the end, it had been Barbara herself who had insisted that Suze go back to Melbourne.

'How's your friend J?'

Barbara loved to hear stories about J. Suze only ever told her the charming ones, not the ones where he left her feeling lonely.

'He's good. He's working on a new collaboration.'

That was certainly one way of describing his blossoming relationship with Ky.

'Good for him. Are you still performing your operations?'

'They're on hiatus at the moment.' Suze always felt a bit

uncomfortable talking about the amateur surgery performances with her mother considering how medicalised her life had been before Greg had died. But Barbara seemed to enjoy hearing about them. It was just as well that she was in Sydney and couldn't actually attend any of the performances, as Suze always made them out to be much better and more entertaining than they actually were. The audience was usually more confused than anything.

'Well, maybe J will bring you in on this new collaboration.'

Suze almost laughed out loud at her mother inadvertently suggesting she have a threesome with J and Ky.

'Maybe,' she replied instead. 'Did you go to your support group meeting?'

'I slept in,' Barbara said. 'I'll make it to the next one.'

'I hope so.'

'I just feel so tired.'

'I know, Mum. Have a Horlicks and try to get some sleep. I'll speak to you on the weekend.'

'Goodnight, love.'

'Goodnight, Mum.'

After she hung up, Suze sat in the dark for a long time. It was hard not to feel that the emptiness of Barbara's life had sucked the life from the room.

Chapter 10

IT WAS LATE on a Saturday afternoon and Charlie was hounding Suze to go to a party, even though he'd only just recovered from his hangover from the previous night's party.

Charlie's appetite for parties was insatiable. He said he needed them to counterbalance the deathly dullness of his job at the bank. ('I can only work with a hangover and the promise of the next one,' Charlie said.)

'Come *on*, Suze.' Charlie tugged on her sleeve like a small child.

'I'm really tired,' Suze told him. She didn't add that she was still hoping J might swing by. It had been ten days since she'd last seen him and two weeks since he'd dropped in. Her resolve to remain aloof and 'chilled' had crumbled and she'd rung him on Tuesday, but he had been on his way out to an art exhibition and said he might come over on the weekend instead. Although she couldn't even admit it to herself, she'd been hovering around the house since 5 pm on Friday. Just in case.

'I promise you'll have fun,' Charlie pleaded. 'Sean throws the best parties. And it's only a few blocks away, in case you really do get tired.'

'Okay.' Suze sighed. She knew that resistance was futile.

'Yay! Now we have to sort out our costumes.'

Suze groaned. 'You didn't tell me it was a dress-up party.'

'Every party is a dress-up party!'

An hour later, they were both dressed up as Courtney Love, in lace-trimmed slip dresses and fake fur coats, with bright red lipstick smeared across their lips and faces.

'Perfect,' he said. 'We just need wigs.'

He opened up his Case of Wonders. As well as wigs, it was full of false noses, sequinned hairpieces and glitter. Lots and lots of glitter. He quickly pulled out three peroxide-blonde wigs.

'Three?'

'One for you, one for me, and one for Emmy.'

Emmy was the mannequin in front of his bedroom window, named after Kim Cattrall's character in *Mannequin*. He regularly changed her outfit, much to the bemusement of people passing by on the street. Last Christmas, he'd dressed Emmy up as a sexy Santa, with lights and fake snow on the windowpane, and one night there had been a whole crowd of people standing outside looking at her. ('It's like living in the Myer Christmas window,' Charlie had said.)

'How do you own this kind of stuff?' Suze asked him, as she held up a diamante bra.

'How do you *not* own this kind of stuff?' he replied. 'Honestly,

Suze. You've been pretty hopeless at having fun lately. Too busy moping around waiting for Lover Boy.'

His words stung. Waiting didn't automatically mean moping. 'Well, you can't talk. You've done your fair share of moping in the past. Dare I mention The Carlosses?'

'Ouch,' Charlie said, pretending to plunge a dagger into his heart. The Carlosses had actually been just one guy called Carlos who he'd met at a party where there'd been another Carlos. Charlie had given both his number and then, when one of them had rung him, he'd had no idea which Carlos it was. And so, the Carlos he spoke to for hours on the phone and then went out with for six months had become known as The Carlosses. 'Anyway, I'm over all that. No more Mope City for me. And no more Mope City for you.'

'Okay,' Suze replied. 'I'm on an express train to Fun City.'

'That's the spirit,' Charlie said, before adding: 'Speaking of which . . .'

He pulled a bottle of vodka out of his backpack. 'Let's get this party started.'

SOMEWHERE BETWEEN THE vodka bottle being opened and them arriving at the party, Charlie decided to wear his fake fur coat backwards like a hospital gown ('Courtney in rehab!' he said), and Suze's tiara lost half its jewels. As they approached the crowded terrace house – identifiable from three blocks away by the number of people dressed as superheroes gathered outside – Suze definitely knew she was drunk from the fact that her eyeballs felt like they were smeared with honey.

'I have Condiment Eyes!' she declared to Charlie, but he was too busy staring at the house.

'Why, it's the Mirror Twin of Moor Street,' he concluded.

And he was right. The terrace was exactly the same as their home, right down to the wrought-iron balustrade on the upstairs balcony, but with everything (front door, hallway, stairs) on the right rather than the left.

'My room is much tidier in this house,' Charlie said, poking his nose in the front bedroom, as they made their way down the hallway. 'But the Mirror Me has terrible taste in soft furnishings.'

'Hey . . .' said a guy in the room. He was wearing a red cap with 'Bubba Gump Shrimp Company' written on it with texta and was boring someone with his vinyl collection.

'Sorry, Mirror Me!' Charlie said with a cheery wave as he continued on into the heart of the party, Suze hot on his heels and laughing hard.

As they pushed their way out into the backyard (which was completely free of whitegoods, functioning or otherwise), Suze was still laughing so hard that she almost missed J on the makeshift dance floor under a Hills hoist covered in tinsel. It was the lining of the suitcase that she saw first. J was wearing it like a cape, edged with silver gaffer tape, and his gumboots had been spray-painted silver. Then Suze realised his face was connected to Ky's, her black hair flying everywhere. She appeared to have come dressed as herself.

'Let's go home,' Suze said.

'Why?' Charlie asked.

'It doesn't matter.'

'Yes, it does,' he replied, looking about frantically, trying to spot the thing that had upset her.

'*Please.*' It was her turn to tug on his clothing.

'Aha,' Charlie said as he spotted J pashing Ky on the dance floor. 'Looks like the cat's found himself a new owner.'

Suze went to leave, hoping to cry-run the whole way

home like she was in a movie, but Charlie grabbed her by both shoulders.

'One Courtney Love to another: you're better than him. You're better than that gothic Cousin It he's mashing his face into. Be strong and stay.'

Suze nodded and they moved back inside, away from the dancing, and onto a long red velvet couch with a guy dressed as Freddy Krueger sleeping at one end ('I hope he doesn't have any nightmares,' said Charlie, 'because then we'd all be in trouble'). They sat in silence for a few minutes, watching the party guests passing through.

'Oh god, there's a cry for help if ever I saw one,' Charlie said about a couple dressed as Prom Night Brenda and Dylan from *Beverly Hills, 90210*. As he commenced a running commentary on every single costume at the party, Suze tried to listen and laugh but her mind (and her heart) was back on the dance floor.

And then J walked into the house.

'Suze!' he said, with a nervous glance at the backyard, where Ky was no doubt waiting for him. 'How long have you been here? I didn't know you knew Doggie.'

'Doggie?'

'Sean's my friend,' Charlie spoke up. 'I invited Suze.'

Sean Doggett. The pieces of the puzzle fell in place.

'Oh, hi, Charlie,' J said. 'Didn't recognise you under that wig.'

'I didn't recognise you under that woman,' Charlie muttered, but J didn't hear him over the music.

'I'm just grabbing some beers,' J said, gesturing to the kitchen to his right. 'Can I get you one, Suze?'

Suze shook her head and J wandered off.

'Thanks for asking,' Charlie grumbled.

'As if you would have said yes.'

'Only because the beers are probably not his.'

A minute later, J passed them again, two beers in his hands, and gave them a slightly sheepish grin.

'I rest my case,' Charlie said, lifting up his slip dress and pulling out a hip flask tucked into the garter around his thigh.

'Charlie!'

'What? It felt very Courtney.'

He handed her the flask and she took a sip. It was cheap vodka, but it warmed the cold feeling in her chest.

A few sips later, she felt brave enough – or drunk enough – to go out to the backyard again. J was standing with some of the superheroes, still holding two beers, with no sign whatsoever of Ky.

'Suze!' he exclaimed, beckoning her over. 'I'm just telling these fellas about the postcards.'

The 'fellas' clearly weren't that interested in J, the postcards or Suze, and they took the opportunity to make their excuses and fade off into the rest of the party.

'Are you still sending them?' Suze asked. Her voice sounded strange, like it was a horse trying to bolt. She mentally pulled hard on the reins to try and control it.

'I actually sent the fifth one on the way to this party. I like it, Suze. It's like pissing in the dark. You don't know where it's landing.'

'But it *is* landing somewhere. And, moreover, it's landing on *someone.*'

'Whoever's getting them probably chucks them straight into the bin. Ky says it's the perfect (non)act of (un)art.'

'For something that's a (non)act, you're talking about it a lot,' Suze replied. She wasn't even bothering to disguise the fact that she was drunk now. 'Where's Ky, anyway?'

'She's around.' Even through the fog of alcohol, Suze

could tell he was pretending to be nonchalant, but really, he was looking around for her, like a lost puppy. 'She's probably disrupting a conversation inside. She's such a wildcard. I never know what she's going to do next.'

I never know what you're *going to do next*, Suze thought. But she must have said it out loud because J was now staring at her.

'What do you mean?'

'Nothing,' she replied, before adding: 'And everything.'

She grabbed one of the beers in his hand and took a big swig, the kind of swig where some of the beer missed her mouth altogether and dribbled down her front. But J hadn't noticed. He'd gone back to looking around for Ky.

'You used to drop by all the time,' she continued, 'but you've only come around once in the last four weeks.'

'Jeez, who's counting? I thought you and I were cool. That we didn't weigh each other down with expectations and stuff.'

'Yeah, I'm cool.'

Suze adjusted her blonde wig. Her head felt so itchy under it, but she kept thinking of how Charlie said she looked really hot. Maybe she had misunderstood. Maybe he had meant overheated.

But before she could prove to J exactly how cool she was, he finally spotted Ky standing on the other side of the yard, talking to a woman dressed as a cotton bud. Or at least that's what Suze thought she looked like.

'I'll be right back,' J said, but the tone in his voice said otherwise. As he walked over to Ky, Suze imagined him stretching his arms out and incanting the word 'brains' like a zombie in a B-grade movie.

Luckily, Charlie swooped in at that moment.

'Let's dance, Sister Courtney,' he said, pulling her onto the dance floor. Suze downed the rest of the beer and threw herself

into the music in the hope of escaping the conversation with J
and the whole situation with Ky.

Charlie was a great dancer. Suze completely trusted him as
he twirled her around and shimmied against her. A couple of
the 'fellas' stopped to watch, probably thinking two girls were
getting hot and heavy on the dance floor, and then one of them
realised Charlie was a man and they started batting the word
'poofta' about like a tennis ball.

Charlie gave them the finger and kept dancing.

'Don't worry, boys, you're not good-looking enough for
him,' Suze said, but it came out more like 'Donworryboyzna
goodlooknuffhim', and one of the guys made a cuckoo hand
gesture in reply and the whole group moved inside.

They continued dancing for a few more songs, but then
'Cotton-Eye Joe' came on and Suze found she had no energy
for a hoedown. She stumbled off to the side of the dance floor
and slumped in a garden chair while Charlie continued dancing.
As she watched him slap his own arse and yell 'Yee-haw', like
he was riding a horse, the full weight of the conversation with
J started to land on her. She had gone to the one place she'd
promised herself she wouldn't go and had revealed how much
his visits meant to her, which was a sure-fire way of ensuring
there would never be any more visits.

Ky led J back onto the dance floor to resume their pashing,
so Suze quickly relocated herself to the kitchen, where she
found a guy wearing antlers on his head pouring tequila shots.

'Oh, hello there, Courtney Love,' Antler Guy said. 'We're
playing lick, sip, suck.'

'Then I'm playing, too,' Suze replied. Antler Guy lined her
up with a shot of tequila and a wedge of lime, as another guy
took her other hand and sprinkled it with salt.

'On the count of three . . .' Antler Guy said. 'One, two, three.'

Suze licked the salt, threw back the shot and then shoved the lime in her mouth. For the briefest of moments, she thought she was going to vomit, but the moment passed and she felt like she'd just woken up from a long sleep.

Everyone else around the kitchen table was wincing. Antler Guy was jumping up and down on the spot. 'Now that's what I'm talking about!' he shouted.

Out of the corner of her eye, Suze could see J and Ky come into the house and make their way to the red velvet couch, where they deepened their exploration of each other's mouth. J was holding Ky's face and it hurt, hurt, hurt.

Suze turned back to Antler Guy.

'I wanna go again,' she said.

BACK IN THE yard, Antler Guy's eyes were kind and Suze noticed he had a dimple on one side when he smiled, which reminded her of a movie star, but she couldn't think of which one.

He stepped closer to her.

'Is it okay if I kiss you?' he said, but 'kiss' was pronounced *kish* and he was looking around her, not at her.

Suze shrugged and he stepped even closer, squishing his face against hers, but his mouth tasted wrong and made her want to vomit, and she couldn't breathe and she wanted to run and yet her mouth had taken on a life of its own, like the Baby Alive doll she'd owned as a kid, whose jaw just chewed and chewed and chewed.

Suze felt a tug on her wig. It was Charlie.

'Time to go home, Courtney,' he said.

'Okay, Courtney,' Suze replied.

'Nooooo, please don't take my Courtney away,' Antler Guy

said, but he was drunk and no longer able to stand without Suze acting as scaffolding. He sank down to the ground.

'Bye, bye, Antler Guy,' Suze said. 'Thanks for playing lick, sip, suck with me.'

'Is that what you call it?' Charlie muttered.

Suze held her breath as they passed through the lounge room. J and Ky were still on the couch but they were no longer kissing. J was lying his head on her lap and she was stroking his hair and that felt even worse to Suze than the kissing.

'I want my fucking postcards back,' she shouted at J, but really, she just wanted *him* back. She wanted him to feel like hers again, not a minion of this she-devil. 'Give me my fucking postcards.'

Charlie grabbed her hand and pulled her out of the house and onto the street. Everything fell away and Suze found herself sobbing inconsolably on Charlie's shoulder as he guided her towards home.

'We'll have to walk,' he said. 'No taxi driver in his right mind will pick us up. And I think the fresh air will do you good.'

'He says he hates *A Room with a View*,' she wailed. 'I thought he was my boyfriend.'

'Well, he can't be your boyfriend if he doesn't like *A Room with a View*.'

'I know! But I thought he was my boyfriend anyway.'

'He was never your boyfriend. He's a cat. He's a cat's arse.'

'He stole my fucking postcards.'

'Yes, yes, he's a bad cat's arse.'

'But I thought he was *my* bad cat's arse,' Suze said and began to laugh and then cry again and then laugh, the whole long walk home.

Chapter 11

SUZE WOKE WITH her head in a vice, and it took her a few moments to work out where she was or even what day it was. And then she remembered the party and J and Ky and the shouting and the crying, and she pulled the blankets over her head.

'How are you feeling?' Charlie said, coming into her room with a glass of aspirin. Just the sound of it fizzing made Suze feel sick.

'Terrible. Just terrible.'

'Regret, thy name is tequila,' he said, gently pulling the covers down and placing his hand on her head. The remnants of the previous night's make-up were still smeared on his face.

'I wasn't so bad,' she said, even though she knew she had been.

'I have two words for you, poppet,' Charlie replied. 'Antler. Guy.'

'Aaaarghhhh,' Suze said, pulling her covers over her head, before poking her head out to peer at him. 'In my defence, Antler Guy definitely wasn't so bad.'

'The clue is in the name, I think. Now take your medicine and I'll tell you the good news.'

Suze sat up and dutifully drank the aspirin, and then braced herself in case it – and everything she'd drunk last night – came straight back up. The moment passed and she lay back down.

'The good news is twofold. One: I did an inventory of our costumes this morning and we managed to come home with everything except the hip flask.'

Suze gagged again, thinking of that cheap vodka. She didn't think the hip flask was a great loss.

'And two: you no longer need to sit around moping in case Lover Boy – sorry, the Cat's Arse – comes around again.'

Suze started to groan, but Charlie placed his hand on her shoulder. 'I know you think this is a bad thing, but really, honey, it's a positive thing. It's like me and The Carlosses. You've given the Cat's Arse far too much power in your life, and it's time to take some of that back.'

He stood up. 'Now, we're going to clean ourselves up and we're going away from this house and out to lunch. My treat.'

After further instructions about make-up removal, showering order and departure time, Charlie left the room. Suze closed her eyes, but all she could see was J's confused and confronted face as he'd finally realised how super (un)cool and (not)chilled she was.

She dragged herself out of bed and considered her reflection in the mirror. If Charlie's make-up had been bad, hers was a horror show, and her short hair was standing on end like she'd been electrocuted. Basically, she looked as bad as she felt.

She cast a bleary eye around her room – it, too, was a manifestation of her internal turmoil, with piles of discarded clothing from last night's struggle to find something to wear to the party. She picked up some of the more ridiculous items and decided to start her own Case of Wonders to prove to Charlie that she was a dedicated citizen of Fun City.

She pulled down the suitcase from the top of her wardrobe and opened it. She traced her finger along the edge of the lining where J had crudely cut the silver fabric. *Just like he did to my heart,* she thought, somewhat over-dramatically, like she was Brooke Logan from *The Bold and the Beautiful.*

She was about to close the case when her finger hit the edge of something made of cardboard. Tucked in the corner of the remaining lining, separated from the set, was a single postcard from Edinburgh Castle. The castle sat high on a hill overlooking a garden with a fountain and lots of people wearing brown sitting in deckchairs on a crisp green lawn.

She turned it over and read:

My only one,

There are only two days left before the flight home. I've tried to enjoy this trip, but it's been impossible to enjoy life when the person who makes it worth living is so far away. I managed to buy some red ribbon from Harrods the other day and your stack of postcards is ready to give to you, along with my humbled heart. When I get back, everything will be different. We will find a way. I promise.

I am yours.

T

Suze looked at the address: Elizabeth Winston, 6 Salmon Street, West Footscray.

She thought of the red ribbon around the pile of postcards that J had. Did the mysterious T ever give Elizabeth the postcards or did he end up keeping them for himself? The cards were in pristine condition, like they had never been touched. Maybe he'd stashed them in the lining of the suitcase and forgotten that he'd ever written them. Or maybe Elizabeth had received them but never read them, or she'd only read them once before hiding them away forever.

Suze pinned the postcard on the cork board hanging over her desk. There were way too many possibilities to consider, especially for someone with an A-grade hangover.

AN HOUR AND a long shower later, Suze and Charlie were sitting in Babka's. Suze had ordered the blinis with her coffee but was still not feeling well enough to eat them. She pushed them around on her plate while she waited for the caffeine to kick in.

'You were crazy last night, Sister Courtney,' Charlie said. 'You kept shouting "Give me my fucking postcards!" What the hell was that all about?'

Suze sighed and then told Charlie all about the suitcase and the postcards and J and (un)art. At the point when she started explaining (un)art, Charlie held his hand up.

'I'm going to stop you there,' he said. 'I think the less I know about non-art, the better.'

Suze went to correct him, but then she closed her mouth and nodded. Charlie leaned back in his chair and, pressing his palms together, brought his fingertips to his lips, like he was considering a deep philosophical question.

'Hmmm,' he eventually said. 'In my humble opinion, the Cat's Arse will never give the "fucking postcards" back.'

'Well, certainly not now that I made such a big fuss about them.'

'Why *did* you make a fuss? Why do they mean so much to you?'

Suze shrugged and finished the last of her coffee. She looked out the cafe window at the people walking along Brunswick Street. They all looked happy and healthy and entirely unlikely to have spent the night drinking tequila shots with a guy wearing antlers.

She turned back to face Charlie only to find him looking at her expectantly.

'Okay,' she sighed. 'If I had to make a guess, it's that it really bugs me that J and Ky don't give a shit about who's receiving the postcards. They're so wrapped up in themselves and their un-ahh—' Charlie held up his hand again. 'I mean, the thing I can't mention, that they're not seeing the impact they're having on actual humans with actual lives.'

'Including yours, right?' Charlie said.

Suze went to shrug again but nodded and bowed her head. 'Yes, Dr Freud. Including mine.'

'He's not worth it, Suze. He's really not worth it.'

In her heart, Suze knew he was right. But her heart had been ensnared with J for so long now, it felt like it might not be able to beat without him.

BUT SUZE'S HEART did keep beating. It kept beating for another two weeks, maybe in the same way a chicken could still run around with its head chopped off.

Her supervisor was returning from sabbatical the next month, which meant she wouldn't be able to fly under the radar like she had with her interim supervisor, a tired-looking man with hair like white fairy floss, who spent most of his time drinking in University House with some professors from the Law faculty. Suze knew she needed to focus on her thesis. She knew that she should be in the Baillieu Library every day. But instead, she was at home, pretending that she was working and not waiting for the doorbell or the phone to ring.

She was pretending to read (and understand) an essay by Foucault when Charlie appeared at her bedroom door.

'The CA is on the phone,' he said. Even though this was what she'd been waiting for, it still took her a second to understand that Charlie was referring to J. 'Do you want me to tell him you're out?'

'No,' she said, tossing the unread essay aside. 'I want to talk to him.'

Charlie raised one eyebrow, but Suze pushed past him and went down the narrow stairs to the phone.

'Hello?'

'Hey, Suze.' His voice was like treacle, sticky and sweet in her ear. 'Sorry I haven't called you in ages. I've been, um, busy.'

'I bet you have.' Suze was surprised by the anger in her voice.

'And, well, I didn't exactly want to see you for a bit after Doggie's party. I mean, what the hell happened to you? Ky said you got a bit Glenn Close, and I had to agree.'

'I wouldn't have thought Ky had seen *Fatal Attraction*. I mean, it's a little lowbrow for her, don't you think?'

'Everyone's seen *Fatal Attraction*, Suze. And Ky enjoys movies as much as anyone. We went to see *Stargate* last night. You should see it. It was pretty good.'

'I thought we said we were seeing that together.' They hadn't exactly made firm plans, because J never made firm plans, but they had definitely talked about it at least twice.

'Did we? I don't remember that. Anyway, I didn't even know we were seeing it until we were actually seeing it. You see, Ky's really into film roulette. We go to a multiplex and buy a ticket to the next session but then walk into whatever cinema we feel like, no matter how far into the film it is. I actually missed the start of *Stargate*.'

'Well, maybe you can come and see the start with me,' Suze said, half-sarcastic, half-pouting.

'Jesus, Suze. Don't be sore with me. You can't *bags* seeing a film with someone. You're not ten years old.'

'No, I'm not ten years old. But I'm also not a toy you can pick up and put down whenever you feel like. If you can't respect me, then please don't ever contact me again.'

'Oh, man,' J replied. 'I thought you were chilled.'

Suze hung up and immediately felt a rush of triumph, followed by a chaser of utter regret. What had she done? Why couldn't she truly be 'chilled'? She wanted to ring J back immediately and apologise and promise to be chilled to the point of frozen, anything to make sure there was still a chance he'd visit her again.

Luckily, Charlie emerged from his room at that moment, slow clapping and stopping her from following that impulse.

'That was an impressive speech.'

The triumph returned, now tinged with rage. 'Yeah, fuck him and fuck Ky and fuck their (un)art and their half-movies and their hair stroking. I'm going to do some disruption of my own.'

And she marched up to her room and grabbed her coat and her bag and the postcard from the cork board and then marched downstairs.

'Where are you going?' Charlie was standing at the bottom of the staircase.

Suze held up the postcard. 'I'm delivering this to Elizabeth Winston at 6 Salmon Street, West Footscray.'

'That's on the other side of the Maribyrnong,' Charlie gasped. 'Do you want me to come with you?'

Suze quickly weighed up the pros and cons. Pros: he would probably wear something outrageous. Cons: he would probably wear something outrageous.

'I think this is something I need to do by myself,' she said.

Charlie held up one finger and quickly nipped into his room. 'For the trip,' he said, re-emerging with a copy of *Who Weekly*.

'How far away do you think West Footscray is?'

Charlie shrugged off the question and handed her a second gift: a packet of Juicy Fruit. 'For courage.'

Suze must have shown her confusion because Charlie quickly added, 'Whenever I chew gum, it makes me feel like a sassy character in an American film.'

Suze nodded and put both gifts in her bag, and, still clutching the postcard, she set off for the western suburbs.

Chapter 12

Thursday 1 June 1995, West Footscray

PHOEBE REACHED DOWN to pick up the postcards she'd dropped, and the girl helped her. Phoebe could smell the chewing gum on her breath and it made her feel queasy.

'Are you Elizabeth Winston?' the girl asked, once they were both upright.

'No,' Phoebe replied quickly. 'No, I'm not.'

'But you live here, right? At Number 6?'

'I do.'

The girl reached out to shake her hand. 'My name is Susan, but everyone calls me Suze.'

'Uh, I'm Phoebe Cotton,' Phoebe replied, giving her hand a firm shake. The girl, Susan, wasn't eating her gum in an obnoxious American-teen-in-the-movies way, but her jaw was moving quickly, like a small mouse.

'Phoebe Cotton? What a great name. Like a character in a book,' Susan said. 'You've been receiving the postcards, but?'

Phoebe nodded.

'And you've probably been wondering why?'

Phoebe nodded again.

'Look, do you mind if I come in to explain? It's kind of a long story . . .'

'Sure,' Phoebe replied, although she didn't feel sure at all. The postcards' arrival had been one thing, but cool girls dressed in black were another thing altogether.

Phoebe led the cool girl into the house, past the telephone table where the light on the answering machine was blinking furiously, and down to the kitchen.

'Would you like a glass of water?' she asked Susan. This was the first time she'd ever had a guest in the house and she wasn't quite sure what to do.

'I'd murder a cup of coffee,' Susan said, still chewing.

Great, thought Phoebe, her toes curling. *First gum and now coffee.*

But she duly put the kettle on and gestured for the girl to sit on one of the chairs at the kitchen table. While she waited for the water to boil, she busied herself by getting out the good coffee set and arranged everything beautifully on a silver tray. Even though this was a weird situation, it felt like it was the right thing to do – the thing that Dorothy herself would have done.

There were still some of Mrs Pap's biscuits left, so Phoebe laid those out, too, despite the risk of 'Puthhhh!' noises. *In for a penny, in for a pound*, she thought.

'Here you go,' Phoebe said, placing the tray carefully on the kitchen table in front of her guest and then laying out the tea coasters.

To Phoebe's immense relief, Susan removed her gum and wrapped it in a small bit of paper.

'Is there anywhere I can put this?' Susan asked, sheepishly. 'I don't normally chew gum, but it helped me with my nerves.'

Phoebe couldn't imagine her feeling nervous – she looked way too cool for that – but she held out her hand in the same way she did for kids in the library to hand over contraband, and she disposed of the gum on her behalf.

The whole gum episode behind them, Phoebe sat down opposite Susan.

'Would you like milk or sugar?' she asked.

'Milk, no sugar.'

They were like two little girls playing tea parties.

'So,' Phoebe said. 'The postcards.'

'Yes. The postcards,' Susan echoed and then launched into a long story about a suitcase and some guy called Jay and a woman called Ky, who sounded like a vampire, and some kind of art project that involved posting the postcards. None of it made much sense.

'It really bugged me that they were sending the cards out into the unknown without any real thought for who might be receiving them, you know?' Susan concluded. 'So I came to try to make amends and give you this postcard. I think this one is the last one that was written.'

Susan handed her a postcard from Edinburgh Castle. Phoebe flipped it over and read the message, while Susan lifted her teacup to her lips and took a careful sip. Not a hint of a slurp. Phoebe instantly felt herself relax.

'To be honest, Phoebe Cotton,' she said, putting her cup down, 'I was expecting to find an old lady whose love affair had been exhumed against her will. Is Elizabeth your grandmother?'

Phoebe shook her head. 'No, my grandmother is Dorothy.

She and my grandfather built this place after the war and, apart from my dad, and now me, they are the only people who have ever lived here. There's not a single Elizabeth in my entire family – at least as far as I know.'

The girl picked up one of Mrs Pap's biscuits and took a soft bite. In the hallway behind them, the phone started ringing.

After a few rings, the girl swallowed her mouthful of biscuit and asked, 'Shouldn't you get that?'

'No, it's fine,' Phoebe replied, hoping that it wasn't Sandy and that she wouldn't leave a message, not while someone else could hear it and know what a terrible friend she was being.

'Hi, Phoebe.' It was Sandy and she sounded defeated. 'I'm in Melbourne now, flying back on Sunday. I'm assuming from your silence that you don't want to see me? I guess so. Anyway. Maybe next time? Or not.'

'Ouch,' Susan said, and gave Phoebe a sheepish glance. 'Sorry, I didn't mean to eavesdrop, but she doesn't sound very happy with you.'

Phoebe shrugged.

Susan noticed she had got icing sugar all over herself.

'You can't take me anywhere,' she laughed. 'Do you mind if I shake myself off in the backyard?'

Phoebe nodded, showed her to the back door, and they both stepped out into the fading daylight.

'Nice garden,' Susan said after she'd brushed the icing sugar off her jacket. 'What kind of tree is that?'

'A mulberry tree,' Phoebe replied. 'It's the only one for miles and quite famous. My grandfather planted it after they built the house, and my grandmother spent decades trying to get mulberry stains out of her hands and clothing. She was like the Lady Macbeth of West Footscray.'

Susan laughed again. 'You're pretty funny, Phoebe Cotton.'

Phoebe had never thought of herself as funny, but she felt immensely proud of herself for being able to make this really cool-looking girl laugh.

'I love how it hangs like an umbrella,' Susan remarked, returning her attention to the tree.

'I used to pretend it was a house when I was little,' Phoebe admitted. 'When you're under its branches, it feels like nobody else in the world can see you.'

Phoebe could feel herself blushing as she talked. She hadn't shared this much with anyone in such a long time.

Luckily, Susan was too busy looking around the rest of the backyard, with the raised vegetable beds and the passionfruit plants and the weeds. Lots and lots of weeds. 'This garden has seen so much love,' she observed.

'Not recently,' Phoebe admitted.

'The love still shines through. *My* garden is mostly dead washing machines and concrete. Are you sure nobody else has lived here?'

'It's always been in the family,' Phoebe replied with a little shrug.

Susan shook her head. 'I guess we might have to accept that the postcards were simply misaddressed.'

'I guess,' Phoebe echoed. 'How many more did you say there were?'

'I don't really know. If I had to guess, I'd say there were about thirty in total. I think J plans to send the rest of them and then that will be that.'

'Well, at least I know it's not forever.'

'Nothing is forever. What will you do with them?'

'When they finally stop arriving, I'll take the whole lot to the post office to be destroyed.'

'You can't destroy them yourself?'

'It's a federal offence to destroy someone else's mail,' Phoebe replied. 'Or something along those lines. There's a form I have to fill in.'

Phoebe thought of Monty and his awkward way of moving, like a newborn foal, long-limbed and barely stable.

'It seems a shame to destroy them,' Susan said with a small sigh.

'But it feels creepy to keep them.'

'Fair enough.'

There was a brief silence, during which Phoebe was filled with a panic that if she didn't find anything interesting to say, Susan would go.

'Would you like some more coffee?' she asked, trying not to sound too desperate.

'No, I should probably head back. No offence, but I don't fancy waiting at that train station after dark.'

On the way to the front door, Susan peered curiously into the rooms as she passed them. At the lounge room, something must have caught her eye because she walked right in.

'Is this an original edition?' she asked, picking up the hardcover Georgette Heyer book from the coffee table where Phoebe had left it the night before.

'I don't think so. My grandmother left an entire bookshelf of her novels here and I can't stop reading them.'

'I've read them all at least three times. This is one of my favourites.' Susan gave the book a deep sniff. 'It smells so good.'

'I'm really enjoying it. Although, I loved *Cotillion* the best.'

'Ah, Freddy Standen. He's my ideal man.'

'I think he's probably mine, too.'

It was official. Phoebe had shared more with this girl in the last fifteen minutes than she had with anyone since Sandy went to Canberra. And now she was walking back out of her life as abruptly as she'd entered it.

Susan held out her hand again. 'It was nice to meet you, Phoebe Cotton.'

Phoebe extended hers. 'It was nice to meet you, too, Susan.'

'Suze. Please call me Suze.'

'It was nice to meet you, Suze.'

'Enjoy the rest of the postcards.'

'I will.'

Phoebe closed the door. She looked at the blinking light on the answering machine and thought of Sandy's message. She knew she couldn't ring her. It was for Sandy's own good, she told herself, even though she knew how much her silence would hurt Sandy's feelings. The reality was that Phoebe's Not Quite Right brain made her as bad at being a friend as she was at being a gardener. She didn't deserve people or plants, and she should probably live the rest of her life completely alone, surrounded by dead washing machines and concrete.

She stared at the closed front door. That girl Susan didn't know what a lucky escape she'd just made.

Chapter 13

THE OPEN MIC night at the Rainbow hadn't even started and Charlie was already complaining about it.

'How long will it go for?' he whined. He'd turned down an invitation to a foam party south of the river so he could hang out with his 'nearest and dearest' (which Suze had thought was another way of saying he couldn't be bothered crossing the Yarra), but he was obviously already regretting his decision.

'It says here "until late",' Sacha replied. She had been diligently studying the program since they'd arrived, turning it from one side to the other, with the colourful glass bangles on her arms delicately knocking against each other, like a human windchime.

'*Ohmygod*. Do we have to stay for the whole thing?' Charlie asked Suze.

Suze didn't respond, because she was too busy looking around for J. When she'd suggested to Charlie and Sacha that they go to the event, she hadn't mentioned that she knew J would be there, that he came every month. Sacha and Charlie would have dug their heels in and refused to come, and she needed both of them with her. She obviously couldn't go by herself – it would look too desperate – but even going with only one friend might have looked like she'd dragged them along to hide her desperation. But coming along with two made it plausible that they had dragged *her* there.

At the sight of J, she felt a jolt of electricity through her body. He was at the bar, buying two pints. She immediately started searching the room for Ky but couldn't see her anywhere.

When she returned her gaze to J, he was heading her way, the two pints sloshing about in his hands. As he neared the table, Suze pretended to laugh at something Charlie said.

'Why are you laughing?' he asked.

Suze just laughed again and then Charlie saw J and started laughing too. Sacha only frowned.

'Hey,' J said, when he got to the table.

'Hey yourself,' Suze said. She was trying to be as chilled as possible. She was Frosty the Fucking Snowman, that's who. 'How are things?'

'Cool,' J responded. He was looking around the room, as if already seeking an exit from the conversation.

'Is that pint for me, young Jonathan?' Charlie asked. 'Or are you double fisting it?'

'I'm double fisting it,' J replied. 'It will save me going to the bar later.' He gestured at the empty chair. 'Is it okay if I sit here for a while?'

'Sure,' Suze said, ignoring Sacha's and Charlie's raised eyebrows.

J sat down on the chair, but perched right on the edge, as if he might need to get up and leave at any moment. Sacha's frown had turned into deep fault lines across her forehead, like her whole skull was going to crack in two.

'I'm going to the bar,' Charlie suddenly announced, standing up. 'Want to come, Suze?'

'Nah, I'm okay.'

'Are you sure?' he asked pointedly. 'I'll buy you a drink.'

'You're too kind,' Suze replied breezily. 'I'll have a vodka and orange.'

'Me too,' Sacha piped up, still frowning.

'I can't possibly carry three drinks.'

'You can get a tray,' J suggested.

Charlie grimaced and then spun on his heels and made his way to the bar.

'How are the postcards going?' Suze asked J, after a short awkward silence.

J gave a world-weary sigh. 'Suze, you've got to stop asking me about it. It makes the act performative, which is the very thing I'm trying to avoid,' he said, like she'd been asking him about the postcards nonstop for the past four weeks instead of enduring a month-long radio silence. 'But since you ask, I'm about to send this little fella.'

He pulled a postcard out of his pocket and handed it to Suze.

'It's the fountain from *Roman Holiday*,' she exclaimed. 'If you throw a coin into the fountain with your back to the water, you're guaranteed to return to Rome one day.'

'What's the point if you're already in Rome?' J asked.

'I need to go to the toilet,' Sacha suddenly said. Apparently, it was now her turn to stand. The table was starting to feel like that game where the moles keep jumping up. She tucked her hair behind her ears – a sign that she meant business – and turned to Suze. 'You should come with me.'

'What is it about you girls needing to go to the bathroom in pairs? It's like you're boarding Noah's ark.'

Suze laughed at J's joke, ignoring the fact that Sacha had stiffened like a board and was now glaring at her.

'Well?' Sacha asked fiercely.

'I went before we left,' Suze replied, with a half-shrug, as she pretended to read the postcard in her hand.

Sacha walked off in a huff, not towards the toilet but to the bar, where Suze could see her immediately start ranting to Charlie, no doubt about how they needed to get Suze away from J.

J had started surveying the room again and Suze felt the panic rise in her chest. Either he was going to leave, or the others would come back, and that would be it. She put the postcard on the table between them and reached over to grip his arm.

'Listen, J, I'm sorry about the whole scene at Doggie's party and what I said on the phone. I was going through some stuff, and I want you to know it won't happen again,' she told him. She was glad that Charlie couldn't hear her capitulate so easily. It was hard enough hearing it herself.

'It's nothing,' J replied, extracting his arm from her grip to pick up one of his pints and take a sip. The word *nothing* was like a knife in Suze's heart. 'I've already completely forgotten about it.'

'Your drink.' Charlie and Sacha had arrived back at the table. Suze gratefully accepted her vodka and orange from Charlie and took a big gulp. She couldn't meet Charlie's eye, because she knew he'd see that she had just crumbled.

'Ah, so you're still sending the postcards?' Charlie said,

spotting the card on the table between them. 'Oh, sorry, I should be calling them by their proper name: the *fucking* postcards.'

Suze started to tell Charlie they weren't meant to ask about them when J overrode her: 'Fine. They're going fine.'

'Did Suze tell you she went to West Footscray to—'

Suze kicked Charlie under the table and at the very same moment a girl with long red hair and a nose stud appeared at the table and interrupted him.

'There you are,' she said to J. 'I thought you'd stood me up.'

'I've been here for ages and didn't see you come in,' J replied. 'Ah, everyone, this is Maeve. Maeve, this is . . . everyone.'

Maeve ignored the rest of the table. 'I've got a table over there with Fitzy and Simon,' she said, pointing to the other side of the room. Suze picked up the strong whiff of an Irish accent.

'Cool,' J said, standing up. He handed her the untouched pint. 'I got you this.'

The girl took the pint with a demure smile that made Suze want to knock the glass out of her hand.

J turned back to the table. 'There's a party at Binnsy's later on if you guys want to come.'

Even though he was addressing everyone, he was only looking at Suze.

'We're busy,' Sacha and Charlie said in unison, at the same time as Suze said, 'Sounds good.'

Now it was Charlie's turn to kick her under the table.

'Cool,' J said again. It wasn't clear which answer he thought was cool. 'See you at the party later, yeah?'

'Yeah,' Suze replied. She watched the two of them make their way through the crowded room, J's hand on the small of the girl's back. *Come back*, she wanted to shout.

'What the hell are you doing?' Sacha hissed the minute J was out of earshot.

'I don't know.' Suze hung her head. She really didn't know what she was doing. All she knew was that she was weak, weak, weak. She turned to Charlie. 'What the hell were *you* doing? Why did you start to tell him about West Footscray? I told you I didn't want him to know.'

There had been something nice about knowing that Phoebe Cotton was receiving the postcards and J and Ky not knowing, although they probably wouldn't even care.

'*I don't know*,' Charlie parroted back at her.

'You're such a child.'

'*You're* such a child.'

'Both of you stop it,' Sacha said sternly.

Luckily for everyone, the MC took the mic and the night began. The first act was an unkempt singer-songwriter obviously going through a bitter break-up.

'*She's a bitch, she's a bitch, she's a stupid fucking bitch*,' he sang, while strumming his out-of-tune guitar.

When the rest of the room clapped politely at the end of the song, Charlie grabbed Suze's wrist. 'One more act like this and we're out of here.'

Suze turned to Sacha, who nodded with great enthusiasm. Her heart sank. She knew that she couldn't go to Binnsy's party, not by herself, and she now knew that the only way to persuade Charlie and Sacha to go was if they got drunk enough, but they wouldn't get drunk enough if they didn't stay at the pub a little longer.

She looked over at J, who had his arm draped casually around the back of Maeve's chair. Maeve was leaning over to whisper something in his ear, probably something lyrical and Irish.

Suze gulped down the rest of her vodka and orange as the next act took the stage.

'Give it up for Laura and her special guest, Monsieur Poupé.'

As a woman took to the stage with a ventriloquist dummy holding a baguette, Charlie grabbed Suze's wrist again and she knew the night was over. But she also noticed that J had left the postcard behind on the table. She picked it up and slipped it in her bag.

BACK AT HOME, Charlie produced a bottle of Bundaberg rum that he'd won in a work raffle and half a bottle of Coke from the fridge.

'Desperate times make for desperate measures,' he said, pouring out the Bundy between three glasses. 'The puppet with the breadstick has already given me nightmares and I haven't even gone to sleep yet.'

'I'll have my Bundy straight. I won't poison myself with that brown stuff,' Sacha replied.

Suze wasn't sure if the Bundy was much healthier without the Coke, but she didn't say anything.

'To a night of art and culture,' she offered instead, holding up her drink.

The others joined the toast and they all drank. The liquid was sweet and syrupy and sightly nauseating, kind of like that Irish girl's accent.

'So what did you think of J's latest squeeze?' Charlie asked, as if reading her mind. 'I thought her nose stud was a bit *obvious*.'

Suze tried to shrug nonchalantly. She was still a little embarrassed by how quickly she had apologised to J, but Charlie didn't even know about that. Not yet. The problem with Charlie was that she ended up telling him all her secrets, even though he weaponised many of them. He'd argue he did it for her own good, but sometimes it didn't feel that way.

'I saw that you nicked one of J's "fucking postcards",' Charlie said, using air quotes.

'I didn't steal it. He left it behind,' she said, her ears hot, as she pulled the postcard out of her bag. Charlie didn't miss a single thing.

'Gotta love a "fucking postcard",' Sacha said. Ever since Charlie had filled her in on Suze's outburst at the party, whenever anything arrived in the mail, even the handknitted jumper from Charlie's godmother in London, Sacha and Charlie would find a way to make the reference. 'Go on. Read it out.'

'Yeah, make a real performance out of it to undo all that non-art bullshit,' Charlie said.

Suze took a swig of the drink that Charlie had just handed her and cleared her throat. The most performative thing she could think of in the moment was to sing it like an aria in an opera. So that's what she did.

My love,

   It's funny how I keep addressing these postcards even though I now know I have no intention of posting them. After a whistle-stop tour of Venice and Florence, we're now in Rome. Yesterday, we visited the Trevi Fountain, and as I tossed three coins into the water, I closed my eyes and thought of kissing you under the mulberry tree.

Suze stopped at the words 'mulberry tree'. What had Phoebe Cotton said? It was the only mulberry tree for miles.

'Is that it?' Charlie complained.

'I thought you said you had to throw one coin backwards,' Sacha argued.

'That was another film, and no, Charles, that's not it, there's more. It's just that . . .' Suze stared at the postcard hard. 'Sacha, can you please hand me the White Pages? I need to make a phone call.'

'You shouldn't be ringing anyone now. It's past the cut-off.'

'The cut-off is ten on a Saturday night,' Charlie said.

'The cut-off is nine,' Sacha argued back. 'No matter which day of the week it is.'

While they continued to argue, Suze quickly flipped to the 'C' section and scanned the Cottons until she found a Cotton, D at Salmon Street, West Footscray. She picked up the phone and dialled.

Chapter 14

PHOEBE HAD BEEN quietly pleased that Suze had called her and even more pleased they had made a coffee date for Saturday on Brunswick Street. After Suze's visit to Salmon Street, things had felt a bit anticlimactic. The postcards, as they had continued to arrive, had lost their spark of mystery. And when Monty had come to Story Time at the library with his niece and Phoebe had explained the whole '(un)art' project, he'd politely pretended to understand, but she could tell he felt a little let down, too.

Now that the case had been reopened, she fanned all the postcards she'd received out in front of her on the kitchen table. There were twelve in total. As she picked up each one, she now looked at them as individual pieces of a larger puzzle, and she felt connected to the world in a way that she hadn't felt for ages.

On Tuesday, she ventured to the post office during her lunch break, hoping Monty might be around. A short, smiling woman behind the counter, who Phoebe guessed was Monty's mother, told her that he was at home, studying for his exams.

'He's going to be a Master of Business,' she proudly told Phoebe.

'That's great,' Phoebe replied. 'Uh, well, thanks.'

She started to leave.

'No, no, no. I mean you can see him now,' the woman said, lifting the flap on the counter and ushering Phoebe through. 'Our home is upstairs. Just go out to the backyard and head up the staircase. Knock loud in case he's sleeping.'

Phoebe obediently followed the instructions, walking across a concrete backyard and up a metal staircase on the other side. She knocked as loudly as she could when she reached the top.

A minute or so later, Monty answered the door. He was wearing striped pyjama pants and a tie-dyed T-shirt that read 'I've been to Bali too'. His hair was standing up on end even more than usual, like he'd just been electrocuted.

'Hello?' he said. He was staring at her as if she wasn't quite real.

'Your mum said I could come up.'

'She probably wanted someone to check I wasn't sleeping.'

'And were you?'

'Of course not.' He seemed mildly outraged. 'I was eating breakfast.'

'It's almost two.'

'What can I say? It's all part of my study strategy.'

'And have you?' Phoebe asked, pointing at the T-shirt.

'Huh?' Monty glanced down at his front. 'Ah, no. I haven't been to Bali. My cousin got to go. This gift was his way of rubbing it in.'

They stood awkwardly, both looking at his shirt.

'Um, can I come in?' Phoebe eventually asked. 'I have an update about the postcards.'

'Of course,' Monty said, slapping his forehead. 'My mum always tells me I'm terrible at manners. Please come in.'

He ushered her into a living area filled with the kind of furniture you'd expect to see in Buckingham Palace – all ornate legs and over-fluffed cushions.

'Would you like a cup of tea?' he asked.

Phoebe shook her head, hoping to keep hot liquid out of the equation altogether. She was dismayed when Monty turned on the kettle anyway.

'So, why do I have the honour of a visit?' Monty gestured towards a chair that looked far too fancy to sit on. Phoebe awkwardly perched herself on the edge of its cushion, and while Monty made himself tea, she explained the phone call from Suze and the mulberry tree connection.

'Hmmm,' Monty said, finally sitting down with an exquisite cup and saucer with gilt edging and a pink rose pattern. As he held it up to his lips, Phoebe braced herself for the slurp she'd come to expect from boys her age, but she was relieved when he instead took a delicate sip.

'Nice cup,' she commented.

'My mum collects them,' Monty explained. 'Because she married an Englishman, she's spent her whole life preparing for the Queen to drop by for afternoon tea.' He put down the cup and stroked his chin thoughtfully. 'So we have to assume that the recipient – what was her name again? Elizabeth Winston?'

Phoebe nodded, impressed and slightly flattered that he'd remembered.

'So, yes, we have to assume that Elizabeth Winston must have lived in your house at some point.'

'Hmmm,' Phoebe said, scratching her head. 'The house has always been in my family, ever since it was built. But I'll check with my dad to see if an Elizabeth has ever stayed there long enough to receive mail.'

'The fact that she didn't actually live there might explain why the postcards were never given to her. You know, because she'd moved.'

'Well, we don't know if the suitcase belonged to the sender or the recipient,' Phoebe argued.

'Then why would the recipient hide them in a suitcase?'

'Because she moved or travelled somewhere and she wanted to take the postcards with her?'

'Perhaps. Or maybe she lost her suitcase on a flight. That happened to my cousin. Another cousin, not the Bali cousin.'

'Your cousins are well travelled.'

'You're telling me,' Monty replied. He seemed downcast about it.

Phoebe glanced at her watch. 'I've got to get back to work.'

'Can you please let me know what you find out?' Monty asked. He wrote his telephone number on the back of a scrap of paper.

'Sure,' Phoebe replied, secretly pleased she now had his number.

Downstairs, she couldn't find another way to get out of the concrete backyard, so she tentatively opened the back door of the post office.

'Come, come,' beckoned Monty's mother. 'There are no customers. Was he studying?'

'Very hard,' Phoebe replied.

Monty's mother smiled.

★

THAT EVENING, PHOEBE waited until dinner had been eaten and the 'Hallelujah Chorus' had been turned off before she raised the topic with her father.

'Dad, I was wondering . . . Did anyone else ever live in the Salmon Street house, other than you, Dorothy and Granddad?'

'Hmmm, let's see,' Phil said, leaning back in his chair. 'There were a series of boarders who stayed in the back room after I moved out. Mostly student nurses from the country doing placements at the Western General, but they were only there for a few months at a time.'

'Dorothy scared them away,' Ellen said.

Phil laughed. 'Truth was, she was much nicer to those nurses than she ever was to Dad and me.'

'True.'

'Was there anyone called Elizabeth?' Phoebe asked.

Phil scratched his head like he was trying to kickstart his memory. 'Not that I remember, but there were quite a few. I didn't meet them all because I was too busy wooing your mother.' He reached over and squeezed Ellen's hand like he was still wooing her, but Ellen didn't seem to notice. Her attention was now entirely on Phoebe.

'What's all this about?' she asked.

'The postcards.'

'I thought that girl's visit put an end to that mystery.'

Phil and Ellen had been amused by Phoebe's story of the strange girl in black and the even stranger (un)art project. All evening, Phil had gone around doing ordinary things like scraping the leftovers into the bin and hanging the tea towel on the oven rail and declaring his actions to be '(un)art'.

'So did I. But then that girl, Suze, rang on Saturday night and said one of the postcards mentioned the mulberry tree, so maybe they weren't misaddressed after all.'

'Interesting,' Phil said, stroking his chin. 'Did you know that some mulberry trees have both male and female flowers and can produce fruit without pollination?'

'Well, now I've heard everything,' Phoebe said.

'You should check with Dorothy,' Ellen suggested. 'You're overdue a visit.'

Phoebe grimaced.

'We can go together,' Phil said. 'There's safety in numbers.'

'Maybe,' Phoebe replied. She knew she didn't have the guts to go and see Dorothy, not with the garden in its current state. Dorothy would instantly know how little gardening she'd been doing from the lack of dirt underneath her fingernails and the missing sunburn on the back of her neck. 'Anyway, I'm meeting Suze on Saturday to talk about it. We're going to Brunswick Street.'

'That's nice,' Ellen said in a tone of voice that reminded Phoebe of *The Muppet Movie* lunchbox incident.

'Brunswick Street? La-di-dah!' Phil said. 'Next you'll be joining an art collective and wearing all black.'

'Don't you mean an (un)art collective?' Phoebe laughed. It felt good to be having dinner with her parents and to not feel like she was on the back foot. She could get used to this feeling.

Chapter 15

SUZE WAS LATE getting to the Black Cat because Sacha had taken ages in the bathroom. Phoebe was already there, reading a book, and Suze was relieved to see it wasn't one of those airport novels with huge gold letters on the cover, but then she immediately chastised herself for being such a snob, especially considering her enduring love of Regency-era romance.

'My housemate Charlie has a crush on one of the waiters here,' she told Phoebe after their order had been taken. Suze had initially ordered a long macchiato, but when Phoebe ordered a hot chocolate, she'd changed her mind and ordered a hot chocolate as well.

'One of my old housemates used to work here,' Phoebe said.

'Someone lived with you in Salmon Street?'

'No, no. I used to live in a share house in Collingwood. I didn't like it much.'

'There's so much politics around the dishes,' Suze agreed. Just that morning, Sacha had berated Charlie for not pulling his weight. She looked at Phoebe Cotton with her long brown hair and dark eyes and tried to imagine her in a share house. Phoebe's quiet and sincere concentration made Suze think she'd raised herself in that house in Salmon Street, that she'd always lived alone.

'So what's your story, Phoebe Cotton?' Suze leaned forward and rested her chin on her hands.

'There's not much to tell. I went to Sunshine High, then did Information Management at RMIT and have been working in various libraries ever since.'

'I'm not asking for your CV,' Suze laughed. 'I want the juice. Boyfriends? Girlfriends? Dramas?'

Suze saw Phoebe shift a little in her seat, and she worried that she might have gone too hard too quickly.

'Then there's even less to tell. No boyfriends. Or girlfriends. Or even pets – unless you count the garden, and we both know I'm not looking after that very well,' Phoebe said quietly, looking down at her hands. She then raised her chin and lobbed the question back at Suze. 'What about you? Are you going out with someone?'

'Nah. I'm too busy chasing unobtainable men to have a relationship.' Suze thought of J and Ky pashing at the party and how utterly obtainable he was for Ky, and she felt that constant knot in her stomach tighten even further. 'My latest is the guy who's been sending the postcards.'

'The (un)art guy?' Phoebe Cotton looked surprised.

'That's the one.' As she launched into a brief summary of her relationship with J (meeting in their second year of uni, kind-of-sort-of-maybe dating in third year, and then Suze's year of exile in Sydney), Suze experienced a little thrill at being able to talk about J without anyone rolling their eyes, like Charlie and Sacha always did.

The waiter arrived with their hot chocolates and Suze's heart leaped with delight at the sight of its foamy top, sprinkled with chocolate. She really should stop ordering drinks she didn't like just to make herself look cool.

'I actually got another postcard from your friend this week,' Phoebe said, pulling it out of her bag.

Suze looked at the card. This one was from Bath, showing an elderly man dressed in a stiff black suit and carrying a bright yellow basket, standing outside a store, maybe waiting for his wife. She held the postcard in her hands and imagined J sending it. Had Ky been with him? Or that Irish bint? She hadn't seen him since the open mic night. He hadn't rung. She hadn't rung either, but mostly because she'd made the mistake of confessing to Charlie about her apology to J, which had resulted in him locking the phone inside an old birdcage for a week, to which only he and Sacha knew the combination. ('For your own good,' Charlie had said sternly.)

Suze broke away from her thoughts to find Phoebe gazing at her expectantly. She realised she was supposed to read the postcard and not just look at the picture. She turned it over.

My dearest Elizabeth,

I dreamed last night that you and I were my real life and everything else — my marriage, my house, my family — was something from a novel or a bad film, something I could just walk away from and forget.

I wish this was true.

Yours, yearning for you and only you,

T

'So, T was married to someone else!' Suze said. Phoebe nodded. 'Did your dad know who Elizabeth was?'

'He said that my grandparents had student nurses boarding in their house in the late sixties. He couldn't remember an Elizabeth, but then he said he didn't meet all of them.'

'Are your grandparents still alive?'

'My grandmother is. She lives in a retirement village in Coburg.'

'So, the next obvious step is to visit your grandmother and ask her if there was an Elizabeth.'

'Um.' Phoebe ducked her head.

'What's the problem?'

'You don't understand. Dorothy is . . . Well, she's hard work.'

'You call her Dorothy?'

'She's not really a Granny or a Nanna or one of those grandmothers who bake and knit and love their grandchildren no matter what.' Phoebe paused and finished the last of her hot chocolate. Suze followed suit, thinking of her own grandmother in Port Macquarie with her soft cheeks and ready hugs. She felt sad for Phoebe Cotton.

'I could come too,' she suggested. 'Maybe a stranger being there will make your grandma behave herself.'

Phoebe didn't look convinced, but she nodded. 'Sure. Okay.'

They made plans to meet at the Western Retreat Retirement Village the following weekend and then went their separate ways – Phoebe on the tram towards the city and Suze back to Moor Street.

She found Charlie and Sacha sitting on the lounge-room floor in front of the bar heater with the Bundaberg rum and a fresh bottle of Coke between them. Charlie was wearing his favourite dressing gown, monogrammed with the name 'Reginald', and Sacha appeared to be dressed as a *Play School* presenter, with a striped T-shirt under a pair of purple velvet dungarees. Groovy Joe was sitting in his usual place under the window, eyeing them all with his trademark disdain.

'I thought you said Coke was poison,' Suze said, as she watched Sacha bring a glass of dark brown liquid to her lips.

'Quiet, Susan,' Charlie chided her. 'This is an emergency convening of the Order.'

Suze immediately shut her mouth and plopped herself down on the floor. The Order of the Wise Ones had met many times over the last few years to council Suze or Charlie about their love lives, but never to council Sacha. This must be serious.

'What's happening?' she asked.

'The worst thing,' Sacha replied. 'The very worst thing.'

There was something in her tone that suggested it really wasn't the worst thing, but Suze nodded nonetheless and prepared herself for the maybe–not-so worst.

But Sacha stood up instead. 'I'll get you a glass,' she said, going to the kitchen, a little unsteady on her feet. It would seem that the Order had been 'convening' for some time before Suze had arrived.

'I thought we had both been kicked out of the Order,' she whispered while Sacha was out of the room.

'She needs us,' Charlie whispered back.

'I need you!' Sacha exclaimed, appearing at the door with a glass.

'What happened? Did Matt . . .'

'Yes, Matt did.'

'Oh, I'm sorry.' Suze was sorry, but she was also surprised. Matt had seemed really into Sacha. 'Did he meet someone else?'

'What? He didn't meet anyone.'

'Then why did he break up with you?'

'He didn't break up with me. It's worse than that.' Sacha poured herself some Bundy into the empty glass and started drinking, obviously forgetting it had been meant for Suze.

'Matt told her that he loved her,' Charlie said solemnly.

Suze blinked. This was not the standard business of the Order.

'Oh,' she said.

'I mean, things were going so *welllllll.*' Sacha fell back so that she was lying on the floor. Her long hair fanned out around her like an angel. Or a drunk girl on the floor.

'The Carlosses once told me that he loved me,' Charlie reflected and then took a big swig of brown drink.

'No, he didn't,' Sacha said from the floor.

'Okay, he didn't. But he said he loved velvet trousers, and I was wearing a pair of velvet trousers at the time, so you know . . .'

'No, I don't know,' Sacha said, sitting up. 'Stop turning this into something about you. This is about *me.* And my *boyfriend.* Who *loves* me.' She fell back down again.

'Sacha,' Suze said, gently placing her hand on Sacha's leg. 'This is a good thing, right?'

Sacha closed her eyes and shook her head. 'No, no. It's a terrifying thing. He thinks he loves me, but he's made a mistake. There's nothing to love.'

Suze was surprised. She had never imagined that Sacha's aloofness was a form of self-protection.

'There's plenty to love.'

'Like what?'

'You're really good at dishes,' Charlie offered.

Suze slapped Charlie on the leg. 'What?' he asked. 'It's true.'

'There's much more to Sacha than her ability to wash dishes. For example, she's a really good friend. She looks after us. She stops us from making too many stupid mistakes.'

'True,' Charlie nodded. 'Just the other day, she stopped me from ringing The Carlosses by sitting on the phone.'

'You tried to ring The Carlosses? In *Brazil*?' Suze wasn't sure which was more shocking: the fact that Charlie wanted to talk to his arsehole ex-boyfriend after he'd dumped him so cruelly, or the fact he was calling Brazil. That would cost over a dollar per minute.

'Tish tosh,' Charlie said, waving his hand. 'It was just a passing moment of madness.'

'How are we back talking about The Carlosses? We should be talking about *meeeeeee*,' Sacha moaned.

Suze immediately returned her focus to Sacha, who had now wriggled around on the floor so that her head was lying in Suze's lap.

Suze began to stroke Sacha's head. 'You're also very funny,' she told her. 'You're a good cook and a good friend. You've got pretty princess hair and a great smile. You also have a great sense of personal style.'

'Except for that rainbow skirt with the bells on the hem.' Charlie shuddered.

'Not now, Charlie,' Suze hissed.

'But even that has its own charm.'

Suze gave Charlie a nod of approval and returned to stroking Sacha's hair. 'And Matt knows he is very lucky to have you.'

'Is he lucky?' Sacha looked up at Suze, eyes brimming with tears.

'He is. Very lucky.'

Charlie passed Suze his own glass of Bundy and Coke and Suze took a long sip. She'd earned both the drink and her place in the Order of the Wise Ones. For now.

Chapter 16

As THEY'D AGREED, Phoebe met Suze outside the Western Retreat Retirement Village the following weekend. She knew Suze's presence wouldn't soften Dorothy's behaviour one single jot, but still, she was glad for the company.

'This is quite nice,' Suze observed, as they walked through the immaculate gardens surrounding the nest of single-dwelling units. 'I thought old people's homes were meant to be depressing.'

'This isn't an old people's home.' Phoebe was quick to correct her. 'This is a retirement village, for people who have retired but can still look after themselves. They choose to live here together. So, whatever you do, don't call it an old people's home around Dorothy.'

'Roger that.'

They were now standing outside Dorothy's small unit and Phoebe's insides started to churn at the thought of having to interact with her grandmother.

'Are you alright? You look like you're going to be sick,' Suze observed.

'I'm fine,' Phoebe said. She did a mental check of the things she wanted to speak to her grandmother about and realised she'd left the stack of postcards back at home on the kitchen table. 'Oh no. I forgot the postcards.'

'We don't need them,' Suze coached her. 'We just need to establish whether or not an Elizabeth Winston ever lived at the address.'

Phoebe nodded and rang the doorbell. It was showtime.

It quickly became obvious that Phoebe was right to worry as Dorothy was in fine form. Within seconds of them entering her unit, she had remarked on Phoebe's need for a haircut and asked why Susan was wearing work boots.

'They're Doc Martens. They're fashionable,' Phoebe quickly explained on her friend's behalf.

'Personally, I prefer a simple court shoe on a young lady. Much more stylish,' Dorothy said. She herself was sporting her usual 'wall of beige' look, with her cardigan, dress, tights and orthopaedic shoes all nuanced variations of the one colour.

'I'm Susan, but you can call me Suze,' said Suze, extending a friendly hand.

'That's very nice. However, I shall be calling you Susan,' Dorothy replied, without accepting the hand. Suze put her hands behind her back. Phoebe thought she could see the hint of a smile on her lips.

The unit was small and very neat. Phoebe had been there many times, but never with somebody outside the family. She now looked at the living area with fresh eyes and was acutely aware of how un-grandmotherly the room was. There wasn't a single family photo or an angel ornament or a mug that said 'World's Best Nanna'. There wasn't even a photo of her husband or son. Instead, there was just a studio portrait photo of Dorothy when she was young, maybe as young as Phoebe was now, framed and hung on the wall above the TV. Her eyes were dewy with youth and promise, unlike the eyes of judgement and crankiness that were scrutinising Phoebe now.

'Well, aren't you going to sit down? The tea will have stewed at this rate.'

Dorothy had already laid out the tea things.

'Should I pour?' Phoebe asked.

'Don't be ridiculous, Phoebe. I'm old but I'm not infirm.' Dorothy carefully poured out the tea. 'Help yourself to lemon, sugar or milk,' she told Suze, as she added a single slice of lemon to her own cup and then took a small sip. While Dorothy was reluctantly respectful of Phoebe's noise sensitivities and never slurped her tea, she also liked to make a big point of the fact that she hadn't slurped her tea, as if it had majorly inconvenienced her. Ellen once referred to Dorothy's behaviour as 'malevolent tolerance'.

Meanwhile, Suze took neither lemon, sugar or milk and left her cup untouched. Phoebe hoped Dorothy wouldn't notice, but of course Dorothy *did* notice.

'Is there a problem with your tea, Susan?' she asked. There was something about her voice that suggested a cobra about to strike.

'No, no, not at all,' Suze said, bringing her cup to her lips. Phoebe automatically braced herself for a slurp, but quickly realised that Suze was only pretending to take a sip.

Luckily for her new friend, Dorothy turned her focus to quizzing Phoebe about the garden.

'Mrs Pap said that the hydrangeas were out of control.'

'In her opinion.'

'I trust her opinion when it comes to my garden.'

'It's a beautiful garden,' Suze piped up. 'You can tell it's seen a lot of love.'

'It's seen a lot of hard work,' Dorothy was quick to reply, but Phoebe could tell she was pleased by the compliment because her face had softened slightly. 'But I suppose that is a form of love. To be frank, I was glad to give it up. It was playing havoc with my knees and back.'

Phoebe wished she really had given it up rather than delegating all the hard, back-breaking work to her instead.

'Goodness, I forgot to put out the biscuits,' Dorothy said, getting up and walking over to the kitchen. 'Don't worry about crunching, Phoebe. They're the soft kind.'

Phoebe blushed and quickly glanced over at Suze to see her reaction, but Suze was too busy quickly tipping her cup of tea into a nearby pot plant while Dorothy was out of the room. She noticed Phoebe watching her and held a finger up to her lips. Phoebe nodded.

Dorothy returned to the table with a plate of shortbread biscuits.

'Would you like some more tea, Susan?' she asked.

'Uh—'

Suze seemed to be floundering, so Phoebe quickly changed the subject.

'Dad said you and Granddad had a few boarders living with you in the late sixties,' she said.

'That is correct,' Dorothy replied, settling back into her chair, the offer of tea forgotten. 'The back room was empty after Philip moved out, so renting it out gave us some extra money as well as someone to look after the garden when we were away. Although it should be said that some were better than others when it came to the garden.'

Phoebe instinctively folded her hands so that her dirt-free fingernails were hidden.

'Did you ever have someone by the name of Elizabeth?' she asked.

Dorothy's face instantly closed up like a drawstring purse. 'No,' she said, and then, 'Yes. There was an Elizabeth, but she was generally known as Libby.'

'Was her surname Winston?'

'Why do you ask?'

There was an extra sharpness to her tone, which for Dorothy meant her words could now probably cut through diamond. Phoebe faltered and Suze jumped in.

'Phoebe has been receiving mail for an Elizabeth Winston at your old address,' she said.

'Why on earth would anyone be sending mail to Libby Winston? She lived there thirty years ago and only for a short time.'

'Do you know where she is now?' Suze pushed on.

'How in heaven's name would I know? She was just a tenant.' Dorothy stood up. 'It's ridiculous that anyone would be sending her anything at that address. You should throw it all away. Now, if you will please excuse me, I need to get ready for my aqua aerobics class.'

Their visit was over. Phoebe wasn't sure if she should feel frustrated or relieved or completely broken. Or all three.

Outside, Phoebe and Suze walked towards the tram stop.

'Hoo-wee!' Suze exhaled. 'Your grandmother's hard work.'

'You're telling me. What was wrong with your tea?'

'I can't stand the stuff. It tastes like dirty sock water.'

'I'm glad you didn't tell Dorothy that. She might have

blown a head gasket. She once said that tea is the nexus of civilisation.'

'Noted for next time. *If* there is a next time.'

Phoebe ardently hoped there would be.

'Still,' Suze continued. 'At least we now have confirmation that the postcards weren't misaddressed. But we're not really any closer to finding Elizabeth Winston.'

'No, we're not.'

'Here's my tram,' Susan said. 'I'll give you a call later in the week.'

Phoebe was left feeling a little disappointed. She'd thought they might go and get another hot chocolate together. She'd really enjoyed the last time. It had been ages since anyone had asked her about her life, other than her mum, but that was more an interrogation than a conversation.

At least there's a phone call to look forward to, she thought as she watched the tram disappear down the road.

ON HER WAY home from the train station, Phoebe dropped by her parents' house. Her mother was sitting on a fold-out chair in the front yard, drinking a cup of tea, while her father dug a trench.

'She's getting me to dig my own grave,' Phil joked as he paused to lean on his shovel and wipe his forehead in an exaggerated way.

'Would you like a cup of tea?' Ellen asked.

Phoebe shook her head and sat down on the front porch step, near her mother. 'I just had some at Dorothy's place.'

'At last,' Ellen said.

'You went without me?' Phil looked disappointed.

'Sorry, I went with my new friend Suze.'

'That's nice,' her mother said, once again in that *Muppet Movie* lunchbox voice.

'So did Dorothy know your mysterious Elizabeth?' Phil asked.

'She said there had been a Libby Winston, also known as Elizabeth.'

Phil slapped his forehead. 'Ah, yes. Libby. Ellen, you remember Libby?'

'She was the one who came for Christmas, right?'

'That's right! The others always went back home for Christmas, but she stayed around. I reckon she was there for a year or so.'

'A year? Dorothy said she was only there for a short time.' Phoebe scratched her head.

'When you're as old as Dorothy, a year is a short time,' Ellen quipped and then sipped her tea, like it was a reward for her joke.

'Do you remember where she went after Salmon Street, Dad?'

'Oh look, not really. She might have gone back to Ballarat. Or Bendigo. One of the "B" towns where she was originally from.'

'And do you remember her having a boyfriend? Someone whose name started with T?' Phoebe was starting to really feel like a police detective. She should be writing all this down so she could type it up in a report for Suze, and maybe even for Monty.

'Nope,' Phil replied. 'Ellen?'

'Don't look at me. I was too busy being nervous around your mother.'

Phoebe struggled to imagine her mother being nervous about anything, but then she thought of Dorothy's face when she mentioned Elizabeth Winston's name and it suddenly was quite easy.

Her cup of tea now finished, Ellen got up from the deckchair. 'I might get dinner on. Are you staying?'

Phoebe shook her head.

'I've got plans,' she replied. It wasn't strictly a lie. She'd planned to get takeaway Chinese food and watch back-to-back episodes of *Twin Peaks* on VHS.

'Is it with that new friend of yours?' Ellen asked.

Phoebe gave a small smile and shrugged. She hoped her mother would read it as a 'yes' without her actually having to lie. The trick must've worked because Ellen returned the smile and retreated into the house, clearly satisfied that her daughter wasn't a complete loser.

Phil returned to his digging and Phoebe watched him for a while. Her father was tall and thin and took up virtually no space. She wondered if growing up in Salmon Street with Dorothy had forced him to grow like that, like a climbing plant seeking the sun.

'I've been thinking,' Phil said suddenly, putting down his shovel again. 'There was some drama around Libby Winston leaving Salmon Street suddenly.'

'What happened?' Phoebe felt a surge of excitement.

'I can't really remember. I'm not sure I even knew at the time.'

'Was there a fight? Did she steal something? Was she on the run as a double agent?'

Phil laughed. 'Sorry, kid. I really can't remember. All my memories have lost their colour, like they're soaked in sepia. Did you know that a sepia is a fish?'

'Well, now I've heard everything,' Phoebe said. But she had a feeling that there was a lot more for her to hear when it came to Libby Winston.

Chapter 17

INSTEAD OF HEADING to the Baillieu Library to study like she was supposed to, Suze faffed about at home for most of the morning and then decided to brave the cold weather and head into the local library to look up Libby Winston in the Ballarat and Bendigo phone books.

Phoebe had rung the night before and told her about what her father had said, and the two of them had talked for ages, theorising about what might have happened to make Libby Winston return to Ballarat or Bendigo so suddenly. Phoebe thought it might have been a pregnancy. Suze thought it might have been textbook heartbreak, or a sickly relative. God knows she knew enough about both of those things.

As she approached Fitzroy Library, she was acutely aware of a number of facts. Fact one: it was J's birthday. Fact two:

every year for the last four years, he'd had birthday drinks at the Napier from lunchtime until closing. Fact three: the Napier was just down the road from the Fitzroy Library. She was trying to pretend to herself it was all a big coincidence, but she wasn't doing a very good job.

The library was full of elderly men and mothers with small children, none of whom were there to look at the White Pages, so she found herself alone in that section. As she copied down all the numbers for the E Winstons and the L Winstons in both Greater Bendigo and Greater Ballarat, she thought about how it was far more satisfying than any of the photocopying or highlighting she'd done at the Baillieu recently.

That job done, she took a vacant spot at a desk along one of the exposed bluestone walls and started copying quotes from those highlighted photocopies into her notebook, another tried and trusted Claytons study technique. After a couple of hours, her hand started to cramp, so she took a break and stepped outside to get some fresh air, despite the drizzle. It was the kind of weather that her stepfather Greg would have referred to as 'the sky on fine-mist setting'.

As she paused to button up her coat, a man entering the library collided with her. It was Daniel Parker, a guy who'd been in one of her third-year English tutorials. He'd asked her to the pub at least four times that year, and even though she'd enjoyed his company well enough, she had been too obsessed with J to ever take him up on the offer.

'How the hell are you?' Daniel asked her. He was tall and spindly, like a human praying mantis, but he had kind eyes behind his heavy-framed glasses.

'Oh, you know,' Suze replied. 'I spent a year back in Sydney leveraging my Arts degree as a waitress and then I came back to do Honours.'

She left out the part about her stepfather dying and her mother being unable to get out of bed for three months.

'That's unusual. You either stay in academia forever or you get the hell out. Nobody ever goes back,' Daniel said.

Suze gave a little shrug. 'I march to the beat of my own drum. How about you?'

'I'm only partway through my life sentence. I just converted my Master's into a PhD at Monash.'

'Wow. That's hardcore. Are you still living on Rathdowne Street?'

'No, I'm in exile out in Clayton. I'm actually meeting some friends on Brunswick Street, but I got in too early so was going to hide in the library for a bit.'

'Yeah, I'm hiding in here too, but in plain sight from myself.'

'Shall we hide together, then? Or better still, wanna grab that drink you've always denied me?'

Suze went to say no, but then she thought about J's birthday drinks just up the road. She imagined him walking in and seeing her there with another guy and finally realising she was The One.

'Sure,' she said. 'How about the Napier?'

As she packed up her papers and notebooks, she was filled with self-loathing and guilt but quickly managed to talk herself around. This was a drink with an old friend in the closest pub! Which just happened to be the pub where J was having his birthday drinks! What a coincidence, (etc).

Daniel was waiting for her at the door. She turned and smiled at him as they stepped out of the library.

'Let's do this,' she said.

★

THE FRONT BAR of the Napier was fairly quiet, just a few old blokes nursing pots of lager. Suze checked her watch. It was only a little after three o'clock. Perhaps the birthday drinks hadn't started yet.

She and Daniel nabbed one of the tables near the door. With every person who stepped into the pub, her pulse raced. This wasn't good for her health. It was also making it very hard for her to concentrate on what Daniel was telling her about his PhD topic, which had something to do with Foucault, systems of thought and post–post-structuralism.

It was only when J's friend Tufty came in wearing his customary Viking horns and headed straight through to the back room that Suze realised the birthday drinks were already underway.

She excused herself, telling Daniel she needed to use the bathroom, and soon found J surrounded by adoring friends at a large table out the back. There was a small pile of badly wrapped gifts in front of him, plus a tray full of shots. Thankfully, neither Ky nor the redheaded Maeve were anywhere to be seen.

'Suze!' J exclaimed with a surprising amount of enthusiasm considering he hadn't bothered to phone her for over a month and she hadn't even been invited today.

'Happy birthday,' she said, blowing him a kiss across the table. 'Sorry, I haven't brought you anything.'

J waved magnanimously at the pile of presents in front of him. 'As you can see, I've been given quite enough already. You've actually arrived just in time to watch me unwrap them all.'

Suze took a spare seat, and someone passed her one of the shot glasses. She sniffed it. Vodka.

'Let me see,' J was saying as he surveyed his gifts. He picked one up – a very CD-shaped present. 'I wonder what this is!'

As he started to tear off the paper, Suze sipped her vodka and worried about Daniel back in the front bar.

'Engelbert Humperdinck's *A Lovely Way to Spend the Evening*,' J said, holding the unwrapped CD up like a trophy. 'Jonesy. You really shouldn't have.'

Suze was fairly certain that everyone at the table agreed that Jonesy really shouldn't have either.

J handed the CD to the girl next to him. Suze became instantly aware of how close she was sitting to him, like she was trying to graft her body onto his left side.

'Let me look,' said the girl, taking the CD from him. 'Oooh, I love "The More I See You".'

'I love the more I see you, too,' J said, with an obvious wink.

Ugh, thought Suze. She downed her vodka and stood up. It was high time she went back to Daniel.

'I'm going to the bar,' she said, her eyes sweeping the table. Nobody had a particularly empty glass, so she added, 'Anybody want anything?'

To her relief, everybody shook their head, and she went back to the bar, her own head held high.

Daniel was reading *Beat* magazine.

'There you are,' he said. 'Did you know there's a band called Menstrual Accident? They're playing the Punters Club on the weekend.'

'Sorry I took so long,' she said as she returned to her seat. 'I got caught up out the back. There's a bunch of people there for Jonathan Wakeman's birthday.'

'That guy? I always thought he was a bit of a dick.'

Suze's face must have betrayed her.

'Sorry, is he a friend of yours?'

'We were kind of seeing each other for a while, but not anymore.'

'*Kind of* seeing each other? How does that work?' Daniel asked, one eyebrow slightly raised.

Fuelled by the vodka and the beer in her system, Suze launched into the whole story, giving far more detail than the breezy top-level summary she'd given Phoebe Cotton the other day, and ending with the whole birthday drinks tradition at the Napier. Daniel's face was so kind while he listened, her guilt became too much for her.

'So you see, I kind of used you,' she said. 'Actually, there's no "kind of" about it.'

'Nah, don't worry about it,' he said. 'I don't mind. I was only looking for a way to pass the time.'

'But you should mind,' Suze told him. 'I really like you, just not in that way.'

'Ha!' he said, leaning back in his chair.

'What?' Suze asked.

'I don't like you in that way either. I'm gay. Sorry, didn't you know?'

Suze almost slapped her forehead with the revelation.

'Charlie's always telling me my gaydar is faulty,' Suze said. 'Can I buy you a drink to make up for it?'

'Nah, I've got to go meet my friends at the Peel,' he said, looking at his watch. 'It's been nice seeing you, Suze.'

He paused and then put his hand on her shoulder. 'I know you're not asking my advice, but I don't think that guy' – he gestured his thumb towards the back room – 'is worth your time.'

'I know, I know,' Suze replied, even though there was still a part of her that really didn't know it at all.

Daniel leaned over and kissed her on the cheek. 'Good luck with your thesis.'

'Good luck with your PhD,' she replied. She watched him

leave and then she picked up the copy of *Beat* and pretended to read it while she finished her lukewarm pint. All the while, she staged an internal debate. On one side, she wanted to go back to the birthday drinks. On the other, she didn't want to see that girl cosying up to J.

She thought of Daniel's words and the fact that J probably hadn't even noticed she hadn't come back, and she decided to leave. She would go to the Co-op and see if Sacha was working so she could sneak out the back to make some STD calls to the Winstons of western regional Victoria. Yes, that's what she would do.

She tried to walk with purpose even though there was the usual pull in her chest as she walked up to Smith Street, away from J and the Napier. *I'm strong*, she told herself, although she didn't feel strong at all. But maybe if she said it enough, it would come true.

Chapter 18

THE ANSWERING MACHINE light was doing its disco dance when Phoebe walked into the house, the latest postcard in her hand. It was another one from Paris, showing a gargoyle overlooking the city, the Eiffel Tower in the far distance. She, Phoebe, was the gargoyle. Libby Winston was the Eiffel Tower.

She pressed the play button on the machine, hoping it was Suze, and was happy to hear that it was.

'I rang the E and L Winstons,' Suze said. 'And none of them were called Libby or Elizabeth. Did you even know Elbert was a name? I didn't. But then I had an idea and I think I've found her, Phoebe Cotton. Give me a call.'

Instead of phoning back immediately, Phoebe decided to eat dinner first and call Suze back later, as a kind of treat. Dessert, even. There was some lasagne her mum had given her in the freezer, but she couldn't be bothered waiting for it to heat up. So, she made her usual salad of chopped ham, lettuce, cherry tomatoes and grated cheese, with a side of potato chips. She cracked open a Diet Coke and ate it all in the living room in front of *Sale of the Century*, her feet on the coffee table and without using any of the coasters. Dorothy would have an embolism if she could see her, and instead of making Phoebe feel anxious or fearful, the thought made her feel rebellious. She felt brave.

After she'd finished her meal, she returned Suze's call but got Charlie, Suze's terrifying housemate, whose every word seemed to be dipped in arsenic. Whenever she called, he pretended like it was the first time, asking her to spell out her surname as he wrote down the message. Suze said it was just his way of joking with her, but there didn't seem to be anything funny about it.

'She's currently indisposed. Will you hold?' Charlie said.

'Yes, I'll hold,' Phoebe replied.

Charlie hummed 'The Girl from Ipanema' while Phoebe waited. This time, she actually got the joke and found herself smiling. Maybe Suze was right about Charlie.

Then she could hear Suze in the background and Charlie saying it was Phoebe Rotten on the phone and Suze laughing and saying, 'Be kind to my friends.'

Phoebe felt a little cut by Charlie's joke, but then simultaneously healed by the fact that Suze had referred to her as a friend.

'Phoebe Rotten makes me sound like I'm in a punk band,' she said when Suze picked up the phone.

'Don't mind him. He's just bitter and twisted because his name is Charles Bartlett-Myers, which makes him sound like a stuck-up school prefect and not the heroine of an adventure novel like Phoebe Cotton. How was your day at work?'

Phoebe took great delight in telling Suze about Des Rollerson wearing shorts and long socks in the middle of winter and Glenda finding all the books on sexually transmitted diseases stacked neatly in one of the cubicles in the women's toilets. As she talked and Suze reacted in all the right places, Phoebe got this strong feeling that she and Suze were actually becoming friends. She hadn't had a real friend since Sandy, and the thought delighted her and panicked her both at once.

'How was *your* day?' she asked.

'I revolutionised my regular study-avoidance technique by introducing highlighter pens. I've assigned different colours to each theme of my Honours thesis so I can mark the margins of my photocopies accordingly. It looks very pretty.'

Phoebe laughed. 'Perhaps we can introduce your different coloured highlighters into our investigation.'

'Speaking of which . . .' Suze launched into the story of her unsuccessful calls to the various Winstons in the Greater Ballarat and Bendigo areas, including a charming conversation with Elbert Winston.

'Elbert was a sweetheart, obviously starved for conversation. I was on the phone for at least twenty minutes, listening to him talk about his gout and his rude neighbour, Mr Howie or somebody. They've been having a decade-long feud about the hedge that separates their property and Mr Howie had a section of it cut into the shape of a cock and balls!'

'Mr Howie!' Phoebe exclaimed in mock outrage.

'Of course, Elbert didn't call it "cock and balls". He was too much of a gentleman. He called them "male bits and pieces", like they were parts of a board game. Anyway, I stayed on the line but nothing else Mr Howie did was as exciting after that. However, I did learn a lot about conveyancing.'

Phoebe laughed, but there was a small part of her that wondered if she was destined to become like Elbert and live alone forever in this house, arguing with various neighbours about her care of the bougainvillea (or the hydrangeas) and whether the side gate was securely fastened.

'But your message said you'd found Libby Winston,' she said, pulling the conversation back to the postcards.

'Okay, so while I was racking up the phone bill at Sacha's work, I rang the regional hospitals and discovered that there is a Libby Winston working in cardiology in Ballarat. It has to be her. Well, it might be her.'

'It might not be her at all.'

'Time will tell. I left a message.'

'What did you say?'

'Just that I was trying to get in contact about a previous residential address and that she should call me immediately.'

'And has she called?'

'No.'

'Well, the message might not be welcome. You know, because of the pregnancy.'

'Or the broken heart and/or sudden family illness,' Suze interjected.

'Of course. And/or the international spy ring.'

'And/or the sizeable drug debt and the hit placed on her by the Mafia. But look, if she *does* ring back, I'll keep the story simple. I'll leave out all the (un)art stuff and just tell her that we've found a bunch of postcards addressed to her.'

'Sounds like a good plan,' Phoebe said. Maybe she should put Suze in charge of the garden, her mother and grandmother, and her career.

★

THE FOLLOWING DAY, Phoebe saw Monty hanging around the library entrance just before closing time. He was standing in front of the rack of community flyers, picking each one up and reading them.

As she approached, she saw he was looking at a pamphlet titled 'You and Your Prostate'.

'I was in the area and thought I'd drop by to see what was happening with the postcards,' he said, hastily returning the pamphlet to the rack. 'Also, to become better acquainted with my prostate, apparently.'

Phoebe laughed. 'We're closing up, but you can wait for me outside if you like. I'll be about fifteen minutes.'

Monty nodded solemnly and stepped outside the library.

Phoebe turned around to see Glenda watching her from behind the information desk. Phoebe braced herself for some reprimand, but Glenda just returned her attention to the reservations list.

Once Phoebe had finished up for the day, she found Monty sitting on a bench opposite the library, waiting patiently, his back straight and his hands folded neatly in his lap. *This is a good person*, Phoebe thought.

The minute Monty saw her, he jumped up and crossed the street.

'Hello,' he said.

'Greetings,' she replied, and then regretted it immediately. She sounded like a character from a *Star Trek* episode.

'Do you want to grab something to eat? We could talk over some pho or something.'

Phoebe immediately panicked. This was why she hadn't been on a date in ages; they always took place over food and that made her tense.

'I had a late lunch,' she lied. She was actually starving. 'Maybe we could just walk.'

The days were finally starting to get longer again, and there was still a little bit light in the sky.

'Sure,' said Monty.

'Is it okay if we start walking in the direction of my house?' Phoebe asked.

'Sure,' said Monty again, with that wide, warm smile of his.

As they headed off down Paisley Street, Phoebe filled him in on Libby Winston and her sudden Salmon Street departure and the telephone message Suze had left at Ballarat Base Hospital.

'Sounds like I should hand over my deerstalker hat to you,' he remarked, clearly impressed.

'Deerstalker?'

'Sherlock Holmes's hat,' he explained.

'Oh no, you should probably give it to Suze. She's the one doing most of the detective work.'

'What's she like?'

Phoebe thought of Suze in her cool outfits and her pixie cut and her clear blue eyes and felt a small flutter of panic, deep inside her chest. What if Monty met Suze and realised what a non-event Phoebe herself was?

'She's your typical Arts student, I guess.'

'Hey, don't forget my minor in Modern History,' he said. 'I was an Arts student too. Well, part of me was.'

'I didn't mean that in a bad way. She's pretty cool, actually.'

'Well, she's a good detective, worthy of joining our squad.'

'We're a squad now?'

'Yeah, we're a squad. Although, I'm not sure I'm a full member,' he said, shyly. 'You haven't called me.'

'Yeah, sorry. I've been busy,' she lied. She'd spent so much time staring at his telephone number, pinned to the fridge with a sunflower magnet, that she now knew it off by heart.

Embarrassed, she stopped and pretended to look in the window of the shop they were passing.

'Are you interested in buying an urn?' Monty asked, and Phoebe realised they were standing outside a funeral parlour.

'Death comes to us all,' she said, and Monty laughed.

'You're pretty funny, Phoebe Cotton,' he said.

Phoebe felt pleased. There was something about Monty that made her a wittier version of herself. Together, they became like a couple from one of those old movies, swapping wisecracks while being deeply and desperately attracted to each other.

She glanced sideways at Monty and wondered if there was any chance he might be even moderately attracted to her. He was busy staring at the urns on display, his brow creased. She noticed he had a beauty spot on his right cheek, like Robert de Niro. He was actually quite handsome, and she felt another flutter in her chest. This was a different form of panic. This was the stirrings of something else. Maybe love.

They started walking again. Ahead of them in the west, the sun was performing its nightly swansong, all oranges and pinks fading into indigo. Phoebe shivered at the beauty of it all.

'Are you cold?' Monty asked, concerned. 'Here, have my scarf.'

He wrapped his scarf around her neck. A woollen hug.

As they walked, they found themselves talking about many other things: Monty's Master's course, Phoebe's work, growing up in Footscray, movies they had seen.

Eventually, they had talked and walked for so long, they'd reached 6 Salmon Street, just as the sun had completed its retreat, with only the thinnest line of burnt orange along the horizon.

'So, this is your house,' Monty said.

'It's actually my grandmother's house, but she's in a retirement village now.'

'Then it *is* your house,' he said. 'Squatters' rights and all that.'

'Squatters' rights?'

'If a person is living in and taking care of an abandoned or neglected property, they can claim legal ownership.'

Phoebe smiled, imagining that Dorothy would argue that Phoebe, herself, was doing the abandoning and neglecting.

'Maybe we can go see a movie some time,' Monty blurted out, completely taking Phoebe by surprise.

Phoebe immediately thought of all the times she'd had to slump down in her cinema seat, her fingers stuck in her ears because someone with a bucket of popcorn had sat right behind her. Popcorn always had a way of seeking her out.

'I never really go to the cinema,' she said, and then mentally kicked herself for effectively turning down his offer.

'Well, maybe you should go with me,' Monty suggested shyly, to Phoebe's intense relief.

'Maybe.'

Phoebe realised that Monty might be waiting for her to invite him into the house, and then she remembered the dishes still left on the coffee table after her evening of rebellion.

But Monty just looked at his watch. 'I've got to get back home. My cousin got engaged and we've got to drop by my aunty's to talk about the ring.'

'Your "I've been to Bali" cousin or your lost suitcase cousin?' Phoebe asked and then instantly regretted it. She'd read an article in *Cosmo* that said women should pretend they're not paying attention if they want a guy to be interested in them. Or something like that.

To her relief, Monty looked impressed.

'Neither. Another one altogether,' Monty said. 'But seriously, your recall is amazing. I should hire you as my personal assistant to keep track of my cousins.'

'I'm the only child of two only children, so that means I have no cousins of my own. But it also means I'm really good with other people's cousins.'

'Seriously? You have no cousins? I don't know if that's a bad thing or a good thing.'

'It's just a thing.' Phoebe shrugged.

'Well, if you ever need to talk to someone about it, you've got my number . . .'

Phoebe's face must have shown her confusion, because he quickly added: 'Which is just a clumsy way of saying, "Give me a call."'

'Okay,' Phoebe replied. 'I will.'

But later, when she found herself standing in front of the fridge, staring at his number, she wondered if she would. Or if she even could.

Chapter 19

SUZE HAD LEFT two more messages at Ballarat Base Hospital, but there had still been no return call from Libby Winston.

'Maybe she hasn't got the messages?' Phoebe suggested as she stirred her hot chocolate in the Black Cat. It was the third Saturday in a row that Suze had met up with her. ('Mark my words, you'll be married before the spring,' Charlie had said.)

'Maybe. Or maybe the reason she left Salmon Street in a great hurry is the same reason she isn't returning my call.'

'What do you mean?' Phoebe asked, leaning in closer.

'It turns out that Jo on the hospital switchboard is quite the gossip. She told me Libby isn't married, doesn't have any kids. So that puts the pregnancy theory to bed.'

'Unless she had an abortion.'

'True. Okay, so pregnancy gets back out of bed. Personally, I'm guessing she's not returning my call for the same reason she left Melbourne in such a hurry: a broken heart.'

'Still?'

'Have you ever had your heart broken?'

'No,' Phoebe admitted. 'I don't think I've ever been in love.'

'Really?' Suze asked, leaning back in her chair to observe her friend. 'I fall in love all the time, and my heart has been broken into a thousand pieces at least five times. Maybe six.'

She counted on her fingers: Sam, Alfonse, Darren, Garry and now J. Although she wasn't sure if she should count J yet. It still felt like there was some hope after he'd rung her late on his birthday, drunkenly telling her how much he'd missed her 'vibe'. He ended the call by saying he might drop by soon. But he hadn't. And Suze was doing her very best not to hang around the house, hoping that he might, but it was much harder than she could admit to anyone, even to herself.

'Four,' she concluded. She wouldn't include J yet.

'Wow,' said Phoebe, her eyes wide. 'I'm amazed you're still standing.'

'My mum left my dad when I was twelve to be with her childhood sweetheart,' Suze told her. 'I guess I learned very early on that love was something you went after.'

'Are they still together?'

'He died last year from bowel cancer. But they had over ten happy years together.'

'And your dad?'

'He remarried within a year. A woman called Deirdre, but she pronounces it Deir-*drah*,' Suze replied. 'They live on the Gold Coast with their two sons, Patton and Sylvester.'

Suze hadn't spoken to her father in over a year. They hadn't been close even when they were living in the same house.

She often thought of her father as an alien being who had never quite committed to his life posing as a human.

'What about your parents?' she asked Phoebe.

'They're pretty boring. Still together. Still happily married, I guess. Mum bosses Dad around, but he seems to like it. He always tells me that he works best under instruction.'

'Are they here in Melbourne?'

'They live ten minutes' walk from Salmon Street. I eat dinner with them every Tuesday night.'

'That sounds kind of nice,' Suze said. 'Like something from a sitcom.'

'I guess . . .' Phoebe didn't look convinced. 'So, what's our next step with the postcards?'

'Well, I've had an idea. If the mountain won't come to Mohammed, Mohammed must go to the mountain.'

Phoebe looked at her blankly.

'We go to Ballarat Base Hospital. I can get my new best friend Jo to tell me when Libby's working, and we can wait for her and then hand the postcards to her in person.'

'Like a subpoena? *You've been served?* Why don't we just post them to her?'

'And miss our only chance to find out the real story behind these postcards? Are you kidding?' Being able to tell the whole story to J and Ky would blow any remaining bullshit about (un)art completely out of the water.

Suze continued, 'So, basically what we need to do here is go on a road trip. Do you have a car?'

'No, I don't even have a licence.'

'Neither do I.' Suze laughed and the two of them high-fived.

'I know someone who has both and who might be willing to drive us,' Phoebe remarked. 'I can ask him.'

'Him?'

Phoebe blushed. 'That guy, Monty, I told you about.'

Suze resisted the urge to tease Phoebe. She sensed that Phoebe even suggesting asking Monty to join them was a big step for her, and Suze didn't want to get in the way.

'Sounds good,' she said.

After they'd finished their hot chocolates, Phoebe seemed eager to order another one, but Suze knew she couldn't afford it. Also, the longer she was away from Moor Street, the more chance there was that she'd miss J if he dropped by. Neither of these were things that she wanted to admit to her new friend, so she invited Phoebe back to her house instead.

As they walked, Phoebe asked how long she'd been living in Moor Street and Suze explained that she'd moved in at the end of her second year of uni but had sublet her room to a guy called Chester the year she'd been up in Sydney looking after her mum. Chester, it had turned out, was a high-functioning heroin addict who'd stolen money and blank cheques from Charlie, but not Sacha, because she was far too scary.

'Basically, anything I do short of murdering my housemates in their sleep can't be as bad as Chester. So I'm set for life.'

'But murdering them while they're awake is okay?' Phoebe asked and Suze laughed.

As they approached the dilapidated terrace house, Suze suddenly felt self-conscious. Would Phoebe Cotton see it as charmingly 'shabby chic' (as Charlie once described it)? Or would she, like Suze, suspect it was only one council notice away from utter demolition? The fact that Emmy was currently dressed in a biohazard suit was definitely a strong case for the prosecution.

Phoebe paused to look at Emmy, obviously confused.

'Charlie,' Suze offered. It was the only explanation needed.

As she opened the door, Groovy Joe shot out like an orange

bullet. Suze guessed someone had forgotten to leave the back window open for him during the day.

Phoebe almost jumped out of her skin. 'What was that?'

'That was Groovy Joe. He acts like he owns the place, but he's not even on the lease.'

As they walked down the corridor, Suze was struck by the usual smell of coffee, incense and faint mildew, and she felt embarrassed. But she needn't have worried.

'This place is cool,' Phoebe said, looking at the milk crate chairs topped with op shop cushions.

Suze prayed to god that she wouldn't glance up and see the peeling paint on the ceiling or notice the fridge in the corner of the living room.

'It's cheap for Fitzroy,' she said. 'Let me show you my room.'

Upstairs, the first thing Phoebe seemed to notice was the suitcase on top of the wardrobe.

'Is that it? Is that Libby Winston's suitcase?'

'It's the suitcase that the postcards were in, yes.' Suze still wasn't sure if it was Libby's suitcase, although she was starting to think that Libby *had* been given the postcards but had somehow lost the suitcase or even given it away.

'Is it okay if I take a closer look at it?' Phoebe asked shyly.

'Of course!' Suze pulled it down and put it on the bed.

As Phoebe opened it, Suze briefly imagined a gold light shining on her face like that scene in *Pulp Fiction*.

'What happened to the lining?' Phoebe asked.

'J happened to the lining.'

'It's a shame.'

'You're telling me.'

'What will you do with it?'

'I had this fantasy of storing my collection of scarves and satin gloves in it, but I haven't started collecting them yet.'

'You're still young,' Phoebe remarked, and Suze laughed again.

But then she had a thought. 'Do *you* want the suitcase?'

'Oh no, I . . . It's yours. You found it.' Phoebe shut the case and carefully closed the clasps.

'Well, if you change your mind . . .'

Phoebe gave her a small smile and walked over to the window. 'I love what you've done with the garden.'

Suze joined her and together they looked down at the white-goods graveyard. She tried to recall how long it had been since J had stayed over and they'd lain on the grass together in the autumn sunshine, drinking Matt's beer. That was the day she'd found the suitcase. If she hadn't bought it, she wouldn't have ended up lugging it home full of his stuff, and things might have gone differently that weekend, and he might have stayed another night. But if she hadn't bought the suitcase, Phoebe Cotton wouldn't be here in her room now. What was that thing her stepfather used to say? *Swings and roundabouts.*

Suddenly, Suze didn't want Phoebe to go, leaving her to pathetically hang about, hoping that J would come by.

'Do you want to stay for lunch?' she asked.

She could see that Phoebe was tempted by the idea, but not sold, so she tried to make the sale. 'Sacha brought home some organic soba noodles and miso paste and I was thinking of attempting some kind of soup.'

It was quite possible that Phoebe had guessed what a terrible cook Suze was, because the smile on her face completely dropped away.

'I mean, I know I'm not exactly a cordon bleu cook. But if I make it hot enough, we can just slurp it down without actually tasting how bad it is,' she offered, in a last-ditch attempt to make Phoebe stay.

'I can't,' Phoebe said, her voice brittle and her jaw tight, and for the first time, Suze saw a resemblance between Phoebe and her grandmother. 'Maybe another time. But thanks for showing me your house.'

'You're very welcome,' Suze replied, trying to hide her disappointment.

And as she led Phoebe to the front door, she felt like she must have offended her new friend in some way, but she couldn't for the life of her think how.

Chapter 20

THE TRIP TO Ballarat provided the excuse Phoebe had been looking for to call Monty, and she'd been relieved when he jumped at the idea.

'A road trip on the Western Highway isn't exactly the stuff of Arthur Conan Doyle,' he had said over the phone. 'But I'll take whatever adventure I can get.'

And now, here they were, in Monty's mum's car, hurtling past Melton, Suze in the back, stretching her long legs across the spare seat.

If Phoebe'd had any trepidation about introducing the cool and stylish Suze to Monty, she quickly discovered there'd been no need to worry. They were polite and friendly to each other but both were far more interested in speaking to Phoebe. Suze had brought a '50s jacket that she didn't wear anymore to give to Phoebe, and Monty had gifted her a badge that said 'Kiss me! I'm a librarian!' that he'd found at a car boot sale.

Phoebe had immediately taken off her sensible wool coat with the shoulder pads 'you could land a Boeing-747 on' (according to Suze) and put on her new jacket, pinning Monty's badge to the fake fur collar. Now sitting in the front seat of the Camry, she felt glamorous and liked – and also a little excited about the message on Monty's badge. Perhaps it was a roundabout way of telling her he'd like to kiss her?

Suze led the conversation for most of the car trip, introducing topics such as 'your favourite subject at school' and 'your first album purchase'. Suze's first album had been by Siouxsie and the Banshees, which made Phoebe feel completely square, but then she'd felt a little frisson when she discovered that she and Monty had both bought (and loved) *1982 with a Bullet*, although it hadn't been Monty's first album. His had been the more disappointing *In the Bag* where none of the songs had been performed by the original artists.

As they entered the outskirts of Ballarat, the car fell silent.

'My sources tell me that Libby's shift ends at three,' Suze said after a while and something deep inside Phoebe tightened. She couldn't tell if it was because she was anxious about how Libby Winston might feel being confronted by her past, or about the fact that this might be the end of the postcard mystery and she'd no longer have a reason to see Suze or Monty.

'We have about twenty minutes,' said Monty, with a quick glance at his black Swatch. 'We can either park the car and head straight to the cardiology ward. Or we can hoon up and down Sturt Street, like Ballarat locals.'

Phoebe laughed at the thought of Monty driving like a hoon. He was such a careful driver, even more careful than her father, whose hands had never once strayed from the ten and two position, and who'd reportedly said, 'I can't drive faster than my guardian angel can fly' on the day Phoebe was born, while Ellen had been labouring intensely in the back seat.

'I guess your idea of hooning is not checking your rearview mirror before turning your indicator on?' she joked.

'Or hand-over-hand instead of push–pull steering,' Suze joined in.

'Hey now, don't bite the hand-over-hands that drove you here,' Monty said, but he was laughing.

He parallel-parked the car in one graceful sweep on a side street, outside a long red brick building with cream trimming and a tower at one end. Phoebe wasn't sure which was more impressive: Monty's parking or the fact that Ballarat Base Hospital appeared to have an actual turret.

'Why haven't either of you got your licence?' Monty asked, as he turned the engine off.

'Oh, I've tried,' Suze replied. 'I've failed the test three times. Just trying to work up the courage and the cash to try again.'

'What about you?' Monty asked, turning to look directly at Phoebe. She noticed how dark his eyes were and felt a jolt of warmth through her body.

'I just lost interest,' she said, quickly turning her focus to undoing her seatbelt.

'In learning or driving?'

'In learning, I guess.'

She didn't explain how the driving instructor had made loud snapping noises with his gum that had almost caused her to crash the car.

'Well, personally, I *like* knowing someone else who doesn't drive,' Suze said. 'We get to feel morally superior in this petrol-guzzling world of ours.'

'Says the girl who just cadged a ride to Ballarat,' Monty remarked.

'Thank you for driving,' Phoebe said, reaching over to touch Monty's arm in reassurance. 'We're very grateful.'

'It's as much for me as it is for you both,' Monty said easily. 'I want to know about these postcards too. Speaking of which . . .'

He opened the driver door and stepped out of the car. Phoebe turned to look at Suze in the back seat.

'Do you think I upset him?' Suze whispered.

'No,' Phoebe whispered back. 'I don't think so.'

Phoebe got out of the car and walked over to where Monty was standing by the red brick wall.

'Do you think I upset her?' he asked in a low voice. 'I was only making a joke and it came out much pointier than I meant it to.'

'No,' Phoebe shook her head. 'I don't think so.'

'I hope not. I want her to like me because she's . . .'

'She's what?' Phoebe's mind was racing at a hundred miles per hour. *She's the most beautiful girl I've ever met? She's much nicer than you? She's my soulmate?* She held her breath.

'Because she's your friend.'

His voice trailed off as Suze joined them on the pavement.

'Libby Winston awaits!' Suze said. 'Let's go!'

Phoebe found she was still holding her breath and she exhaled.

THE THREE OF them found the cardiology ward, thanks to the intel from Jo at Reception.

'We're here to meet Libby Winston,' Suze told the nurse behind the counter.

142

'You actually just passed her. That's her now, waiting at the lifts.'

The three of them, like one person, all turned to look in the direction that the nurse was pointing and they began to walk hurriedly towards the lifts.

'Excuse me,' Phoebe said, but her voice came out small, like a cartoon mouse.

'Excuse me!' Monty echoed, his voice louder and deeper, but still not reaching the woman who was stepping into a lift, beyond the reach of her pursuers.

'Libby Winston!' Suze shouted, her voice the loudest and most forceful of them all.

Libby Winston turned to face them, with a bright smile. She was around Phoebe's parents' age, maybe a few years older, with her short hair turning silver around her temples. She had one of those faces that was as open as an invitation, exuding kindness and understanding. Phoebe could imagine strangers choosing to sit next to her on long bus journeys just so they could tell their life story and/or spill their deepest darkest secrets.

'Yes?' she said in a cheery, professional voice. 'How can I help you?'

Phoebe opened her mouth and then closed it again, suddenly acutely aware of how awkward the situation was.

Monty stepped in. 'Is there somewhere private we can speak to you for a moment? We won't take up much of your time.'

'Sure,' Libby replied, ushering them into an empty patient room, like there was nothing awkward or unusual about this situation at all. Maybe this kind of thing happened to her all the time. 'But I have to warn you: I've got to be in Clunes in half an hour, so we'll need to keep it short.'

Suze went to sit on the bed, but Libby stopped her. 'Sorry,' she said, holding up her hand. 'Someone just made that. As my mother always said, "Be mindful of the work you leave other people."'

The three of them nodded, one person again. Phoebe noticed how smooth the blankets and sheets were on the bed and how neatly they were folded over the mattress. With Libby in her hospital uniform, Phoebe imagined that if anyone burst into the room at that moment, they would think this a typical tableau of a doctor delivering the worst news to a family, the empty bed behind them.

'So?' Libby was staring at each of them in turn, obviously wondering who was going to talk.

Phoebe stepped up to the plate. 'My name is Phoebe and I live in West Footscray. On Salmon Street. Where you used to board.'

Libby Winston's eyes widened. 'Salmon Street?'

Phoebe took that as a sign to continue. 'We, um, found some postcards addressed to you,' she said. 'And we wanted to return them to you.'

'Postcards?'

'Yes, postcards.' Phoebe pulled the small pile out of her backpack and handed them to Libby.

As Libby read the first one, her face resembled an Etch-a-Sketch being shaken: suddenly there were all the feelings and then there were absolutely none. She sat down on the very bed she'd just stopped Suze from sitting on and continued to look through the postcards.

Phoebe raised her eyebrows in surprise and quickly glanced at Suze and Monty. They were all in silent agreement: this was the first time Libby Winston had ever seen these postcards. T had never given them to her.

'Where did you find these?' All of her bright professionalism was gone, and her voice was now soft and low.

'Um,' Phoebe said, suddenly wondering whether she should launch into the whole (un)art project story after all, in the interests of full disclosure, but Suze stepped in first.

'We found them in the lining of a suitcase,' she told Libby. 'There are a few more, but someone else has them.'

'And how long have you all been living at Salmon Street?'

'It's just me who lives there,' Phoebe explained. 'It's my grandparents' place. I've known the house my whole life, but I've only been living there for the last year or so.'

'You're Edward and Dorothy's granddaughter?' Libby asked.

Phoebe nodded.

'Ah,' she said, with a long, soft sigh. 'I should have known from your eyes.' She smiled slightly. A small smile, like a secret she had with herself. 'How are they both?'

'Granddad passed away about fifteen years ago and Dorothy is living in a retirement village.'

'Oh,' Libby said with the kind of sigh that felt like a feather floating slowly to the ground. 'I'm so sorry to hear that.'

She returned her attention to the postcards in her hands.

'I have to go,' she said, mostly to the postcards. And then she stood up suddenly, like someone pulling themselves out of a very deep and complicated dream before it had finished. She went to give the postcards to Phoebe, but Phoebe put her hands behind her back.

'They're yours.'

'Thank you,' Libby said, and then held up the cards. 'You said there are more?'

'I think there's about thirty in total,' Suze offered, but Libby ignored her, eyes locked on Phoebe.

'Do you think I could get the rest?' she asked Phoebe.

'I think so. It just might take some time to get them all.'

Imbi Neeme

Phoebe definitely knew this wasn't the time to start talking about (un)art.

'Here. I'll give you my number.' Libby pulled a pen and notebook out of her bag and wrote down a telephone number, carefully ripping the page out for Phoebe. She passed the pen and notebook over. 'Can I have your number too?'

'Sure,' said Phoebe.

'So, you're living in Salmon Street now?' Libby asked, as Phoebe wrote her name and phone number down.

'I'm looking after the place while the family decides what to do with it. Dorothy wants to sell it, but my dad is too attached to it, just not enough to live in it.'

'Ah, yes. I remember that garden.' Libby's face lit up, like she'd just recalled a precious memory. 'Although, I have to admit it was a beast to look after. I think I murdered the hydrangea when your grandparents were away on one of their trips.'

Phoebe smiled. 'You'll be glad to know it's still alive,' she said. 'Despite my worst efforts.'

Libby gave her one last, long look and then said, 'It was nice to meet you, Phoebe. Call me when you have the rest of the postcards.'

And then she left, without even a sideways glance at Suze and Monty.

The three of them stood frozen in her wake.

'Well,' said Phoebe.

'Well,' said Monty and Suze in unison.

Phoebe went over to the bed and tried to smooth the wrinkled sheet where Libby Winston had just sat, but she couldn't return it to its previous pristine state.

★

146

IN THE CAR, the conversation quickly turned to Libby Winston's reaction to the postcards.

'Did you see her face when she heard your grandfather had died?' Suze said.

'I felt bad that she had to hear it from a bunch of meddling kids,' Monty remarked.

'Meddling kids? Have we moved from Conan Doyle to Scooby-Doo?' Phoebe was quick to observe.

'Holmes and Watson were strictly a two-person partnership. Mystery Incorporated means there's room for all of us. Plus, we have the opportunity to expand, depending on the mystery.'

'Bags being Velma,' Phoebe said. Velma definitely grew up to be a librarian.

'Bags being Shaggy,' Suze said. Phoebe was surprised. She thought of Suze as being more like Daphne. But bagsing Shaggy was actually pretty cool.

'I'd like to say I was Fred, but I think I'm probably Scooby,' Monty admitted, as he pulled the car into a petrol station.

As she watched him walk around the car to the petrol bowser, Phoebe found herself thinking how wonderful it would be to hug him.

Instead, she wound down the car window.

'Here,' she said, waving her purse at him. 'Let me give you some petrol money.'

'Yes,' echoed Suze from the back seat. 'We should totally give you some petrol money.'

'I wouldn't dream of it,' Monty said with a little wave of his hand. 'You are my guests.'

As they watched him go inside the station to pay, Suze leaned forward and said in a whisper, even though she didn't need to whisper, 'To be honest, that's a relief. I didn't have any money to give him.'

Phoebe felt sad for her friend, but she was also glad Suze had confided in her in that moment. She knew Suze was proud when it came to money, always trying to pay her own way and do her bit. But she also knew Suze was broke. Even though her librarian wage wasn't exactly competitive, at least Phoebe didn't have to count her coins to work out if she could afford another hot chocolate as she'd seen Suze do once or twice.

'Oh, thank god,' Suze muttered. 'I'm starving.'

To Phoebe's dismay, Monty was walking back to the car with a huge packet of chips, some lolly snakes and a packet of bubble gum held aloft, like they were trophies he'd just won.

'I got us some Scooby Snacks!' he exclaimed as he climbed back into the car. He pulled open the chips packet with a flourish and held it out to Phoebe. 'Want one?'

Phoebe shook her head, hoping her quiet refusal might make the others think they didn't want any either. But instead of putting the chips away, Monty offered them to Suze in the back seat, who took a huge handful.

'Zoinks!' she said, and then started eating the chips one at a time, crunching loudly.

'Scooby-Dooby-Doo!' Monty exclaimed, taking his own handful and shoving them in his mouth, causing Phoebe's whole body to clench like a fist.

As soon as Monty started the engine, she switched on the radio, desperately wanting to drown the eating sounds out, but her brain couldn't let go of the sounds, wouldn't let go of the sounds, and she couldn't concentrate on anything that anyone was saying anymore. The song 'Creep' came on the radio and she immediately cranked up the volume, focusing all her attention on the lyrics, wanting to lose herself in the music. But the chips bag kept being passed between the front seat and the back seat and the crunching continued, mouthful after endless mouthful – the bag was as bottomless as the Magic Pudding – making Phoebe's body grow tighter and tighter, and her brain feel more and more like an overwound clock. When the song finished, Monty turned down the volume and he and Suze continued to chatter, while Phoebe remained silent, unable to find a way back to them or their conversation.

And she realised that she was the creep, and she was the weirdo, and that she really didn't belong here, not in this car with these normal people who were just doing normal people things, while she, the abnormal person, nursed a deep, burning fury at them.

And not for the first time, nor the last, she wished she had a normal brain.

Chapter 21

At home, Suze found a couch in the lounge room. An actual couch in their house!

'Did we win the lottery?' she wondered out loud.

'Sash and I found it in someone's hard rubbish,' Charlie said, appearing at the kitchen doorway. 'I've made Tuna Surprise to celebrate. The surprise is there's no tuna in it.'

'That really is a surprise,' observed Suze with a laugh, as she happily sank onto the couch. Such luxury.

'Where's Sacha?'

'Out with Matt.'

'Even though he loves her?'

'Even though he loves her,' Charlie said, with a sigh.

Later, as they sat on the couch and ate their Tuna Surprise – Black & Gold pasta ('More porridge than pasta,' said

Charlie) and Dolmio pasta sauce ('Top shelf!' said Suze) – Charlie asked Suze about her day.

She told him about the trip to Ballarat and the meeting with Libby Winston, but she left out how weird Phoebe Cotton had been on the car ride home. Trying to start a conversation with her had been like trying to light a fire with wet wood, and she'd refused any offer of chips or bubble gum, not even when she and Monty had started a competition to see who could blow the biggest bubble. It had reminded Suze of the day she'd tried to get her to stay for noodles, when Phoebe had suddenly disappeared into herself, leaving nothing but an empty shell and Suze to wonder if she'd said or done something wrong.

'And now I have to contact J to try and get the rest of the postcards,' she explained, trying to give the impression that calling J was the absolute last thing she wanted to do, even lower on her list than getting a pap smear, because she knew that anything else would not be acceptable to Charlie.

'That wanker,' Charlie said and then launched into a story about how he had seen J and Ky at a party the night before, where the two of them had walked backwards in slow motion through the crowd and had refused to talk to anyone the entire time they were there. 'I mean, they ran into the drinks table and had to edge their way around it, still facing backwards. It was ridiculous. *They* are ridiculous.'

Suze nodded as she pushed the remaining pasta around her plate with her fork, but she felt a small pang of jealousy. It *was* ridiculous, but she also imagined what fun it would've been, how J's eyes would have shone when they came up with the plan, how triumphant they would have felt after they'd pulled it off. She remembered the time that she and J had gatecrashed a party on Greeves Street on their way home from an amateur surgery gig and had set up a triage station outside the bathroom, completely confusing many of the drunken guests and delighting some of the stoned ones.

'So why do you think this Lizzy Watson was so weird with you?' Charlie asked.

'Libby Winston? I don't know. It was like she could only see Phoebe.'

'What was her relationship like with Mr and Mrs Rotten?'

'Who?'

'Phoebe's grandparents.'

'She didn't really talk about them, although she seemed upset that Phoebe's granddad had died. To be honest, she showed much more interest in the garden. She said she looked after it when they went travelling.'

Charlie put down his fork and sat up straight. 'Travelling? To Europe?'

'She didn't say.'

'Do either of their names begin with T?'

'No,' Suze responded. 'They're Edward and Dorothy.'

'But Ted is short for Edward and that starts with a T. Of course, not all Edwards are Teds. Just as not all Charleses are Chucks. But still, it's worth considering.'

He sank back down into the couch, evidently a little bit pleased with himself. 'I think I might be the greatest detective that ever lived.'

'Steady on,' said Suze. She was thinking about the disdain with which Phoebe's grandmother had talked about Libby Winston when they'd visited her at the Western Retreat Retirement Village. Charlie really might be onto something.

THE NEXT MORNING, Suze waited until eleven before she rang J. Nobody picked up, but that was to be expected. J said that his housemates never answered the phone, and Suze always imagined that it was like that scene in *The Accidental Tourist* where the phone rings and rings and everyone ignores it and just continues eating their dinner.

She then rang Phoebe, but Phoebe didn't pick up either and the call went to the answering machine. Suze opened her mouth, closed it again and hung up. She realised that Charlie's theory about Phoebe's grandfather being 'T' was not the kind of thing she should reveal in an answering machine message. Also, after that awkward car ride back from Ballarat, she wanted to check that Phoebe was alright before she dumped anything more on her.

Charlie emerged from his room with an armful of magazines.

'I don't know what you're doing today, but my plan is to drink instant coffee and read up on Farrah Fawcett and Lee Major's marriage breakdown. Would Madam care to join me?'

'Mais oui,' Suze replied, readily accepting the pile of magazines. They were old copies of *Woman's Day* and *New Idea*. 'Where on earth did you get these?'

'I have my sources,' Charlie said mysteriously, as he disappeared into the kitchen.

Suze looked down at the magazines and felt the usual internal battle: in the right corner, her thesis; in the left, the chance to catch up on decade-old celebrity gossip.

'Oh, the humanity,' Charlie cried out from the kitchen. 'We're out of International Roast. It's either dandelion root tea or that awful Ecco stuff that Sacha buys.'

Luckily Suze was saved from making that impossible decision by the sound of the front door opening.

'It's Sacha!' Charlie exclaimed, clapping his hands. 'Hopefully she's been out to the shops to get coffee!'

But Sacha hadn't been to the shops to get coffee. Instead,

she looked like she'd been dragged backwards through a hedge. Her face was pale and she was wearing the same clothes as yesterday.

'What the hell happened to you?' Charlie demanded.

'I slept over at Matt's house.'

Suze and Charlie quickly exchanged looks. Sacha never slept over at anyone else's house. She had an unwavering preference for sleeping in her own bed. Even when her ceiling was leaking, she just moved her bed to the other side of the room.

'And?' Charlie asked, leaning forward.

'He said he loved me again, and I . . .'

You told him to shut up? You ran screaming from the room? You killed him?

'I told him that I loved him too.'

She dropped next to Suze on the couch, like a sack of very sad potatoes.

'Oh honey,' Charlie said, sitting down too and putting his arm around her. 'That's wonderful.'

'It is.' Sacha turned to Suze. 'Isn't it?'

She sounded so uncertain that Suze found herself nodding so enthusiastically that she was in danger of dislodging her skull from her spine. 'It is.'

'Let's celebrate!' Charlie said, leaping up. 'It's a multi-pronged celebration: Sacha and Matt love each other, I've made an important breakthrough in the Case of the Fucking Postcards, and we have a new couch.'

What about me? thought Suze. *What have I got to celebrate?*

Charlie must have read her mind because he said, 'Plus, it's been exactly four weeks since young Susan here saw the Cat's Arse, aka Jonathan. That's practically a month.'

Suze hadn't told Charlie about going to the birthday drinks at the Napier, so it really wasn't something worth celebrating.

But she smiled and nodded, nonetheless.

'How about lunch at the Standard?' Sacha suggested.

Suze's face must have fallen at the thought of the cost because Charlie immediately added, 'My shout.'

Sacha stood. 'I'll get changed.'

'And maybe brush your hair?' Charlie suggested gently.

'And I'll brush my hair,' Sacha echoed.

'We leave at noon,' Charlie pronounced. Suze looked at the clock on the wall. If she got dressed quickly, she could maybe squeeze in some reading for uni before they left and make lunch her reward.

'Foucault, here I come,' she said, standing up.

Charlie held out one of the magazines. 'Perhaps "Loni's Heartbreak over Burt" might be a wiser choice for a Sunday?'

'Actually, no,' Suze said, resisting temptation. She was determined to have something to celebrate at the lunch, even if it was only that she had achieved the absolute bare minimum of thesis research.

But the ringing phone had other ideas.

Charlie reached over and picked up the receiver. 'The Loni Anderson Heartbreak Society. How may I help you? Babs! So good to hear your voice. Your daughter is right here.'

Suze took the phone. At the end of the day, the urge to be the Good Daughter was greater than the urge to be the Good Student.

'Hi, Mum,' she said, sitting back down on the couch.

'Hello, love.'

Charlie swivelled his body around so his feet were resting on Suze's lap. Out of nowhere, Groovy Joe appeared and jumped onto Charlie's chest. Suze felt the strongest sense of home she'd had in years and years, and she wanted the same for her mother.

'Are you having a happy Sunday?' she asked.

'Not exactly,' Barbara responded. 'It was our wedding anniversary yesterday.'

Suze slapped her forehead. She'd known it was coming up and that it would be a hard day for Barbara, but somehow the knowledge had fallen in between the cracks.

'Oh god, I'm so sorry I forgot.'

Suze remembered how she and Barbara had spent the day last year, looking at the wedding photos, watching the wedding video, reading the wedding cards. They had both cried so much it was hard to believe that they hadn't been swept away by all their tears.

'It's okay, love. It gave me a good reason to go to the support group.'

'Did you like it?'

'I guess so. We talked about how a person's life is made up of all these dates, these milestones, big and small, and how it all gets reduced to two days in the end: date of birth and date of death. I've been feeling responsible for holding on to all of the days I shared with Greg and all of the little things that made him *him*: the way he drank his tea and held his pen, the way he folded his T-shirts, the look on his face when he tasted something sour, that dance move he only did when he was at weddings . . . It's like holding too many oranges.'

'Oranges?' Suze had no idea where her mother was going with this, but she was just so glad her mother had actually gone to the support group meeting.

'There are only so many oranges a person can hold comfortably while still being able to appreciate the oranges and not dropping them everywhere. So, it's better for me to focus on the important things: Greg lived, I knew him, I loved him, and he loved me. Those are the oranges I choose to hold. I was so lucky, Suze.'

'You were, Mum. You really were.'

After their conversation, Suze continued to sit on the couch. Both Charlie and Groovy Joe had their eyes shut and she didn't want to disturb them, even though she still felt an itch to study.

'What was that about oranges?' Charlie asked without opening his eyes.

'It's hard to explain,' Suze replied. 'Something about appreciating things more. That between the dawn and the sunset, there's the whole sky, and everything underneath it, but we can't possibly carry it all and appreciate it at the same time. Or something.'

'That's deep,' Charlie said, his eyes now open. 'But it still doesn't explain the oranges.'

'We can talk about it more over lunch,' Suze said, pushing his feet off her lap.

'Or not,' Charlie said.

'Or not,' Suze agreed.

As she climbed up the stairs, she thought of her stepfather's face the last time she'd seen him, obscured by an oxygen mask, his eyeballs yellow and dry, his gaze unfocused. She had been carrying around that image for so long now, it had almost become her default memory of him. As she reached the top step, she focused hard on conjuring another memory: the time her team had won the netball championship. Greg had been so proud. Later, Barbara had told her that when Suze had made a particularly good intercept, he'd turned to all the strangers around him and said, 'That's my stepdaughter.' She hadn't seen his face at that moment, but she could imagine it. And, in imagining it – in holding that single orange – she could feel his love, even now.

Chapter 22

IT WAS ONE of those mid-July days where the sky was so vibrant and clear that winter was hiding in the shade. Phoebe stood in the backyard of Number 6 Salmon Street with the sun on her face and remembered Dorothy's mantra, back when she was in charge of the garden: 'Never waste a blue sky.'

She'd woken with her insides feeling like an off-balance load in a washing machine. She felt embarrassed by how she'd behaved in the car on the return trip from Ballarat.

Then there was the meeting with Libby Winston. There had been something about it that had left Phoebe feeling that there was more to the story, still to be discovered.

And finally, there was Monty. The more she saw of him, the more she liked him. But the more she liked him, the more vulnerable she felt, like a hermit crab without its protective shell. And after yesterday's performance, he was unlikely to like her back, strange and silent and sullen as she had been in the car.

Life had definitely been easier without people in it.

Phoebe rolled up her sleeves and got to work. After a few hours of weeding and pruning, she stepped back to admire the fruits of her labour. The effort she'd put in that morning had made a difference, but not enough of a difference considering how hard she'd worked. Her back was aching and her fingernails had so much dirt under them, they looked like a reverse French manicure. And that anxious feeling inside her – the washing machine one – was still there. She realised that she needed to talk to someone.

She went back inside the house and picked up Sandy's number, which had been stuck to the fridge with a Williamstown RSL magnet. She hadn't been able to ring her, nor had she dared throw the number away. The thought of Sandy in this moment felt like a familiar blanket she wanted to wrap herself in. She wanted to go back in time, to before Sandy went away to Canberra, back to their high school library, the smell of books, the dust dancing in the afternoon sunlight. And Sandy's laugh.

Would Sandy take her call now?

In for a penny . . .

She dialled the number.

Nobody answered, not even an answering machine.

She put down the receiver and then picked it up again and dialled the Moor Street number.

Suze answered the phone after only a couple of rings. There was music in the background and the sound of other voices. She sounded happy to hear from Phoebe.

'I tried ringing you earlier, but I didn't leave a message,' Suze said.

'I was doing some gardening.' There was the loud pop of a champagne cork being released, followed by cheers. 'Are you having a party?'

'We're celebrating!' Suze exclaimed. 'Sacha's in love, we have a new couch and Charlie made a . . . We're just celebrating life, really. With Passion Pop!'

'The nectar of the Gods,' Charlie shouted in the background.

'I should let you go,' Phoebe said.

'No, no, it's fine. I want to talk to you. I'll just move outside.'

After a minute or so of muffled chaos and Charlie complaining about tripping hazards, the noise of the party dropped away, and Suze's voice was clearer.

'How are you feeling? You were very quiet in the car ride home yesterday.'

'I was just tired.'

'Are you sure? I was actually a bit worried about you.'

'I'm really fine,' Phoebe said, even though she knew she wasn't – not really. And the fact that her stupid eating-sound issue had caused her new friend to worry made her feel even less fine.

'Okay,' Suze replied in a tone that suggested she was putting the issue reluctantly aside, but only temporarily. 'I think Monty's very nice.'

'He is, isn't he.'

'He seems to really like you.'

Phoebe felt herself blush. 'Do you think so?'

'I know so! Seriously, you don't ever seem to see it, but he looks at you a lot.'

'Hopefully not when he's driving, because that would be dangerous.'

Suze laughed. 'You'll need to get your licence so you can

keep your eyes on the road while he gazes adoringly at you, then.'

All this talk about Monty and his eyes and his gaze was making Phoebe feel like a shell-less hermit crab again, fleshy and vulnerable. She quickly changed the topic.

'What did you think of Libby Winston?'

'She wasn't at all what I'd imagined. I thought she would have long dark hair and flashing eyes like one of those heroines in a romance novel, but she was more like everyone's favourite aunt.'

'Her reaction to the postcards was a little odd,' Phoebe said, remembering the Etch-a-Sketch of emotions on Libby Winston's face as she'd flipped through the cards. 'I definitely think that she had never seen them before.'

'I agree,' Suze replied. 'I think we can all agree that T never gave them to her. But here's the thing, Phoebe . . . Charlie has a pretty good theory about who T is.'

'He does?' Phoebe felt flattered that Charlie would waste his thoughts on anything even vaguely related to her.

'You might not like it, but . . . well . . . have you ever considered that T might be your granddad? I mean, Ted is short for Edward.'

'Nobody ever called him Ted. Not that I know of.'

'Not that you know of,' echoed Suze, as if she was making a very important point. 'Do you remember the look on her face when she found out he had died?'

'The death of anyone is upsetting,' Phoebe argued. 'Especially if you shared a house with them for over a year.' Although she hadn't exactly been friends with anybody in the Share House of Cereal, she knew she would feel sad if she heard one of them had died.

'Sure, okay. But Libby also said she'd looked after the Salmon

Street house while your grandparents were away on trips. Do you know if they ever went to Europe?'

Phoebe felt some of the warmth leave her body. Her mind had occasionally fluttered around the idea it might have been her grandfather who wrote the postcards, but it had never quite landed on it.

'Yes,' she replied. 'They did.'

Her grandparents had done a lot of travelling in the '60s and '70s, mostly before Phoebe had been born. She knew they'd gone to Europe at least a couple of times. There used to be a photo of Dorothy standing at the Trevi Fountain in Rome hanging in the front room of Number 6, although it wasn't there now. Maybe Dorothy had taken it with her to the retirement village.

'I mean, think about it,' Suze continued. 'He knew he could give her the postcards when he got home from Europe because she was already living in his house. And then – get this – what if Libby's sudden departure from Salmon Street happened before they got back from the trip and that's why the postcards were never delivered?'

Phoebe swallowed again. 'I guess it's a possibility.'

'What do you know about your grandparents' marriage?'

'What does anyone know about their grandparents' marriage?' Phoebe replied, her eyes immediately drawn to their wedding photo on the hallway wall. Phoebe had never thought it was odd that Dorothy had left it behind. At least, not before now.

'Good point.'

They talked about how Suze planned to get the remaining postcards off J and agreed to meet the next Saturday morning for another hot chocolate on Brunswick Street.

'Phoebe,' Suze said just before they hung up. 'I hope I didn't upset you with Charlie's theory about your granddad.'

'It's okay,' Phoebe replied. 'I didn't really know him. I was only nine when he died.'

'Also, I really think you should ask Monty out.'

'What?' The blush returned.

'Seriously. I'm no good at reading men when it comes to my own love life, but I can see that he really likes you, but he's probably even shyer than you are.'

'I don't know . . .'

'I tell you. I *do* know. Promise me this: the minute you hang up, give him a call and ask him out.'

'I . . .'

'Promise me.' Suze's tone was so firm that it felt even more legally binding than a Year 10 pinky promise.

Phoebe relented. 'Okay. I promise.'

She pressed the receiver down and before she knew it, she was dialling Monty's number, still etched in her memory from staring at it so much.

After a few rings, Monty answered. Phoebe was relieved it wasn't his parents. She might lose momentum if she had to have a conversation with his mother.

Monty sounded happy to hear from her. 'Hey,' he said. 'Phoebe C!'

In the background, Phoebe could hear Monty's mother saying something and Monty put his hand over the receiver as he said something back. After a few moments, he returned to the call.

'Sorry, I can't talk long. We're going to my aunty's house.'

He sounded annoyed about having to leave and that gave Phoebe courage. It also meant she'd have to seize the day.

'That's okay,' said Phoebe. 'I was just . . .'

Her heart was pounding in her ribcage so hard she thought it might be making an escape attempt.

'. . . I was just ringing to see if you wanted to do something together next weekend.'

'As a date?'

'I guess so.'

'That would be nice. I know you don't really do movies, but there's a Scottish double feature next weekend. *Braveheart* and *Trainspotting*. They're calling it *Trainheart*.'

'Sure,' Phoebe said, her heart now beating like a jackhammer. The cinema was going to be hard for her, but she could do this. Once again, she was in for that metaphorical penny.

Monty's mum was in the background again, saying something. 'Alright, alright,' Monty told her and then returned to Phoebe. 'You'd think it had been years since she last saw her sister. We literally saw her three days ago.'

They agreed to talk mid-week about which session to go to and then Monty was gone. Phoebe slunk to the floor, her insides set to spin-cycle now.

The postcard from Nottingham that had arrived the other week, which was now in the hands of Libby Winston, flashed into her mind. The picture had shown a statue of Robin Hood, strong and true and brave, his back straight and his bow drawn. He had done something wrong (stealing) to do something right (giving to the poor). She was fairly certain Robin would have been fine with going to the cinema on a date, even if the whole place would be filled with popcorn-crunchers and soft-drink-slurpers. She, too, could do the wrong thing to do the right thing. Maybe.

Chapter 23

'THE BEEP IS coming. You know what to do.'

The first time Suze had rung J's number and got his answering machine, she had thought the message was pretty cute. But as this was her sixth attempt to catch him since the weekend, the message was starting to annoy the shit out of her.

'Morning!' Sacha said as she passed Suze on her way to the kitchen. She was wearing Matt's *Goodies* T-shirt and a huge grin – a solid sign that her lovefest with Matt was continuing. Charlie had quickly developed a theory that aliens had taken the real Sacha and Matt and replaced them with the lovey-dovey parents from *Family Ties*. ('Soon they're going to start trying to teach us valuable life lessons,' said Charlie.)

'Morning,' Suze said, although she knew it was already afternoon.

She had a meeting with her supervisor, Claire Portelle, in just under two hours. She'd been hoping to get J on the phone as a way of diverting her nervous energy about the meeting back towards her love life (or lack thereof).

'Ugh,' she said, lying down on the couch and putting a cushion over her head.

'What's up with you?' Sacha said, passing back through the living room with a glass of orange juice.

'I'm meeting my supervisor this afternoon.'

'The real one or the fake one?'

'The real one.'

'She's back already?'

Suze nodded. 'Quite frankly, I'm terrified about what she'll say when she sees my lack of actual progress.'

'She's just a person. Also, she can't kill you, because it's against the law. But she could hurt you psychologically. She probably has a PhD in mental cruelty.'

'You're not helping.'

'I'm trying to build up your expectations so that when she's actually much nicer than you remember, it will be a huge relief,' Sacha said in a matter-of-fact tone. 'You'll thank me later.'

Suze doubted it. She couldn't remember this kind of advice being served up on *Family Ties*.

'I EXPECTED TO see more words than this,' Claire told Suze sternly as they sat facing each other in her cramped office that smelled faintly of cigarettes and despair. She was holding the first chapter of Suze's thesis. 'This isn't a first-year essay you can pull an all-nighter for the night before it's due.'

'I have another three thousand words,' Suze assured Claire. She didn't tell her that those three thousand words were just transcripts of quotes she'd pulled from all her photocopies, and that counting each of those three thousand words had been another extremely productive use of an afternoon.

'Then it will be easy for you to give me two more chapters by the end of the month,' Claire replied. Suze did a quick calculation in her head. Ten days. She had ten days to write two chapters. That was possible. Maybe. But probably not.

Suze felt truly chastised. Somehow, she'd come full circle with her education. Gone were the freedoms she'd experienced in her first year, skipping lectures and slipping essays through the slot in the door of the office seconds before the deadline. Gone, too, were the gentle chats with her interim supervisor, which had gently skated over almost every subject under the sun except her actual Honours topic.

Now she felt like she was back in the principal's office, being told she needed to do better.

But still, the fact remained: she needed to do better.

She left the campus and walked dolefully to Lygon Street where she stood in front of the noticeboard outside of Readings. So many people searching for someone or something – a place to live, a housemate, a band member, a car. Someone even wanted to start a kazoo orchestra.

'Are you thinking of moving out of Moor Street?' a voice asked behind her.

She turned around to face J, handsome as ever. Her traitorous heart did that thing where it stopped for the briefest of moments at the sight of him and then fluttered back to life.

'Oh, no,' she replied. 'I was just thinking of starting a kazoo orchestra, but it looks like someone else has beat me to it.'

She pointed in the vague direction of the notice on the board behind her.

J had some slight stubble, a star painted on his cheek like

a beauty spot, and he was wearing a deep purple jacket that resembled her grandmother's shagpile carpet from the 1970s. She quickly checked behind him. No sign of Ky.

'Wanna get a drink?' J asked, and she found herself nodding, even though she knew she probably should be spending her money on groceries or even the electricity bill.

They went into Jimmy Watson's, but it was full of academics drinking their way through the late afternoon, so they walked across the road to Trotters and ordered coffee instead. Suze would have preferred a hot chocolate, but there was no way on earth she was going to order one of those in front of J.

'So, what's the goss?' J asked her once their drinks had arrived.

Suze told him about her meeting with Claire Portelle, but his eyes glazed over in the way they always did when she talked about her studies. He had barely scraped through a Classics degree, and he'd once confessed to her that he only passed Latin because he'd memorised the whole textbook for the exam while drinking pints of VB at Naughtons. To this day, if he got drunk enough, he would start reciting Cicero's Catilinarian Orations.

'What's *your* goss?' Suze shot back at him, and he perked up right away. Suze remembered what Charlie had said about J: he was always happier when he was talking about himself. She had defended J at the time, but now she was starting to see that Charlie was right after all.

While J launched into a whole story about him and Ky and an (un)art festival they were trying to set up in Meredith, Suze found herself looking at him in a different way, as if she was Charlie or even Phoebe Cotton. She began noticing how arrogant he was, how oblivious he was to the feelings of anyone else in the story, like he and Ky were the only people on the planet that mattered. She thought of Libby Winston's strange reaction to the postcards and wondered how Phoebe might be feeling about the possibility her grandfather had written them.

Suze interrupted J during a pause in his story. 'You know we went and met with Elizabeth Winston?'

'Huh?'

'We – I mean, me and Phoebe Cotton, the person who lives at the address on Salmon Street, the person who's been receiving those postcards – well, we found Libby, I mean Elizabeth, and we went to Ballarat to meet with her and return them.'

'Who?' J seemed even more confused.

'Elizabeth Winston. The person the postcards are addressed to,' Suze said, somewhat impatiently. She couldn't believe he didn't know who Libby Winston was, and, in that moment, she realised he might never have read the postcards or even properly looked at them before sending them. 'She asked if she can have the rest. So, can I have them back?'

J opened his mouth as if to speak and then suddenly leaped up and ran outside, and for the briefest of moments Suze thought he was running to get the postcards. But then she realised he was running after Ky, who had just walked past Trotters. She watched them talking through the window and they both turned towards her. J's face was apologetic. Ky's was indifferent.

'I was filling in time while I was waiting to meet up with you,' Suze heard J explaining to Ky as he led her into the cafe.

Now if that wasn't a statement that summed up J's entire relationship with her, Suze didn't know what was. She'd merely been a way for him to fill in time until Ky came along.

'Hi, Ky,' Suze said.

Ky greeted her with something that was half-smile, half-grimace.

'Suze was just telling me how she went and met with the person those postcards were addressed to.'

Ky's immediate response was, 'That's not very (un)art.'

J nodded. 'That's exactly what I was about to tell her.'

Suze knew that wasn't true. He would've most likely said 'Huh' again if Ky hadn't interrupted them.

'Elizabeth Winston would like the rest of the postcards.'

'Elizabeth who?' Ky asked.

'Seriously?' Suze responded, starting to lose her patience. 'Neither of you ever looked at the name on the postcards?'

'Writing is simply a sign of a sign,' Ky said, with a slight wave of her hand.

'Derrida would disagree,' Suze replied, and Ky gave her a look that almost resembled respect. Suze felt glad that some of her highlighting had actually started to sink in. If only Claire Portelle was around to witness it. 'Anyway, Libby Winston, the person who the postcards were addressed to, would like to have the rest of the postcards back.'

J nodded and started to open his mouth, but Ky interjected. 'I wouldn't think so. Your intervention has changed the course of this (un)art (non)act. J, I forbid you to hand over any of those postcards or to post any more of them.'

Forbid? Suze thought. What kind of relationship were they having? Was J like the gimp in the basement in *Pulp Fiction*?

J just nodded again.

'So, what are you going to do with the postcards, if you're not going to return them to their rightful owner?' Suze challenged Ky.

Ky thought for a moment, while J looked at her, a small dog waiting for his next command.

'We shall burn them,' she decreed.

'But it's illegal to destroy mail that isn't yours,' Suze blurted out, now channelling Phoebe Cotton.

'These were never posted, so they can't be classified as mail,'

Ky replied, her tone as even and steady as the ground beneath them. 'In any case, ownership is a construct. Nothing belongs to anyone, except our actions, words, thoughts and intentions. And our intention is to burn them in a giant fire, but in a way that nobody will realise the significance of what we're doing.'

J nodded once more, and Suze groaned.

'These postcards are real things written for a real person who wants them returned to her,' she said.

'In a way, burning them *is* a way of returning them to her, returning them to the same place to which we all will ultimately return,' J said and Suze looked at Ky, half-expecting her to pat him on his head or throw him a Scooby Snack.

'Fine then,' Suze said, standing up. 'I think you're both full of shit, but fine.' She turned to J. 'You can pay for my coffee. You owe me about a hundred of them.'

And she walked out of the cafe, head held higher than it had been in a very long time.

Chapter 24

ALL WEEK, PHOEBE had planned to take a bath on Saturday morning and shave her legs ahead of her date. Even though it was winter and she was likely to wear jeans, she still wanted to feel prepared.

But when she woke up on Saturday morning, the pilot light in the gas system had gone out and she couldn't get it re-lit, no matter how hard she tried.

Luckily, her dad had swooped in, like the conquering hero, with his toolbox and some croissants, and had it all sorted out within the hour.

Phil drank a cup of tea very quietly and Phoebe delicately ate a croissant while the bath filled and her day's plans got back on track.

'You doing anything fun today?' her father asked. Phoebe

deliberately hadn't mentioned her date to Phil and Ellen at dinner the other night. She had been feeling nervous enough without her mother coaching loudly from the sidelines. But she knew she could trust her father not to overreact.

'I'm going on a date,' she said.

'Good for you,' Phil responded.

They sat in silence for a while. 'Is it with the guy you met at the post office?'

Phoebe was surprised. 'It is. How did you guess?'

Phil shrugged. 'Your face always lit up when you talked about him. What's the latest with the postcards?'

Now it was Phoebe's turn to shrug. 'Not much.'

She'd been trying not to think about Charlie's theory that T might be her grandfather, and it had been easy enough, with her impending date to worry about instead. But the theory had still been gnawing away at her.

'Dad,' she said, after she finished the last of her croissant. 'What do you know about Dorothy and Granddad's marriage?'

'Well, I know that I was their biggest mistake,' Phil joked, but then he obviously saw that she was being serious, and he changed tack. 'Not much, I guess. Marriage was different back then. It wasn't the big quest for true love that it is now. Not many people were talking about soulmates.'

'So they didn't marry for love?'

'To be honest, I don't know. After the war, your grandfather went to work in the tiny town your grandmother was from, and I think she saw him as her ticket out of there. She fell pregnant with me very soon after they married – although your mother has a theory that Dorothy was pregnant *before* they were married – and they tolerated each other for the next thirty years.'

'Tolerated?' Phoebe asked.

'I never got the feeling that they were particularly close. They had a good partnership, but more of a business one than a romantic one. They never held hands or kissed each other hello or goodbye, even with Dad travelling all the time for work.'

'Do you think . . .' Phoebe paused and then rallied. 'Do you think Granddad ever had an affair?'

Her father was arranging some crumbs on the table into a group. His complete focus on them made her think of someone raking one of those Zen gardens.

'Not that I know of,' he finally said and then looked back up at her. 'Why do you ask?'

'Because Dorothy didn't take their wedding photo with her to the Western Retreat,' Phoebe said. She didn't want to tell her father about the postcard theory, not while it was still half-formed.

Her father laughed. 'If I know anything about your grandmother, it's that she is the least sentimental person on the planet. It wouldn't have been a deliberate oversight. She probably hasn't even realised she left it behind.'

After her dad was gone and she'd sunk deep into the bath, Phoebe thought about a thirty-year marriage 'tolerating' each other, in the same way she tolerated her work colleagues with their apples and celery sticks and tea-slurping. What kind of life would that be? Would it be better than being alone?

As much as she yearned for a relationship, she'd never been able to imagine herself in one. When she thought about the future, she could only see herself, sitting alone in a room with her books and her bad TV shows, eating pasta for one. How could she possibly endure a lifetime of sharing meals with another person, enveloped in a cloud of red fury at every single noise they made? And moreover, who would put up with *her* when she judged them so hard for just being a person and merely eating, a basic human function required for survival?

She hadn't endured a single meal with Monty, let alone a lifetime of them, sitting opposite each other every night. The closest she had come was the car trip back from Ballarat. Her toes curled at the thought of it.

She sank her head under the water.

AS SHE WALKED up to Russell Street from Museum Station, Phoebe's nervousness and excitement battled with a deep sense of dread. Monty had been at a cousin's bar mitzvah in the eastern suburbs and was driving into the city to meet her at the cinema.

He greeted her in the foyer, tickets in one hand, and – to Phoebe's dismay – a huge box of popcorn in the other.

'I should probably get a drink, too,' Monty said, glancing back at the queue at the candy bar. 'Popcorn makes me thirsty.'

Popcorn makes me murderous, Phoebe thought but didn't say. She tried to smile instead. 'I'll shout you a drink. You go grab us some seats.'

Her new hope was that the queue for the candy bar would take so long that he would have finished half the popcorn by the time she got to the cinema. But when she rejoined him, her stomach lurched; Monty had sat right in the middle of the theatre, the worst possible place for popcorn. And indeed, there was a tight ring of people, all with identical boxes, surrounding him. Worst of all, Monty's box was still untouched.

'You haven't eaten your popcorn,' she noted, trying to keep her voice as light and breezy as she could manage. Her whole body felt tense, like she had died and rigor mortis was setting in.

'I was saving it for the movie. And for you,' he said, with a shy grin.

To her great relief, Monty wasn't a shoveller. He ate the

175

popcorn one piece at a time, without a loud crunch and with minimal squeak. But still. *Popcorn.* And the downside of not being a shoveller was that they were halfway through the movie and his popcorn was still going, while the people around them had long since finished.

She tried to concentrate on the feeling of his arm against hers, the nearness of his warmth. All she wanted to do was slink right down in her seat and shove her fingers in her ears, but she also knew that it wasn't the most attractive way to sit in the cinema, and there was no way he was going to hold her hand if she was sitting like that. But then again, there was not going to be any handholding while he was eating the popcorn either.

Around the two-thirds mark, he placed the box on the cinema floor and excused himself.

'Bathroom,' he whispered in explanation.

Phoebe saw her chance. She stretched out her leg and casually kicked the box over with her foot, spilling the remaining contents all over the floor.

When he returned, she pointed at the mess. 'Sorry,' she whispered. 'I knocked it over.'

'That's okay,' he whispered back. 'I'd had enough.'

And he took her hand. She felt immensely glad and immensely guilty at the same time. And for the rest of the movie, with his warm smooth hand in hers, her happiness felt like a snake eating its own tail.

It was dark when they came out of the cinema. 'Do you want to go somewhere?' Monty asked. 'We could get cake on Degraves.'

Phoebe knew that Degraves Street would be crowded and loud, so she agreed. As they went to cross Collins Street, a car ran a red light and Monty grabbed her hand to pull her back and then continued holding her hand, and Phoebe's heart nearly exploded with happiness. It was happening. It was really happening.

But then, at the cafe, they sat at a table outside on the pavement, next to an old man eating a roll with his mouth open. She couldn't hear the noise, but the motion of his jaw and the sight of the food swilling about inside his gummy mouth set her teeth on edge and made her want to shout.

She was thinking of an excuse to change tables when the waiter delivered their Italian hot chocolates and some small cakes shaped like horns.

Monty held the two cakes up to his head. 'Look at me, I'm an Italian Viking,' he said. 'Hang on, did Italy even have Vikings?'

But Phoebe couldn't focus on what he was saying. The man had moved on to eating a bowl of minestrone that must have still been too hot, because half of what he was putting in his mouth was instantly falling out. What had the doctor said? 'Just move to another room.' Phoebe knew it was only a matter of asking Monty to swap seats – he was so polite, he probably would do it without question – but she couldn't. She was worried he'd think she was being weird because, well, she knew she *was* being weird. So, instead, she tried to move her chair so the man was in the very edge of her periphery, but somehow, her brain wouldn't let her turn away completely. She had to keep looking back at him, to see if he was still eating the soup. How deep was that bowl? How long would it take him to finish it? How on earth could a person that old have such trouble eating soup? Surely he'd eaten soup hundreds of times before and had learned to eat it without slurping?

Meanwhile, one of Monty's legs had started jiggling against the table leg and she could feel the vibrations through the table and she wanted to put her hand on his leg and tell him to

Imbi Neeme

stop because it was making her feel physically ill, but she didn't know him well enough yet, and she wasn't sure if she would ever know anyone well enough to be able to ask them to stop jiggling their leg.

'Is everything okay?' Monty asked, now concerned.

'I might be coming down with something,' she lied. She was feeling like Maxwell Smart in the closing credits of *Get Smart*, with a hundred doors slamming shut between the two of them.

'You don't have to have one of the horns,' he told her. 'Or even the hot chocolate. We can just leave. I'm sorry. I should have never suggested this place.'

Phoebe felt awful. How could she tell him that this terrible situation had nothing to do with him, or even with the old man at the next table, but that the problem was *her*?

'No, it's okay. I'm happy to be here with you,' she said but then instantly regretted it as his jiggling intensified and a waiter brought the old man a steaming bowl of spaghetti. Suddenly, all she wanted to do was run screaming from the cafe, or to at least flip the old man's table over, sending the spaghetti and soup and bread everywhere.

But she knew she couldn't do either of those things. Instead, she tried to focus on her hot chocolate, which was as thick as tar, and not sweet like the hot chocolates she was used to.

Monty did his best to keep up the conversation – mostly about the film they had just seen – but when it became clear that Phoebe's attention wasn't on the conversation, he, too, focused on drinking his hot chocolate, and soon they were finished and back out on the footpath and heading towards the car, and Monty's leg was no longer jiggling, it was just walking, and the old man was far behind them.

But there were still all those closed doors between them, and

178

Monty didn't take her hand and she didn't offer it and when he dropped her off at Salmon Street, there was no attempt to make further plans, and there was certainly no kiss.

She'd blown it.

Chapter 25

'HONEY, I'M HOME,' Suze called out as she stepped through the door of the Moor Street house.

'Honey, I'm homo!' Charlie called back from the couch, where he was stretched out, reading an article about how to get his body 'bikini ready' before summer. Groovy Joe was sitting on his feet. 'How was your day at the office?'

'Fine.'

It had been a reasonably productive day at the Baillieu, even for a Sunday. She'd started to string the transcribed quotes together, creating a framework for the two chapters that were due. It wasn't particularly good, but it meant she had something to give to Claire Portelle by the deadline, which was now in eight days. But who was counting.

'Did Phoebe ring?'

'No,' Charlie said, still reading.

'Shit,' Suze said.

Sensing gossip, Charlie put the magazine down immediately. 'Trouble in paradise?'

'No.' Charlie's face fell. 'I tried ringing her last night, and again this morning before I went to the library. I wanted to ask how her date with Monty went.' Charlie perked up again. 'Also, to tell her about the postcards.'

'The *fucking* postcards?'

'The one and the same.'

She gestured for Charlie to move his legs so she could sit on the couch in between him and Groovy Joe, and she told him about her conversation with J and Ky, feeling the indignation at their callousness rise again in her chest.

'Maybe you were right about him all along,' she concluded. 'J *is* pretty full of himself.'

'Like a balloon filled with gas generated from his own arse?' Charlie suggested.

Suze laughed. 'Exactly like that.'

'Well . . .' Charlie leaned forward, like he was about to share a tasty morsel of information, but he was interrupted by a door being slammed very loudly on the first floor and the sound of someone stomping down the stairs. It was Sacha, wearing a face like a thundercloud.

'Hi Sash,' Suze said, but Sacha didn't respond. She just walked by them and out the front door, slamming it too.

Suze looked at Charlie, hoping he had an explanation.

Charlie rolled his eyes. '*Definitely* trouble in paradise. Matt went to a wedding yesterday and didn't invite her because he knows she's not into weddings, but apparently he was supposed to invite her so she could decline with great force and angrily remind him that she's not into weddings. At least, that's what

I've gleaned from the very loud telephone conversation she's been having with him.'

'What happened to our *Family Ties* parents?' Suze remarked.

'Our days of living inside an American sitcom are over, honey. It's all telekinesis and pigs' blood from here on.'

'Ugh,' Suze said, thinking of that final scene in *Carrie* and hoping she would be like Sue Snell, who'd stayed at home and survived. They shared a name, after all. She had begun wondering if there were any gay characters in the film that Charlie could play when she suddenly became aware of him staring at her.

'*Ahem*,' he said. 'Before Sacha interrupted us with her minor temper tantrum and you skipped away with your mind pixies, I was going to tell you that Ky's share house is having a party this weekend.' He obviously noticed the confused expression on Suze's face, because he launched immediately into an explanation. 'Dan, who works at the Standard, used to go out with Slasher, who works with Franco, who lives with Ky. Apparently the lease is up, so they're planning to have a big bonfire and a wild house party . . .'

Suze imagined Ky and her housemates setting the whole house on fire because they had no further use for it, without thinking that someone else might want to live there, that someone else might own it. No doubt, they would strip themselves naked and circle around the flames incanting some obscure druidic text.

She realised that Charlie was staring at her again.

'What?' she asked.

'Try to stay with me, Susan,' Charlie tutted. 'The point of all this is it seems to me that this will be the "great fire" of which Young Kylie doth spake. So we should stormeth the castle and get the fucking postcards back.'

He raised his fist and shook it in the air.

Suze groaned. 'I can't go to the party. I've got those chapters due next Monday.'

'Then I'm setting you a new deadline,' Charlie said sternly. 'You need to get those chapters to Claire by 5 pm on Friday.'

Suze paused to think it through. It was Sunday today. If she really knuckled down and had a few more semi-productive days at the Baillieu, she might be able to pull it off.

'Deal,' she said, bending down to pick up the phone from the floor.

'Honestly, I should have been coaching you the entire year,' Charlie said. He picked up his magazine and lay back down on the couch again, stretching his legs across her lap. 'I would make a *great* supervisor.'

'Yeah, yeah, yeah,' Suze said dismissively, as she rested the phone on top of his legs and dialled Phoebe's number. Secretly, she entirely agreed. He really would make a great supervisor.

Phoebe answered the phone after just a few rings.

'Wanna gatecrash a party with Charlie and me on Saturday night?' Suze asked. 'Monty can come too.' Then she gave Phoebe a quick summary of the meeting with J and Ky and their refusal to give back the postcards.

'What is wrong with those people?' Phoebe asked, in an uncharacteristically feisty way that made Suze smile.

'Well, Ky is about a hundred flavours of callous, but J . . .' she paused. 'I thought better of J.'

'I didn't!' Charlie piped up beside her.

'If you're going to listen in on my phone calls, you can at least keep your opinions to yourself,' she said to him, before returning to Phoebe. 'But yes, Charlie would like it stated for the record that he never thought better of J.'

A memory of lying with J in the Exhibition Gardens came

into her mind – her head on his chest, listening to the steady rhythm of his heart while he played with her hair. That was back when she thought they might be becoming boyfriend and girlfriend, before she'd had to move back to Sydney. What a fool she'd been. She touched her hair now, imagining his hand through it. What a fool she still was.

'Now that the record has been updated, I am retiring to my quarters,' Charlie said, throwing his magazine aside and extricating himself from the couch. Suze waved him off and then stretched out in his place.

'That's better,' she said, more to herself than to Phoebe. 'So . . . how did the date go with Monty?'

'I don't know,' Phoebe replied, her previous feistiness replaced with her usual brand of uncertainty. 'I think I might have blown it.'

'I'm sure you haven't.'

'I have. It was never going to work, anyway.'

'Don't be like that. That's not true.'

'It *is* true.' Phoebe almost sounded like she was going to cry. 'There's something about me that I haven't told you.'

Suze felt a frisson of intrigue. The mild-mannered Phoebe Cotton had a secret? Her mind exploded with possibilities: a teen pregnancy and a secret child, a criminal past, a strange fetish, an extra nipple.

'I don't like the sound of eating,' Phoebe said.

Suze felt let down. This was not even close to being frisson-worthy. 'Okay . . .'

'Ever since I was a little girl, I've had to put my fingers in my ears at mealtime. I can't stand the sound of slurping, crunching or munching. They all hurt my brain. It's like . . . it's like my brain doesn't work properly.'

'That sounds hard,' Suze said. She tried to think of any

noises that she didn't like. 'The sound of polystyrene annoys me.'

'Ugh. I hate that too. But for me, it's deeper than annoyance. Sometimes, it's like this great rage, like I've become the Incredible Hulk, but just on the inside.'

Suze tried to imagine Phoebe in a great rage but couldn't. But then she remembered how quiet Phoebe had been in the car on the way back from Ballarat.

'The chips in the car,' she said.

'Yes, the chips in the car.' And then Phoebe launched into a whole story about going to the movies with Monty and the popcorn.

'I can't imagine watching a movie in a cinema without popcorn,' Suze said.

'You and ninety-nine per cent of the population it would seem. Which is why I generally avoid cinemas,' Phoebe replied. 'But I was trying to be bolder. Like Robin Hood. Like you.'

Suze felt deeply flattered by this statement. She'd never considered herself to be bold, but she wasn't sure she got the Robin Hood reference. 'Why don't you get really bold and just tell him?'

'I can't. It's embarrassing and unreasonable. He won't like me anymore.'

'You've told me,' Suze pointed out. 'And I still like you.'

'That's different.'

'It is, and it isn't. If you can't be honest with each other, then the relationship can't work, no matter what shape it takes.'

She thought of J and his slippery, noncommittal answers. And look how well *their* relationship was working.

'Thanks for the pep talk, Suze.'

'Any time,' Suze said.

She placed the receiver back in its cradle and thought about

Saturday night and knew, deep in her heart, that she was excited about seeing J again, despite everything, and she really hated herself for it.

'Do you think I'm strong?' she asked Charlie, as he made his way to the kitchen.

'Why? Did you accidentally crush the phone with your own brute strength?' Charlie replied. 'Yeah, you're strong. Mostly.'

'I don't think I'm strong.' She was weak. She knew she was weak.

'That's probably the thing that's stopping you from being stronger,' Charlie observed.

'And that's probably the wisest thing you've ever said.'

'What about the time I told you not to buy those parachute pants?'

Suze laughed. 'I think you'll find it was *me* telling *you* not to buy those parachute pants.' She picked up his discarded magazine and headed up to her room. She would read just one article before she got back to her thesis.

Oh, who was she kidding. She'd read the whole lot.

See? she said to the universe. *Not strong. Weak.*

Chapter 26

'SEE? THAT WASN'T too bad,' Phoebe said to her reflection in the hallway mirror after she'd finished her call with Suze. Her heart was still racing but her breathing was returning to normal.

She thought back to the time she'd almost managed to tell Sandy about her broken brain, but the fear of how that revelation might have affected her one and only friendship had stopped her. It was the same night that Sandy had confided in Phoebe about how fat she felt and that her goal was to lose another five kilograms by the Year 11 ball. That was the closest Sandy had come to revealing her own secret, but Phoebe had missed the significance, mostly because she hadn't thought Sandy was fat at all, and she'd had no real concept of how much five kilograms was, having never been that bothered about her own weight.

She had also been far too busy being bothered by the loudness of other humans simply being humans.

Phoebe had long suspected that this had been Sandy's breakthrough – the fact that she'd effectively told her secret to Phoebe – but Phoebe hadn't heard it, hadn't been listening hard enough, hadn't been enough of a good friend and given Sandy the support she needed rather than hiding away with her in the library.

She shook her head, as if to shake these thoughts completely out of it. And then, to keep any further thoughts away, she returned to the couch where she curled up (feet definitely on Dorothy's upholstery) and read for the rest of the night, one ear cocked for the phone, in case Monty might ring. But he didn't ring. And nor did she ring him. Deep down, she knew she was avoiding him. Now that Suze had made her promise to tell him about the eating thing, she was caught between disappointing her friend and revealing too much of herself to the boy she liked. And rather than make the decision, she was avoiding it altogether.

EVEN THOUGH MONTY had told her that he had to help out at the post office this week, Phoebe still found herself hoping she'd see him at Story Time on Wednesday.

'Your boyfriend hasn't been in for a while,' Des Rollerson observed afterwards in the staffroom, with a knowing look at Jasmine. 'Everything okay?'

'He's not my boyfriend,' Phoebe snapped, which just increased the levels of knowingness on Des's face. 'Anyway, he's working today.'

Phoebe thought of Monty standing behind the post office counter, like he had on that first day she'd met him, looking as awkward as a teenage boy at a school dance, and she found she missed him in a way she hadn't allowed herself to miss anyone for years, not since Sandy moved to Canberra.

During her afternoon tea break, she went out to the payphone across the street and rang the post office number. He answered after only a couple of rings.

'Good morning, this is the post office speaking. I mean, this is Montgomery Smith speaking. Is there something I can help you with today . . . please?' he asked.

Phoebe almost burst out laughing.

'For the record, it's afternoon,' she said, and then she paused, because she realised that she hadn't worked out what she was going to say. So she just said, 'It's Phoebe.'

'Thank god. I really stuffed that up, didn't I?'

'No, no. You were fine.'

'Would you mind telling my mum that? She's been riding me pretty hard today. I told her she can take my life, but she'll never take . . . MY FREEDOM!' he replied, quoting *Braveheart*.

And their conversation was off and running, like that horribly awkward night had never happened. Phoebe's whole body started to relax in a way it hadn't been able to since she first saw Monty holding that box of popcorn in the cinema foyer. And she suddenly felt foolish. Popcorn. Such a small thing. Such an innocent thing. What the hell was wrong with her?

'So why have you rung?' Monty eventually asked. 'You don't normally ring during working hours.'

Phoebe remembered he was at work. 'Sorry, you probably have customers.'

'None as important as you. Anyway, it's really quiet so I'm in the back room allegedly sorting out the parcels, while Mum mans the counter.'

'And I'm ringing you from the phone box across the road from the library.'

'What's new?'

'A lot.' She quickly updated him about the postcards and the party.

'I'm in!' Monty exclaimed. 'I mean, if you want me to come.'

'Of course,' Phoebe said, trying to sound nonchalant. Secretly, she was thrilled and relieved that she hadn't had to go through the agony of asking and him potentially saying no.

She glanced at her watch. 'Oh boy, I better get back to work.'

'And I'd better get back to sorting these parcels.'

'Good luck. I'll see you Saturday.'

'Looking forward to it,' Monty said, and Phoebe felt happy and anxious all at the same time.

As she went back into the library, she saw Glenda look pointedly at her watch and she tried not to roll her eyes. She had literally only taken one minute more than she was due for her break. She wished she could alert Glenda to the number of minutes she'd stayed back longer than her required shift or the hours she'd spent preparing materials at home, unpaid.

She joined Jasmine behind the information counter. Jasmine was helping an elderly man find a book on crystal healing, which seemed at odds with his corduroy trousers and cardigan.

'My wife has cataracts and doesn't want to have the surgery,' he was telling Jasmine. 'My granddaughter used crystals to get herself a car, so my wife wants to give them a try.'

'She got herself a car using crystals?' Phoebe couldn't help interjecting.

'It's about the power of positive thought, or at least that's what she told us. I told her that the money she saved and the small inheritance she received from her other grandparents got her the car, but she insisted it was the crystals. Which, one could suppose, means the crystals killed off her maternal grandmother in order to give her a car?'

As Jasmine led him off to the non-fiction section, Phoebe tidied up the desk and thought about the crystals and whether she could use them to wish away her sound sensitivity and make her normal.

'Ahem,' a voice said, and she looked up to find her father standing in front of her. She instantly glanced over at Glenda to see if she had noticed Phoebe had a personal visitor, but she was busy helping another patron and uncharacteristically had her back to the information desk.

'Good afternoon. How can I best assist you?' Phoebe asked in her most professional voice.

'I'm looking for a book about books,' Phil replied, in his best meeting-with-the-bank-manager voice.

'What are you doing here?'

'I was passing through Footscray and thought I might give you a lift.'

'I don't finish for another hour.'

'Well, I can wait. Is there a computer free?'

Phoebe laughed. 'Only if you booked it three weeks ago.'

'Well, I'll just go loiter in the non-fiction section.'

'Seriously, Dad, you don't have to wait. I am quite happy to catch the bus home.'

'And I'm quite happy to wait,' he said with a smile.

Phoebe watched him walk over to where Jasmine was still helping the elderly gentleman find books on crystals and wondered what was going on. Her father had never dropped by the library like this. And to hang around an extra hour to save her a ten-minute bus ride was very odd, especially when she'd only just seen him last night for dinner.

But she didn't have time to wonder about it too long because Glenda was suddenly by her side.

'Who was that?' she asked.

For a second, Phoebe was tempted to say he was a stranger, but then she realised the lie would be revealed when she left with him.

'It was my dad,' she replied. 'He's looking for a book on crystal healing.'

'Really?' Glenda asked, and Phoebe wished she'd thought of a better lie.

AT THE END of her shift, Phoebe found her father sitting in a corner, actually reading a book about crystal healing. She hoped Glenda had seen him.

'My new best friend Cedric was telling me all about it,' Phil said. 'It says here that malachite will align my kidney chakras. Or something.'

'Would you like to borrow the book, sir?'

'No, I'd like to burn it, but I expect that would get you in trouble with your scary-looking manager.'

Phil was looking over at Glenda, who was evidently wishing them both a fiery death for daring to talk in the library.

'Let's get out of here,' Phoebe said, grabbing his arm.

PHIL WAS QUIET on the car ride home, but instead of the usual easy silence, there was a heavy quality to it, like something pushing gently, yet firmly, down on Phoebe's chest. When they arrived at Salmon Street and Phoebe went to get out of the car, Phil put his hand on her arm.

'Wait a moment,' he said.

Phoebe sat back in the passenger seat and folded her hands in anticipation.

'I've been feeling bad,' he said. 'I wasn't as honest with you as I could have been the other day. When you asked about your grandparents' marriage, you took me by surprise and I didn't actually tell you everything.'

Phoebe swallowed.

'At my dad's wake, my uncle Stephen – Dad's brother – got very drunk and told me that Dad and Dorothy had had an "understanding". As long as Dorothy or her friends or the neighbours didn't know anything about his affairs, and there was enough money for her to live her life the way she wanted, then he could do what *he* wanted. That's why he spent so much time travelling for work.'

Phoebe scratched her head, trying to digest this latest bit of information.

'So,' she finally said after a long pause. 'Do you think he had an affair with Libby Winston?'

Phil's brow furrowed. 'It seems like it would have been against the rules. Libby Winston was living right under your grandmother's nose. But that's not to say it didn't happen.'

Phoebe looked at the dark facade of Salmon Street and thought about her grandparents' marriage.

'What was Granddad like?' she asked. All she could remember was a man who liked to tell bad jokes. Her mother used to call him 'The Perennial Christmas Cracker'.

'A good man, but with appetites far different from Dorothy's. He loved food and wine and parties. She preferred the company of plants. But somehow, even though they were polar opposites, they made their relationship work. I think they loved each other in their own way – but it wasn't exactly the stuff of your romance novels.'

'They're *historical* romance novels,' Phoebe said. 'And they were originally Dorothy's.'

'Well, I never saw her read one. She was always in the garden, never wanting to waste a blue sky.'

'I always think of her saying that whenever the sun is shining.'

'And do you waste those blue skies?'

'Regularly.'

Phil gave a small laugh and then sighed. 'All those flowers and plants thriving outside in the garden, but growing up inside that house, it always felt empty and cold, like I could never be truly comfortable or warm. I like it much more now that you live here.'

Phoebe was surprised. She'd barely changed a thing since she'd moved in – she often felt like she was a caretaker in a museum, trying to preserve everything for the family. She'd never considered that the family hadn't wanted it to be preserved.

Chapter 27

'WITH GREAT CELEBRATIONS come even greater hangovers,' Charlie said, handing Suze the traditional aspirin as she lay almost comatose on the couch. The vodka had been Charlie's idea of celebrating Suze submitting her chapters to Claire Portelle. Suze would've been happy enough with an early night with a hot water bottle, but Charlie had insisted. ('You've been *soooooooo* boring lately,' he'd said.)

Suze eyed the half-drunk bottle on the mantlepiece and groaned. 'What *was* that stuff?'

'Poland's finest.'

'Why aren't you suffering as much as me?'

'You're out of shape, friend, whereas I'm still match fit.' Charlie pretended to flex his muscles, clearly pleased with himself. 'I'm hoping that I can build my amazing capacity for drinking cheap spirits into my KPIs at the bank.'

Suze drank down the aspirin and closed her eyes, before opening them again as she asked, 'Where is Sacha? I thought this house meeting was her idea.'

'She's probably putting the finishing touches on the new chores roster. Love hearts over the i's and whatnot.'

'Smiley faces in the margins.'

'Bubble-writing headings.'

'Elephant stamps.'

'Scratch 'n' sniff stickers.'

The two of them grinned. There had been many iterations of the chores roster over the years, but the decorations had been consistent and they somehow made the roster even more officious.

Upstairs, they heard the sound of Sacha's bedroom door opening and Matt's voice booming out. 'Hear ye, hear ye, house meeting, house meeting.'

'When did he become a house member?' Charlie whispered.

'Maybe that's what the meeting's about?' Suze whispered back. 'Next, he'll be in the Order of the Wise Ones.'

Charlie's hand flew up to his throat in mock horror just as Sacha and Matt reached the bottom of the stairs.

Sacha looked uncharacteristically sheepish.

'Um, the thing is . . .' she started. 'I've really enjoyed sharing a house with you both, but . . .'

There was a long pause while Sacha swallowed and Matt looked at the ground. Suze felt a tightening inside her chest.

'Matt and I have decided to move out together.'

Charlie gasped loudly. And whatever had started gripping Suze's chest was now fully clenched.

'But I thought Matt would move in with us,' Charlie

exclaimed, like a child who had just been told Santa wasn't real.

'We've decided to be a grown-up couple living in a house that doesn't have a fridge in the lounge room or seventeen dead washing machines in the backyard,' Sacha said in a slightly haughty way that made Suze feel sad. She loved the home they'd built together despite all those things, and she'd thought Sacha did, too.

'I'm not taking Sacha away immediately,' Matt hastened to reassure them. 'We're going to take our time to find the right place, and we'll be able to give you at least two weeks' notice when we do.'

'Can't we come with you?' Charlie whined. 'We could be your wayward teenage children.'

'You've certainly made me feel like the mother of wayward teens,' Sacha said. 'But no. It's time for us to nest and for you to spread your wings.'

'I don't want to be a bird,' Charlie said, pouting. 'I want to be a wayward teen.'

'Suze, you haven't said anything,' Sacha said. 'Are you okay?'

Suze wasn't okay. The news, the hangover, the impending party, J, Ky, her anxiety about what Claire Portelle would think of her chapters – it was all quickly piling up in her head, like a Tetris game that had gone out of control.

'I need to go back to bed,' she said. 'I'll say something later.'

She stood up and made her way up the stairs to her room, aware that the three of them were watching her and worrying, but she didn't care. She was going to rest her aching head and hope that, while she was asleep, one of her worries would resolve itself. Or if not that, then at least the aspirin would kick in.

★

SUZE AWOKE TWO hours later, her mouth dry but her head feeling better. She looked at the ceiling. She needed to ring her mother, but she didn't want to go down to the lounge room if the others were still around. She wasn't ready to talk to them just yet.

She opened her door slightly and listened out for signs of life in the house but heard nothing, so she crept quietly down the stairs. On the telephone table was a note. It read: *We've gone to the Vic Markets. We'll bring you back a borek.*

It was signed with one of Sacha's trademark love hearts. Suze crumpled up the note and swatted it to the other side of the room.

Her mother took longer than usual to answer the phone. Normally, Suze got the sense that Barbara was sitting right beside it, always waiting for her daughter to call.

'Hello, love.' Her voice sounded bright.

'You sound chirpy.'

'I'm about to go out.'

'You what?'

'I know! I've got my outside shoes and lipstick on.'

'Where are you going?' Suze's surprise at this news elevated her out of her own misery for a second.

'One of the women in that support group invited me to her book club.'

'Oh wow, you've kept going to the support group! That's great, Mum. I should let you go. We can talk later.'

'Fiddlesticks. I don't have to leave for another half an hour. What's up with you?'

'Everything.'

'Oh dear.' And in that second, Suze caught a glimpse of how her mother used to be, back when she'd felt more like Suze's parent than her responsibility, and she found herself telling Barbara everything.

'Well, of course you need to get the postcards back,' her mother concluded. 'As for the rest, you know you always have a home here with me in Bondi. You could even transfer your studies to UNSW or Sydney.'

Suze had a flash of life with her mother before she'd moved back to Melbourne and knew it wasn't an option. Not yet. Right now, even though Barbara seemed to be doing better, they might still pull each other down, like drowning sailors. Also, she wasn't sure if she could get back into *The Bold and the Beautiful* after such a long break.

'I'm really glad you're going out, Mum,' she said.

'So am I,' her mother replied. 'I've even finished the book – something about a mandolin. It's a novel with an Italian protagonist set on a Greek island written by a British writer with a French name. Why is modern literature so complicated?'

'Because life is complicated, I guess,' Suze replied, secretly pleased that her mother had engaged with something a little more literary than *TV Week*.

'Good luck with your mission tonight. And ring me any time. And I mean *any* time.'

'Thanks, Mum. I love you.'

'I love you, too.'

Suze sat with the phone for a long time after the call, until Groovy Joe snaked his way around her ankles, his subtle way of letting her know that he was hungry. She stood up and got him some food, made herself some toast, and withdrew to her room.

She had just started to wade into a piece by Hélène Cixous for the next chapter of her thesis when there was a knock on the door. It was Charlie.

'Are you okay?' he asked, as he sat down on the edge of her bed.

'Yeah.'

'I couldn't help but overhear your conversation with your mum.'

'I thought you were out.'

'No, I was lying face down on my bed wishing Sacha had never met Matt.'

'Change is the one thing we can rely on.' It was something her stepfather Greg used to say all the time, and saying the words made her feel close to him and miss him all at once.

Charlie sighed and lay down next to her. 'I really thought we would grow old in this house and eventually it would just collapse on us and we'd all be buried together.'

'There's a cheerful thought.'

'It's more cheerful than the thought of house interviews.'

'That's true.' Suze remembered the humiliation of all the interviews she'd endured before she'd found Moor Street. In one house, a blonde woman working in marketing had sneered at her shoes, and one of her near-identical blonde housemates had questioned her life choices. ('Why on earth would you study English when you speak it every day?' she had asked.)

'We could try and get a place together,' Suze suggested.

'With your earning power, we'd end up in Preston,' Charlie shuddered.

'What about keeping the lease on this place and finding someone else for the big bedroom?'

'Are you kidding me? The white-goods graveyard and the fridge in the lounge room aren't exactly an easy sell, at least not to the type of people we probably want to move in with us.'

'I guess not.' Suze let out a loud sigh.

Charlie sat up. 'Whatever happens, wherever we live, we'll always be friends. You know that, right?'

'Yes,' Suze replied in a small voice.

'And if I find a place first, you can always crash on my floor until you find a place of your own.'

'Your floor? I thought you'd be a gentleman and offer the lady a bed.'

'What lady?'

Suze laughed and pushed Charlie off the bed with her foot.

'That proves my point entirely,' Charlie said from the floor of her room, his voice slightly muffled. 'Hey, there's my hip flask.'

He crawled under her bed and emerged seconds later, the empty hip flask in his hand.

'So it did make it back to the house after all,' Suze said. 'Never leave a man behind, etcetera, etcetera.'

'You did good, soldier. And this might just be the weapon you need for tonight's mission to save the fucking postcards from the Great Fire of Fitzroy.'

He picked himself up from the floor and grabbed the half-drunk bottle of Polish vodka from the mantlepiece. He held it aloft.

'Liquid courage, baby.'

Suze groaned and lay back on her bed. Maybe a future of not sharing a house with Charlie was a good thing – for her liver at the very least.

Chapter 28

PHOEBE KNOCKED ON the door of the Moor Street terrace, while Monty hung back behind her, cautiously eyeing the mannequin in the front window. Tonight, the mannequin was dressed entirely in clingwrap and was wearing a hat made of tinfoil.

'What's that?' Monty asked.

'It's Charlie's personal project.'

'Is Charlie Suze's boyfriend?'

Phoebe laughed. 'Wait until you meet him and then ask that question again.'

She was feeling a kind of giddiness that she hadn't felt for years, maybe not since she and Sandy had used all their pocket money savings to spend the day at Luna Park.

The door was flung open and there were Suze and Charlie

dressed to the nines. Suze was wearing a '70s-style silver snakeskin dress and Charlie was wearing a pink camouflage jacket and trousers, with a feather boa. Monty gave Phoebe a quick look as if to say *Aha*.

'I tried to talk him into wearing something else, but he insisted,' Suze said.

'This is a covert operation,' Charlie said, flinging the end of his boa over his shoulder dramatically. 'It's important to keep a low profile. The feathers will help me hide in nature.'

He then looked at Monty properly, who was standing awkwardly to the side on the footpath.

'And who is this tall glass of water?' he asked.

'I'm, er, Monty,' Monty replied, holding out his hand.

'And I'm delighted,' Charlie said, shaking Monty's hand very slowly. 'Well, my name is actually Charles Bartlett-Myers, but you can call me whatever you like.'

'Settle down now, Charles,' Suze said. 'He's spoken for.'

'All the good ones are taken,' Charlie sighed, relinquishing Monty's hand.

Phoebe blushed at this, and Monty gave a little smile and looked at the ground.

As they walked to the party, Charlie gave them all the lowdown on the history of Ky's share house. 'It's been a share house since time immemorial and every room has either been set on fire or hosted an overdose at one point or another. The owner, who's lived overseas for the last twenty years, is finally selling it and so the lease that has been passed between generations of high-functioning junkies and Arts-degree dropouts is finally ending.'

'The end of an era,' sighed Suze.

'Legend had it that one of the Farriss brothers – or maybe it was one of the Daddos – lived there,' Charlie continued.

'They're quite different, the Farrisses and the Daddos,' Suze pointed out.

'It was one of the Brother Sets,' Charlie said, with a dismissive wave of his hands. 'Anyway, the current line-up of tenants is Franco, who's okay but the worst-groomed gay man that ever walked the planet. Seriously, he's an ape in a pair of jeans. Then there's Jess, who plays in a Viking metal band by night and works as an accountant for PricewaterhouseCoopers by day; and Sven, who apparently works at the Fitz, but I can't verify that because I never go to the Fitz.'

'He had a bad caesar salad there once,' Suze offered.

'Which instantly precipitated a necessary lifetime ban,' Charlie said.

'Which has lasted five months so far.'

'Five months *is* a lifetime, Susan,' Charlie sighed, before turning back to Phoebe and Monty. 'And finally, there's Kylie Anne Reynolds, who was a rising netball star at Camberwell Girls', but who these days prefers shitting on perspex as a form of art, along with embracing the mononymity of *Ky*.'

'I didn't know that Ky was into netball,' Suze said.

'You know it makes sense, girlfriend. Those netball bitches are nasty,' Charlie replied. 'They'd sooner strangle you with their long ponytails than look at you.'

Phoebe silently disagreed. She had played – and loved – netball in high school. She and Sandy had even played for the local team in Year 10, before her friend's illness had stopped her from doing anything at all. And neither of them had ever strangled anyone with their ponytails. She was therefore glad when Suze spoke up.

'I do not accept your premise,' she said. 'I know plenty of perfectly decent netball players, myself included.'

'I rest my case,' Charlie said, one eyebrow raised.

They had now reached Rose Street. It was immediately obvious which house was having the party by the number of people spilling out of it onto the footpath.

Phoebe felt her internal switch turn itself to spin–dry mode. It had been so long since she'd gone to any kind of party, let alone an 'End of an Era' Fitzroy house party. Monty must have noticed, because he reached over and took her hand, and she felt instantly fortified.

They worked their way into the house and out to the backyard, where she and Monty shared one of the wine coolers Charlie offered them because Monty was driving and Phoebe didn't actually like wine coolers. Suze and Charlie were taking turns swigging from a hip flask. Suze had offered Phoebe some, but it smelled like turps.

The four of them huddled in a corner of the yard, near the bonfire, which turned out to be just a fire in an oil drum. Near them, a man wearing Viking horns was ripping out pages from a physics textbook and throwing them in the fire. It surprised Phoebe that Suze and Charlie weren't mingling, but she was secretly pleased that they seemed happy to hang out with her and Monty.

'I've never seen half of these people before,' Charlie observed. 'Did they bus them in from St Kilda?'

'I feel so out of place,' Monty said, looking down at his bright white sneakers. 'Like I've just stepped off the set of *Seinfeld* and onto the set of *Dogs in Space*.'

'I couldn't have put it better myself,' said Charlie, his admiration evident. Phoebe felt proud that this almost-maybe-boyfriend of hers had earned the admiration of such a terrifying person, even if the remark had been at the expense of himself.

'Ohmygod,' Suze suddenly said. 'Is that *The Carlosses* over there, talking to Steve?'

For a moment, Phoebe saw a completely alien emotion appear on Charlie's face. Was it uncertainty?

'The Carlosses? I thought he was still in Brazil,' Charlie said.

'It looks like he's back. Are you okay?'

Charlie's face resumed its usual default expression of vague disdain. 'Of course I'm okay,' he said, a little testily. 'That was all so long ago. I was over him before he even finished breaking up with me.'

But his eyes were completely focused on the group of people Suze had pointed out. Phoebe wasn't sure if all of them were The Carlosses, or some of them, or just one of them. It was confusing.

'Heyyyyyyy, Soooooooooooz.' A guy appeared out of nowhere. He was dressed in a wizard's hat and, from the way he was swaying, was already quite drunk. He draped himself around Suze like a cheap fur coat and kissed her square on the mouth. 'How the hell are you?'

'Um, not as drunk as you, apparently,' Suze replied, trying to gently extricate herself from his embrace.

Phoebe could see that the guy, if he hadn't been so drunk and dressed as a wizard, was actually quite handsome, with bright blue eyes and the kind of smile you'd see in a toothpaste commercial. But there was something about the size of his teeth that reminded her of the donkey in the hat on the postcard from Scarborough.

Charlie stepped forward. 'Kindly unhand my friend, Jonathan. You're making her feel uncomfortable.'

'I just wanna talk to her,' he said, trying to shoo Charlie away with his hand. 'Suze, can I talk to you? You've always understood me better than anyone else. Certainly much better than *Kylie*.'

He practically spat the name, and it was then that Phoebe put two and two together and finally realised who this person was.

She stood on her tiptoes to whisper in Monty's ear. 'It's J,' she said, and Monty's eyes widened.

Phoebe thoroughly expected Suze to push the drunk wizard off her and demand to know where the postcards were, but she was surprised to see her friend melting into him instead.

'Is everything okay?' Suze asked J in a low voice.

'No, it's not. Everything is fucked,' he replied, before throwing his arms up into the air and shouting, 'FUCKED!'

A few people turned around at this sudden outburst, but when they realised it was the wizard guy, they quickly returned to their conversations.

'Please, Suze, I just wanna talk to you. I've missed you so much,' he pleaded, his voice now quiet like hers.

'Okay,' Suze replied. She took his hand and led him away to an old couch covered in a tarp at the far end of the long yard, shooting an apologetic look over her shoulder at her friends as if to say, *What else can I do? The man wants to talk.*

'Stay on mission!' Charlie called after her, drawing a rectangular shape with his fingers.

'Uh, what was all that about?' Phoebe asked Charlie.

'You've just witnessed the full and destructive power that Jonathan Wakeman has over our young friend Susan,' Charlie replied with a sigh. 'It doesn't matter what a dick he is or if he's dressed like the Wizard of Earthsea, all he has to do is click his fingers and Suze comes running.'

He said all this while still gazing longingly at the group of people who were evidently known as 'The Carlosses'.

'I should go over to say hello. That's the polite thing to do, right?' Charlie asked and then left before either of them had a chance to reply. They watched him walk over to the group and embrace a tall, bronzed Adonis with curls to die for.

Phoebe and Monty remained next to the fire and talked

about everything and nothing, but Phoebe kept finding herself glancing over at Suze and J, still sitting on the old couch which seemed to be sagging under the weight of their conversation. J was talking to Suze and stroking her hair. Suze was completely still, except for the occasional swig from her hip flask. Phoebe felt strangely deflated, like she'd found out one of her sporting heroes had been taking steroids all along.

Monty kept looking over at them, too. 'What do you think we should do?' he asked. 'Do you think we should just go and leave Suze to it?'

'I don't want to leave without her,' Phoebe replied. 'I don't feel good about what's going on with her and J.'

'The situation doesn't look too bad to me,' Monty replied, eyeing the two of them at the end of the yard. 'But maybe we could go over and check.'

This time, Phoebe took his hand, glad to feel his fingers instantly tighten around hers. 'Okay, let's do it.'

Chapter 29

SURE, SUZE HAD seen J drunk before, but never like this.
Usually, he just got more confident and argumentative after
a few beers, and then started speaking in Latin after a few more.
But this was a whole new level. He was emotional and open
and almost clingy – the complete opposite of 'chilled'. She felt
torn between joining him in that same slushy state and staying
as sober as possible and looking after him. She chose the middle
road, taking the occasional swig of vodka from the hip flask that
Charlie had insisted she carry. She was pacing herself, like a
runner doing a marathon.

J was telling her about Ky and their recent (un)performances
with some guy called Magnus who had just come back from
New York and who now spoke with an American accent, even
though he'd only been there for a couple of months. 'And now

he's here at this party, wearing a beret, like he's a member of the French underground.'

Says the man in the wizard's hat, thought Suze.

'Ahem,' a voice said, and Suze pulled away from J and looked up to see Phoebe and Monty, eerily silhouetted by the fire behind them, like they were a physical manifestation of her conscience paying her a visit.

'Where are the postcards?' Phoebe asked. There was a pointiness in her voice that Suze hadn't heard before.

'The postcards?' repeated J, like a drunk parrot.

'Yes, the postcards,' Phoebe said. 'We've come to get them.'

'The postcards are gone,' another voice said, and Ky emerged from the shadows, like a villain in a Bond film. 'J burned them, didn't you, J?'

Ky was accompanied by a tall man with a goatee, thick black glasses and, yes, an actual beret. He was ostentatiously (Suze thought) smoking a cigarillo and Suze half-expected that he would open his mouth to reveal a full set of silver teeth.

'Yes, I did burn them,' J answered in an almost indiscernible whisper as he hung his head.

'Seriously, what is wrong with you people? They weren't yours to burn,' Phoebe said to them both sternly and Suze felt proud of her, like a mother bird watching her child stretch its wings for the very first time.

'As I keep telling you people, ownership is an arbitrary construct,' Ky replied, with a dismissive wave of her hand. 'Those postcards didn't belong to the writer or the person they were addressed to any more than they belonged to the person who manufactured the postcards or sold them in their shop, or the person who found them in a suitcase from an op shop. J had just as much — or as little — right to destroy them as anyone else. Wouldn't you agree, Magnus?'

She turned to the tall man and he nodded, his teeth still disappointingly hidden.

Phoebe seemed deflated. But when Monty put his arm around her, Suze felt glad for her friend. Phoebe looked so pretty in her floral shirt and her 501s. Had Suze told her she looked pretty? She couldn't remember. And were they 501s? She actually couldn't see whether there was a zip or buttons on the jeans, and she was about to lean forward to ask, and to also tell her that she looked pretty, when Ky started barking at J.

'I need the house key back.'

Ky was a yappy little black dog that thought she was much bigger than she was. Suze wanted to pat her on the head.

'Because you want to give them to Pepé Le Pew here?' For a moment, the old J flickered to life, like an engine almost turning over.

'No, you doofus, I need it back because we're vacating the house and have to return all keys.'

'Oh,' said J, slumping back onto the couch. 'I already put it on the hook by the door.'

'Wait . . . what?' Phoebe said. 'When it comes to the end of a lease, you are both model tenants, but when it comes to returning someone else's property, you burn it?'

'To quote Goethe, contradiction makes us productive,' Ky said and then left. The tall man did a strange salute to them all before following her.

'What did that mean?' Phoebe turned to Monty, who just shrugged.

'Don't look at me. We didn't cover Goethe in "South-East Asia and the Modern World",' he said.

Next to Suze on the couch, J had slumped even further, to

the point of being almost completely swallowed by the sagging cushions, but his hand was on her leg, and she felt the promise of its warmth.

'Well, we're going home now,' Phoebe said.

'Okay,' Suze replied, but then she realised that Phoebe and Monty were staring at her, and she knew that they expected her to go home with them, too. 'I'm, um, going to stay for a bit longer.'

'I really think you should come with us,' Phoebe insisted.

'No, you should stay,' J said, his hand tightening on her knee. The way he was gazing at her with those big blue eyes was just like how he used to look at her, back when they were (kind of) together, except now with much more alcohol involved.

Suze shook her head at Phoebe, who stared back at her grimly. Suze knew she had disappointed her friend and that she was letting herself down, but fuck it, she was doing it anyway.

'Well, we're going to stand over there for a while in case you change your mind,' Phoebe said, pointing to where they'd been standing before, near the fire.

I'm weak, Suze thought, as she watched them walk away. *So weak*.

But then J put his head on her shoulder and her insides turned to marshmallow.

'I'm glad you're staying,' J said.

And Suze was glad too.

PHOEBE AND MONTY hung around the party a bit longer, and Phoebe made two more entreaties to Suze to leave with them, but Suze kept refusing, her eyes deliberately avoiding Phoebe's. The last time Phoebe tried, she brought Charlie over with them as reinforcement, which Suze felt was deeply unfair, like bringing a machine gun to a knife fight. But Charlie merely peered down his nose at Suze and J and shook his head.

'These two are like those bits of Lego you can't break apart,' Charlie said to Phoebe. 'She's a lost cause.'

'She's only a lost cause if we give up on her,' Phoebe said, turning back to Suze, and grabbing her arm, she tried to pull her up. 'Come on. Let's go.'

Suze shrugged her off. She couldn't work out what was annoying her most about Phoebe right now: her persistence or the fact she was probably right. But she didn't care what was right; she wanted to follow her heart, goddammit. A robot like Phoebe would never understand.

'I'm sorry I'm not perfect, Phoebe.'

'You don't *need* to be perfect, Suze. You just need to come with me. You're better than this.'

'No, I'm not.'

'Yes, you are.'

'How do you know? You've only just met me. You don't *know* me. You don't know my *heart*.' Suze clutched at her chest like a character in her mother's daytime soap operas.

'I know your heart,' J said next to her, but his eyes were closed and he could have been talking about someone else.

'Jonathan Wakeman, you wouldn't know a heart if it walked right up to you and said, "Hello, I'm a heart,"' Charlie said.

'Ouch,' said J, his eyes still closed.

Suze couldn't stand her friends looking down at her and J like this, judging them, when they themselves were hardly masters of their own lives.

'Talk about lost causes,' she said to Charlie. 'I saw you kissing The Carlosses' arse like he'd never broken your heart. Where's your spine? You probably wouldn't recognise it if it walked up to you and said, "Hello, I'm your spine."'

'Well, that doesn't make a lick of sense,' Charlie said, but Suze could tell he was thrown a little.

'And you, Phoebe Cotton!' she said, turning to point at Phoebe dramatically. 'You're standing there being all judgy-judgy, thinking you're perfect and I'm not. But you're not perfect. You're nowhere near perfect. Have you told Monty about your big secret? Have you told him that your brain is broken and you want to kill people for eating popcorn?'

Even through the haze of alcohol, Suze was able to see something in Phoebe shut down, like a blind had been pulled down over her face.

'Let's go, Monty,' Phoebe said, now pulling on Monty's arm instead of Suze's.

Suze watched the two of them walk away, J's head on her shoulder. Charlie was watching them too.

'I don't know what that was about, but it seemed like a dick move, Susan,' Charlie said, turning back to glare at her. 'Now if you'll excuse me, I apparently have some arses to kiss.'

'Lost cause!' Suze shouted after him.

'Thank god your parents have gone,' J remarked, his eyes still shut. Suze laughed and tried to ignore the pit of writhing snakes in her stomach.

A few hours – and many drinks – later, J was still sitting with her on the couch. He'd got up a few times to go to the bathroom or the kitchen, and each time Suze had braced herself for him to not come back, but he had come back, albeit a little drunker and a little sadder.

When Ky had started dancing with Pepé Le Pew (as J kept calling him), her arms flapping like a crow about to attack its prey, J had grown agitated and Suze had dragged him from the backyard, through the rest of the party, to the front of the house.

They sat side by side in the gutter. The street was cold and quiet away from the party and the fire, and Suze started to shiver. She pulled her coat tighter around her and pushed the collar up so it covered her neck and ears.

'She's broken my heart,' J told her, his head in his hands. 'I didn't think I had a heart anymore, not after Stephanie, but somehow she found it and broke it.'

Suze didn't need him to spell out who 'she' was, but this was the first time she'd ever heard him mention Stephanie. But she didn't need to wonder for long, because J launched into the whole story about Stephanie Winger and how they'd gone out for five months in Year 12, but then she'd left him for someone on the footy team, and he'd driven his car into a tree 'kind of on purpose'.

'That's where I got this scar,' he said, lifting his head and pointing at the scar on his forehead, the one Suze had always looked at but had never asked him about. She'd had enough vodka to turn his face towards hers and to stroke the scar gently.

'Poor J,' she said. In her mind's eye, she could picture a younger J, sad and desperate, getting into his car, his chest bursting with emotions he was unable to process. 'Where is Stephanie Winger now?'

J fell back into himself, like a balloon that was rapidly deflating. 'Engaged to a financial analyst in Sydney. And now Ky is leaving me, too.'

'I didn't think you did the boyfriend-and-girlfriend thing,' Suze said.

'I don't. What Ky and I had was much deeper than that. We're soulmates, Suze. Soulmates!'

He buried his head back into her shoulder and started making the sound of a lawnmower that wouldn't start. Was he actually crying?

Suze was taken aback. This was as far from 'chilled' as she'd ever seen J, and in direct response, she felt strangely calm. Half of her wanted to compound this reversal of fortune by leaving J to cry alone in the gutter. But the other half still wanted to be with him.

The weaker half won, of course. She lifted his head from her shoulder and turned to him, cupping his face in her hands.

'You're going to be okay,' she said. 'There will be other soulmates.'

Like me, she hoped.

He stared at her with his big, beautiful blue eyes that had always felt to her like swimming pools on a very hot day.

'Suze, beautiful Suze,' he murmured. 'You have always understood me best.'

And he leaned in and kissed her. His mouth tasted like an ashtray doused in beer, but his lips felt soft and familiar, and she, too, leaned into the kiss, pathetically grateful that she got to kiss him again, even if she knew she was taking the scraps from Ky's table.

'Let's get out of here,' she said, but in all honesty, she didn't know where to go. She knew Charlie would have an absolute fit if he found J in their house, and that Sacha would probably never speak to her ever again.

J, in the meantime, had ideas of his own.

'I need to go home,' he said. He tried to stand up but fell back down and Suze realised he was not going anywhere on his own two feet. He lifted his hand and called, somewhat pathetically, more a question than a command, to the empty street: 'Taxi?'

'Okay, let's get you to Brunswick Street and find you a cab,' she said, pulling him to his feet, a sinking feeling in her heart. He was going home, to that place where she couldn't follow.

'Suze, beautiful Suze,' he repeated.

'Yeah, yeah, beautiful Suze,' she said.

It didn't take too long to hail a taxi on Brunswick Street, but the driver wasn't pleased at the look of J as Suze helped him into the back seat.

'He's too drunk,' the taxi driver said. 'I've already had to clean vomit off the seats twice this week.'

'He won't vomit,' she promised. 'Please? He needs to get home.'

The taxi driver grunted.

She kissed J on his forehead. 'Do you have enough money?'

'I have lots and lots and lots of money,' J said. 'Lots!'

'Good. Now give the nice man your address. And ring me in the morning.' She knew he wouldn't ring her in the morning, but she said it anyway.

'What?' the taxi driver said as she went to close the door. 'You're not coming with him? I'm not taking him by himself.'

'Please,' she pleaded.

'No, either you come with him to make sure he doesn't spew all over my upholstery, or you find him another cab.'

'You can come with me!' J exclaimed, clapping his hands like a delighted child.

He didn't need to ask twice. Suze quickly ran to the other side of the taxi and climbed in.

Finally, she was going to J's house.

Chapter 30

A s she sat in the back seat of her parents' car on the way to the Western Retreat Retirement Village, Phoebe regretted ever having mentioned the Fitzroy party to her parents. At their last Tuesday night dinner, she'd used it as evidence of her blossoming social life, but now it just felt like a symbol of her failure. She didn't even want to think about it, let alone talk about it. But her mother had other ideas.

'So, were there many people? What was the bonfire like? Did your friend get the postcards back?' Ellen asked.

An image of Suze swigging from the hip flask and then dissolving into J like she was the aspirin to his water flashed through Phoebe's mind. And then she remembered Monty asking about Suze's popcorn comment, which caused all of Phoebe's *Get Smart* doors to slam shut simultaneously and resulted in a very long and extremely awkward silence on the drive home.

She found herself reverting to her former teenage self with colourless answers. 'I guess so. Okay. And no.'

'That's a shame. So, will you see this boy Montgomery again? He sounds very nice.'

'Probably not,' Phoebe replied, and then instantly wanted to take the words back. When it came to her mother, it was like waving a red flag at a bull.

Ellen immediately twisted around in the front passenger seat to look directly at Phoebe. 'Why not?' she demanded. 'What's wrong with him?'

'There's nothing wrong with Monty.'

'Well, there's nothing wrong with you either.'

There was everything wrong with Phoebe. *Everything*. And now that Suze had blurted out her secret about her Not Quite Right brain to Monty, he knew it too.

'Leave her alone,' Phil said. 'Let her do things in her own time.'

Ellen turned back to Phil. 'But she doesn't do anything in any time. She uses the eating noises as an excuse to keep moving from room to room, away from people.' Ellen twisted back to face Phoebe. 'Was that it? Did Monty eat popcorn at the movie with his mouth open? You can't go on like this, shutting the world out with the "Hallelujah Chorus".'

'Please don't trivialise it, Ellen,' Phil said. His voice was tight – this was the closest to anger Phoebe had seen him get in a long time. 'You don't know what it's like to be Phoebe. And for that matter, I don't either.'

Ellen huffed and turned back to the front. *Great,* thought Phoebe. *I've lost all my friends and now I'm breaking up my parents' marriage.* She slumped down in the back seat, hoping to disappear altogether.

★

AT THE WESTERN Retreat, Phoebe presented her grandmother with some flowers from the Salmon Street garden.

'Evidence that not everything in my garden is dead,' Dorothy said, as she arranged them in a vase. 'Although it would probably take a nuclear winter to kill that hydrangea bush.'

'Now, now, Mum,' Phil said. 'It's not really your garden anymore, now is it?'

'From what Mrs Papathanasiou tells me, nor would it seem to be Phoebe's garden,' Dorothy snapped, placing the vase of flowers in the centre of her small round dining table. 'Now, we'd best be going. We're late for morning tea.'

Phoebe shot a look at her father. Nobody had said anything about a morning tea. She'd thought they would just hang out in the unit so Dorothy could snipe at them at close range, as was her birthday tradition. There was a part of Phoebe that needed that, like a form of self-flagellation after the disaster of the night before.

'It's time that the people of the Western Retreat met my family,' Dorothy said, surprising Phoebe. She'd known that Dorothy had a very busy schedule of aqua aerobics and pottery classes, but she'd never thought about the fact that there were other people there, and that Dorothy might actually talk to them.

As they followed Dorothy out of her unit and along a flower-lined path leading towards a large brick building, Phoebe noticed that Dorothy had a dab of pink lipstick on and a dark green scarf tied around her neck to offset her usual 'wall of beige' look.

'This is the lounge,' she said, leading them into a large, sunny room filled with small tables and chairs and elderly people. 'When I first moved in, they had long tables like a cafeteria but a group of us campaigned for cabaret-style seating.'

'But without the actual cabaret,' Phil said.

'Actually, Philip, we have had a sufficient number of cabarets performed in this space to earn the label,' Dorothy scolded him, while Phoebe stood wondering who the 'us' was in that campaign.

'Here we are,' Dorothy said, stopping at a RESERVED sign perched on a crisp white tablecloth next to a huge bunch of red roses. Phoebe cast her eyes around the room. None of the other tables had red roses or white tablecloths.

'Dorothy!' A man wearing a tartan bow tie rushed over and Phoebe braced herself for her grandmother's displeasure.

But instead, Dorothy smiled graciously and gave a little nod, like a queen greeting a loyal subject. She looked far happier to see this person than she had to receive flowers from Salmon Street.

'This is my son, Philip, my daughter-in-law, Ellen, and my granddaughter, Phoebe. And this,' she gestured back to Mr Dicky-Bow. 'This is Mr Grange.'

'Please, call me Harold,' the man said to them with a magnanimous smile. 'Would you mind if my friend Carol and I join you fine folk?'

Once again, Phoebe braced herself, ready for her grandmother to bristle at this man boldly inviting himself and his lady friend to sit at their table.

'It would be my pleasure,' Dorothy said instead, her smile widening even further.

Phoebe looked over at her father to share her surprise, but Phil was too busy staring at Dorothy, his mouth ever-so-slightly agape.

Harold waved over a woman wearing a powder-blue dress with matching eyeshadow and bright red lipstick, evidently Carol.

'Happy birthday, Dorothy,' Carol exclaimed, springing forth

to kiss Dorothy on both cheeks. Clearly, Carol had no idea who she was dealing with. 'Did you like the flowers?'

Phoebe looked back over at Dorothy, expecting her to demand everybody stop all this fuss immediately, but yet again, her smile endured.

'They're beautiful,' Dorothy said, once more with that royal nod. 'Thank you so much.'

'Shall we go and get you scones, Mum?' Phil asked. Surely this was the time for Dorothy to snap out of this reverie and tell her son that she was perfectly capable of serving herself.

'Why, that would be lovely.' By this stage, Dorothy's demeanour was so serene, she'd certainly be on track for recognition as a living saint. But then she added, 'However, I suggest you exercise moderation with the cream on your own plate, Philip. You've put on some weight.'

Perhaps the sainthood wasn't exactly in the bag, Phoebe thought. But still.

'Are we in an episode of *The Twilight Zone*?' Phoebe whispered to her father, as they walked over to the buffet, with Ellen following behind.

'It seems that the role of Dorothy Cotton is *not* being played by Dorothy Cotton for today's matinee,' Phil muttered back.

'You two,' Ellen hissed, but she looked just as confounded. 'It seems like your grandmother is better at making friends than you are, Phoebe.'

'Now that was unnecessary, Ellen,' Phil said, putting his arm around Phoebe, as if that might protect her from further such remarks.

'You're right,' Ellen said. She reached out and patted Phoebe on the arm. 'I'm sorry, Phoebe. It's just . . . This is all so confusing.'

Even though her mother's words hurt her, Phoebe knew

it was true. She looked back at the cabaret-style table where Dorothy was chatting, and even laughing, with Harold and Carol. Phoebe had never known Dorothy to have friends before – on Salmon Street, she'd only had allies (Mrs Pap) and enemies (the smiley Mrs Whitehouse, who was always very friendly to Phoebe, but who apparently had crossed Dorothy one time too many). But even then, Dorothy's friendship resume was better than Phoebe's, who'd had nobody since Sandy, and who had even less than nobody after the previous night's disastrous party.

'You'll find your people,' Ellen said, patting Phoebe again on the arm and then handing her a plate.

Phoebe wanted to tell her mother that she thought she *had* found her people, but she'd been wrong.

'This is a pretty good spread,' Phil remarked, as he filled one plate with scones (no cream) and the other with chicken sandwiches cut in small triangles.

'You'd certainly hope so considering the cost of living here,' Ellen said in a low voice.

Phoebe stared at the food. She wasn't really hungry, but it was always easier for her if she was eating when other people were eating. It gave her something to try to focus on.

'I bet you're glad it's all soft food,' Phil whispered to Phoebe. 'And I bet the residents are, too. Did you know that dentures used to be a common wedding gift in the British Isles?'

'Well, now I've heard everything,' Phoebe whispered back, finally settling on an egg sandwich and a slice of Swiss roll.

As they walked back towards the table, Dorothy was holding court with Carol and Harold and another couple who had stopped by the table. They were hanging off every word in the story she was telling, which was evidently coming to its conclusion.

'. . . and that's how I came to hate raisins,' she said, and the group erupted into laughter. Harold placed his hand on Dorothy's knee, as if to support himself through his fit of hilarity.

'Ah, there you are,' Dorothy said, smiling up at Phoebe and her parents. Phoebe couldn't help but notice that Harold's hand was still resting lightly on Dorothy's knee.

Yes, here we are, she thought, even though she didn't quite believe it.

HER PARENTS CLEARLY hadn't seen Harold Grange's hand, because raisins were their hot topic as they walked back to the car.

'Why does she hate raisins? Why didn't I know she hated raisins? What's the difference between a raisin and a sultana anyway?' Ellen wanted to know.

'Let me address your questions one at a time,' Phil replied. '*Why does she hate raisins?* I do not know. *Why didn't you know she hated raisins?* Again, I do not know. As for the difference between raisins and sultanas, I think that comes down to the grape varietal and the drying method.'

'You're very quiet,' Ellen said over her shoulder to Phoebe, who was trailing behind.

'I'm just tired,' she lied. The truth was she was falling into a deep funk. If she'd dreaded going to the Western Retreat for Dorothy's birthday, she was dreading returning to an empty house and even emptier life more.

'Why do you think Dorothy is never like that with us?' she found herself asking her parents in that same tone of voice she might have once used to ask why Santa hadn't brought her a Cabbage Patch doll for Christmas.

'Beats me,' said Ellen.

'Because she loves us best,' Phil replied, turning to look at her. Phoebe's face must have betrayed her confusion because her father quickly added, 'I know it sounds strange, but it's true. It took me decades of being her son to realise that she just wanted the best for me, for me to be the best version of myself.'

'Well, it worked,' Ellen said, now touching Phil's arm. 'I can't imagine a better version of you.'

Phoebe wanted to say 'Well, now I've heard everything' because really, now she had heard everything. Her grandmother was making friends and maybe even had a boyfriend. Her mother was being soppy. And her father seemed to think that Dorothy's barbed comments were a form of love. She wanted to go back to the time before the postcards, where life was quiet and simple, and it was just her and the Regency romance books. But somehow, even though she wasn't sure if she would ever see Suze or Monty again, she knew that her life could never be that quiet and simple again.

Chapter 31

SUZE WOKE WITH a terrible headache and the crushing weight of J's arm across her body.

It took her a few seconds to remember where she was and how she'd got there. And then she remembered the party, the couch, Ky, Pepé Le Pew, Phoebe and Monty looming over her like spectres, the gutter, and the taxi ride to Clifton Hill.

They'd crept down the side of the house so they wouldn't wake J's housemates, out to the granny flat where J lived. After that, J had lain down on the bed while Suze used the bathroom, and by the time she had come out, he was completely asleep. So she had stripped down to her T-shirt and undies and had lain down beside him, disappointed that he was asleep, but also relieved that she, too, could now rest her vodka-addled head.

Now, she eased J's arm off her and propped herself up so she could have a proper look around.

It was a large room, with a small ensuite, and a microwave, kettle and sink in the corner – the kind of thing she supposed was called a kitchenette. It was reasonably tidy, not the explosion of dirty clothing and half-drunk cups of tea that she had seen in the rooms of other guys J's age. Instead, there was a basket of dirty washing by the door and, next to it, another basket full of carefully folded clean clothes. Suze imagined J folding his clothes with such care and felt a rush of affection for him.

Above the bed, there was a framed poster of *Betty Blue*. In Suze's experience, it was synonymous with boys who thought they were intense and arty and fantasised about a beautiful – yet broken – woman typing up their brilliant manuscript, but she forgave J for it because next to it was a poster of that Robert Doisneau photo of the couple kissing in Paris. It was one of her favourite photos ever.

She rolled onto her side and gazed at J's face, relaxed and almost angelic in sleep. He had slight stubble and there was some dry spit around the edges of his mouth, but he was still handsome.

He opened his eyes, very slowly, and looked at her.

'Suze,' he said groggily. 'What are you doing here?'

'I had to be your chaperone in the taxi, remember?'

He shook his head. 'I don't remember at all.' He sat up in the bed and looked around, like he was seeking evidence. 'Did we . . . did we wake up my, um, housemates?' he asked, slightly panicked.

'No, we went down the side of the house,' she assured him. 'Nobody was woken up.'

He lay back down, obviously relieved. *These housemates of his must be formidable*, she thought. She had always imagined that they would have a chores roster way more extensive and rigorous than Sacha's, without the rainbow stickers. And that they would have labels on all the food in the fridge and the pantry.

'So, what else happened last night?'

'You were quite upset,' she told him. 'About Ky. And about Stephanie?'

'Oh god,' he said, slapping his forehead. 'I must have been drunk if I was talking about Stephanie.'

'Stephanie must have left quite a mark,' she said.

'It was just a high school thing,' he said with a dismissive wave of his hand.

'And Ky?'

'A misunderstanding.'

Suze wasn't sure what the misunderstanding was, but J had closed his eyes.

'Did anything happen between us?'

'No. Well, not much.'

'A shame,' he said. 'I don't normally invite women into my lair.'

Suze immediately thought of the neatly folded laundry and almost laughed out loud, but she saw that he was being serious.

'Thank you for looking after me,' he said, turning onto his side and gazing at her with those blue eyes of his. Those beautiful, beautiful eyes. 'Truly.'

She could feel herself sliding back into him and she was about to just let go and let herself fall when there was a knock on the door.

J sat bolt upright.

'Jonathan?' a female voice asked. 'Are you there?'

It was one of his housemates. She sounded older than Suze had imagined. No wonder they were so uptight.

'Coming!' J called out and, grabbing a robe, pulled it around himself and ran to the door. He opened it only a sliver so Suze couldn't see who was on the other side.

'What?' he asked. Suze was surprised by his tone. For someone he was so terrified of, he was sounding quite testy.

'I've just come to get your dirty washing,' the woman said. Suze felt her eyebrows shoot up to the ceiling with surprise. 'Did you see the clean pile I left you?'

'Yes, I did,' he said, opening the door wide enough to push the basket of dirty clothes through. 'I'm just . . . busy.'

'Sorry, I didn't mean to bother you. There's sausages and eggs for breakfast if you want it.'

'Thanks, Mum,' J said, trying to swallow the name so Suze didn't hear it. 'Maybe later.'

'Good-o,' the voice replied. 'I'll leave it on the warmer for you.'

Oh my god, Suze thought. *J's housemates are his parents.*

J shut the door and walked back to the bed, his eyes not meeting hers. He knew he'd been sprung.

'Yes, um, so yes, in case you're wondering, I still live at home,' he said. 'I have my own space, so it doesn't really make sense wasting money on rent.'

'Or meals or laundry or utilities,' Suze observed.

'I pay my own telephone bill,' he said.

Well, whoop-de-do, Suze thought. She remembered how often she'd been skint but somehow J had managed to get her to pay, and all that time he'd been living at home, having his mum cook his meals and do his washing, like a little prince.

She looked at J and it was like a light had been switched on and she saw him properly for the first time. Like *really* properly.

'Have you ever lived away from home?'

'Of course I have,' he replied. 'You know that.'

She thought of his three years at Ormond College and remembered when he had taken her as his guest to a meal in the dining hall, just after they'd first met. It had been a room full of little princes.

'I mean, other than Ormond,' she said.

'I count Ormond.' (Suze didn't.)

Suze stood up, pulled on her trousers and started wandering around the room.

'What are you doing?' J asked.

'Getting to know you,' she said.

She opened his wardrobe and saw one section contained all his performance/(un)performance costumes, all hanging neatly, evidently dry-cleaned, judging by the wire hangers and plastic covers. She wondered what Ky would think of this.

She went over to his bookshelf, but rather than the expansive collection of Charles Bukowski and Jack Kerouac she had expected, it was a handful of John Grisham paperbacks, the complete works of Aristotle and a self-help book called *Think Like a Winner.*

'Does this work?' she asked him.

J shrugged. 'I haven't read it.'

She continued around the room, stopping to admire the careful way the Robert Doisneau poster had been tacked to the wall.

'I love this photo,' she murmured.

'Ky says they're only models posing,' J said.

'Ky's been here?' Suze turned around, surprised.

'No,' he replied, hanging his head. 'I asked her to come and stay the night with me, but she told me that I wasn't being chilled.'

'Ha,' Suze said, mostly to herself. She continued her inspection, this time focusing on a set of Star Wars collectibles, still in their boxes.

'They're going to be worth an absolute mint one day,' he said, but she didn't say anything. She just moved on to the next part of the room.

As she skimmed through his CD shelf, she was aware that this was probably the most chilled she'd ever been around J, and she realised how little she actually cared about whether or not he was noticing. *And that*, she concluded, *is the true meaning of being chilled*.

After noting the large number of Billy Joel and Dire Straits albums in his collection, making a point of pulling out *Brothers in Arms* and staring at it very intently, she finally turned around to face him. He was still sitting in bed, the sheet pulled up to his chin, looking warily at her, like she might attack him at any moment.

'I think you should take me out for breakfast,' she told him.

'My mum's already cooked for me,' he said, with a little shrug.

And there it is, she thought. The words that finally meant the spell was broken. J was no longer a sex god, the object of her fantasises. He was just a guy who lived at home and pretended that nailing offal to the wall was an act of Supreme Art, even though he was probably wearing underpants ironed by his mother under his costume. And all that would be okay if he didn't live his life pretending otherwise.

'Okay,' she shrugged back. 'I should head off.'

'Do you want to catch up later? I could drop by.'

'I've got plans,' she told him, slipping on her shoes and collecting her costume bits and pieces. 'Maybe another time.'

'But wait,' he said. 'I have something to give you.'

And he got out of the bed and rummaged around a drawer in the desk in the corner of the room. He pulled out a small stack of postcards. On the top was a postcard of a European town, all lolly-coloured houses and turrets and castles on hills.

'What? You didn't burn them?' J really was full of surprises.

'I burned some others that my parents sent me when they went to New Zealand. I knew Ky wouldn't check.'

'But why didn't you burn them?'

'Because it's a federal offence to burn someone's mail. You told me that,' he said. 'Also, I can't go to jail. I'm too good-looking.'

Suze couldn't tell if he was joking or not, and she concluded it was a little bit from column A and a little bit from column B.

Chapter 32

THE MINUTE PHOEBE stepped through the front door, her eyes sought out the answering machine to see if the light was blinking.

It wasn't.

She thought back to only a month or so ago when she would ignore the answering machine for days at a time, sometimes as long as a week. But these days, it was a lifeline between her and the world. The pull that the little red light had on her eyes was like a magnet. Even when she knew the phone hadn't rung at all, she still found herself checking it. Just in case. She hated how dependent she had become on an ugly box of electronics.

As she made herself a cup of tea, she thought about how *complicated* relationships of any kind were. She thought about her parents talking in the car on the way to Dorothy's birthday lunch, the small pricks of tension, the unspoken currents of conflict between them that had smoothed them down over the years, like rocks in a river.

And there was Monty. Maybe Suze was right and it really was time to tell him the truth about the eating noises and how they made the *Get Smart* doors close between Phoebe and the rest of the world.

'Maybe you'll eventually grow out of it,' her mum had once said, more out of hope than anything. That was after that trip to their GP.

For a while, Phoebe had believed her, and she'd waited for the sounds to hurt her brain less, but they never did. If anything, things got worse, and her shame about her Not Quite Right brain had only grown deeper. She wasn't confident that Monty would look at her the same way if he knew how flawed she was, how difficult it was to be around her. What she was really like.

She thought of Suze and how comfortable she seemed in her own skin and her own life. Or at least that's what Phoebe had thought until last night. The image of Suze so completely caught in J's tractor beam was something she couldn't unsee.

And then Suze's words came back and whipped around her like a squall. She'd taken a risk and had confided in Suze in a way she'd never been able to confide in Sandy, but it had blown up in her face.

Yes, relationships were complicated, she concluded.

Her mum was always telling Phoebe that she was shutting out the world, but Ellen had no idea how much she'd been trying to let the world in and how much pain it was causing everybody.

Now it's time to actually shut the world out, Phoebe thought, as she took the phone off the hook, grabbed a family block of chocolate from the pantry and disappeared inside her latest Georgette Heyer book for the rest of the afternoon.

TWO DAYS LATER, Phoebe still hadn't replaced the receiver. She knew she was being childish, maybe even cruel, but she also knew she was doing the best thing for everyone. They'd thank her eventually. They really would.

And in any case, they probably weren't trying to call her anyway.

Luckily for Phoebe, she'd been easily distracted by work. There had been a few primary school visits and the librarian who was the education officer had been sick, so Phoebe had had to step in, quickly discovering the preschool voice she used to control the normal Story Time crowd had zero effect on eight-year-old boys. Meanwhile, Glenda was on the rampage because someone, possibly even an adult, had stuck chewing gum underneath one of the computer stations. Phoebe knew it hadn't happened on her watch – she would have been onto any gum chewer at the slightest movement of their jaw – but she couldn't tell Glenda that because it would mean revealing too much of herself.

Instead, she inadvertently revealed herself another way by whipping her head around every time she detected any tall man coming through the front doors.

'Is there something troubling you, Phoebe?' Glenda asked her one day as they were unpacking the interlibrary loans together and Phoebe had almost given herself whiplash when a tall Chinese guy had walked into the library. 'You're not your usual self.'

Phoebe had no idea what Glenda considered to be her 'usual self', but she was grateful for her concern. But instead of bursting into tears, like she wanted to, she just shook her head. 'No, I'm okay. Thank you for asking.'

As she stacked the books on the Reserved shelf, she thought about how all these friendships – Sandy, Monty, Suze – felt like books she'd borrowed and loved but had to return.

EVEN THOUGH PHOEBE was exhausted, she dragged herself to her parents' house for their regular Tuesday night dinner because she knew that having to explain why she wasn't going would take more energy than actually going.

'I tried calling you on Sunday but the line was always busy,' Phil said, once they'd finished dinner and the stereo had been turned off. 'You've obviously been having a bit of a gasbag with those new friends of yours.'

'Just like you and Sandy did back in the day,' Ellen said, with a heavy whiff of nostalgia. Ellen had obviously forgotten that she'd spent most of the '80s in a state of utter fury that Phoebe was still on the phone. 'Have you heard anything from Montgomery?'

Just the mention of Monty's name was like a little knife in her heart.

'No,' Phoebe said. 'Anyway, after meeting Dorothy's gentleman caller, Mr Grange, I'm setting my sights on men with bow ties.'

Her father laughed, but Ellen just said, 'Oh, Phoebe.'

But it wasn't in the usual disappointed tone. This time, her voice was full of sadness.

'We might meet up this weekend,' Phoebe said, although she knew that was impossible with the phone so firmly off the hook. 'Anyway, I'm busy at work right now. I've started planning the activities for Halloween and Christmas.'

'But it's the first day of August,' Phil said.

'That's practically December,' Ellen moaned, and the conversation thankfully swerved away from Phoebe's personal life and moved on to the speed at which the year was going. 'We should probably start negotiations with Dorothy about where to hold Christmas. I'm not sure I can stomach cabaret-style seating for Christmas lunch.'

Every year, there was an extended power struggle between Ellen and Dorothy about who was hosting Christmas. Now that there was a third venue in the mix, it had become almost impossible.

'Would you like some dessert, Phoebe?' her father asked, changing the subject again. 'I can make you peach Melba. Well, it's just ice cream and tinned peaches, but we can pretend it's fancy.'

'Um, okay,' Phoebe replied. She wasn't in the mood for going home to an empty house. In fact, she suddenly had the urge to stay the night in her childhood bedroom and never return to Salmon Street.

'Did you know that the soprano Dame Nellie Melba had two dishes named after her? One was peach Melba and the other was Melba toast.'

'Well, now I've heard everything,' Phoebe replied.

'I wonder if anyone has ever made peach Melba toast. That'd be fun. It reminds me of that game we used to play during long car rides, do you remember? When we joined all the names.'

Phoebe nodded. She could still remember the string of names they'd come up with and she recited it out loud. 'It was Big Ben – Ben Elton – Elton John – John Major – Major Tom – Tom Hanks – Hank Williams – William Shakespeare – Shakespears Sister.'

'There was a little bit of cheating in there. William is not the same as Williams,' Ellen remarked, opening up an old argument.

'Phoebe and I made up the game, so Phoebe and I made the rules. You're like a football ref calling a cricket match.'

Ellen laughed. 'I'm not sure that's the same.'

Phoebe sat back in her chair and half-listened to her parents talk. She thought, as she often had, that her parents' relationship was like a symphony, with instruments coming in and out, the music rising and falling. And while the moments of silence could be the most powerful, the music that followed was always the sweetest. And yet today, it may as well have been the soundtrack to *The Piano* again, such was the gaping hole it had opened up in her chest.

Chapter 33

THE FIRST PERSON Suze wanted to talk to about her most recent experience with J was Phoebe. This surprised her and didn't surprise her at the same time. Phoebe was a bit like Groovy Joe, who had wandered into their lives, slowly spending more and more time in the house, until one day they realised he lived there and they couldn't imagine the house without him.

But she couldn't get through to Phoebe, no matter how many times she tried to call her.

After the third day of trying, she called Telstra to report a fault on the line.

'They think the phone's just off the hook,' she told Charlie, who was sitting on the couch next to her, this time reading an old copy of *Woman's Day* with a woman wearing a crocheted hat on the cover.

'I'm not surprised,' Charlie muttered.

'What do you mean you're not surprised?'

'You don't remember? Oh, Susan. That's really too much,' Charlie admonished her.

'Remember what?'

'At the party, you said some things to young Phoebe Rotten that seemed to upset her, although I, personally, couldn't see what the big deal was. It was something about eating noises.'

'Oh god.' Suze grimaced as the memory swam back into view. Phoebe and Monty looming above her. The look on Phoebe's face, like all her confidence had been whipped out from under her, like a tablecloth beneath a tea set, but where the trick goes wrong and the tea set falls on the floor and shatters into a thousand pieces. Phoebe had confided in her, and she'd broken that confidence after a few slugs of vodka. Well, more than a few. But still.

'Yeah, whatever was going on there, it obviously upset Phoebe. *Ergo* . . . phone off the hook.'

'I'm such a dick,' Suze moaned.

'Give her some time. She'll calm down.' Charlie returned to his magazine. But Suze wasn't sure about that. Her stomach was now tied up in a thousand knots, each one tightening with every thought about every terrible word she'd said to Phoebe Cotton.

A FEW DAYS later, Charlie knocked on her bedroom door.

He was excited. Suze knew he was excited because he never smiled after he'd climbed the stairs. 'It's Mr Tall, Dark and Handsome on the phone.'

'Who?' She couldn't imagine that Charlie would ever refer to J that way.

'Phoebe Rotten's special friend.'

Suze was surprised Monty had her number.

'I didn't know your surname, but I remembered Charlie's was "Bartlett-Myers" and I looked him up in the phone book,' Monty explained.

'I wouldn't tell Charlie that if I were you,' she laughed, thinking that she wouldn't tell Charlie either. His ego would explode.

Monty went on to tell her how he hadn't been able to get through to Phoebe all week either.

'I haven't been able to go see her at the library because I'm on a work placement,' he added. 'I'm really worried about her, Suze.'

'I am, too.'

'What do you think has upset her so much? She was very quiet in the car on the way home from the party. I asked her about what you said. You know, about popcorn, and she shut down completely.'

'Uh, yes, well, that,' Suze said, feeling sheepish again. 'I shouldn't have mentioned that.'

'So what was it about?'

'I've said more than enough. But you should go and visit her at home when you get a chance. And maybe she'll explain it to you herself.'

'Okay,' Monty said. But he sounded wary, and after the phone call, Suze found herself hoping Phoebe would be able to just tell him about her sound issues and they could all move on.

Everyone had their quirks and kinks. Suze wished she could help Phoebe understand that. Certainly, she'd just discovered J was a whole basket of weird.

★

'I CAME INTO the Co-op today with some white chick with dreadlocks,' Sacha told Suze over dinner that night. They were sitting in the lounge room, Sacha and Charlie on the couch like the King and Queen of the House, and Matt and Suze sitting on the milk crates, like their humble servants.

'Oh, yeah?' Suze said. She was so used to pretending to Sacha and Charlie that she didn't care, but as the words came out, she found that she really didn't care.

Suze watched Charlie exchange a knowing look with Sacha. Sensing some kind of interrogation, Suze stood and collected the plates.

'It's my turn to wash up,' she said.

But Charlie followed her into the kitchen.

'Something happened on Saturday night, didn't it?' he asked, as she ran the water for the dishes. 'You disappeared off into the night with him and you haven't mentioned him since. Not even once.'

'Let's just say the spell has finally been broken,' Suze said.

'Amen to that.'

'Also, he gave me back the postcards,' Suze added.

'What? I thought he'd burned them.'

'Turns out he's less of an anarchist than he – or Ky – supposed.'

'Quelle surprise,' Charlie said. 'Does Phoebe Rotten know about the postcards?'

'I still haven't been able to get through to her,' Suze admitted.

'Quelle surprise double. You should go around to her house and apologise for . . . whatever it was you did.'

'That's exactly what I told Monty to do.'

'To apologise for what you did?'

Suze laughed. 'No, to go to her house.'

'You should go together. A two-pronged attack. I could come too. A third prong. A very big third prong.'

'Stand down, John Wayne Bobbitt.' Suze laughed again. 'We'll let you know if your services are needed.'

MONTY AGREED TO go together ('There's safety in numbers,' he'd said, although they both knew it was Phoebe that they were really worried about). He picked her up from West Footscray Station the following Saturday morning and they drove to Salmon Street.

The street was an explosion of people washing cars and mowing lawns, but at Number 6, the house was completely quiet and the blinds were drawn.

As they'd discussed in the car, Suze knocked on the front door, while Monty hung back at the gate. Suze knew it was best if she talked to Phoebe first because she knew exactly why Phoebe was upset with her and she could apologise immediately, hopefully clearing the air enough for Phoebe to then be able to talk to Monty.

'Phoebe?' she called. 'Are you there?'

Deep inside the house, she could hear a noise, maybe a radio, but she knew that didn't necessarily mean someone was home. People left the radio on all the time in empty houses – at least, they did where she grew up.

'Phoebe?' she called again, knocking harder. She beckoned for Monty to give it a try.

'Phoebe, it's Monty and Suze,' he called out, after some impressively loud knocking. 'We're worried about you.'

'Can I help you?'

A short elderly woman was standing at the gate wearing gardening gloves.

'We're Phoebe's friends,' Suze explained. 'We haven't heard from her for a while. We're worried about her.'

'I think she probably is too busy,' the woman said. Her accent was thick, maybe Italian or Greek, Suze thought.

'Maybe,' Monty said.

'Do you know if she is in?' Suze asked.

'I don't know,' the woman shrugged. 'I mind my own business.'

Suze didn't believe for a moment that this woman minded her own business. If she did, she wouldn't be standing there trying to suss out who they were.

'We might just wait here for her,' Suze said, sitting down on the front porch step.

'I think you're trespassing, and I will call the police.'

'We're waiting for our friend,' Monty explained.

'It's private property.'

'And we're her friends.'

'If you were her friends, she'd answer the door,' the woman said, evidently impressed with her own logic.

'So, she is home?' Suze asked.

'I mind my own business until my very big and very strong son arrives to visit me very soon,' the woman said, backing off. She retreated back to her house across the road, where she continued gardening, one eye fixed firmly on them.

Monty sat down next to Suze on the step and they both smiled and waved at the woman every time she stopped pruning and looked over at them.

'At least we know Phoebe's safe,' Suze remarked. 'Nothing's going to happen to her with that woman around. Or her very big and very strong son.'

'Do you think Phoebe's really home and not opening the door to us?'

'I don't know.' Suze really didn't know. She didn't even know if it was worth waiting there on the step. If Phoebe didn't want to talk to them, they couldn't force her. 'I wish I could go back in time to the party and stick a sock in my drunk mouth.'

'You were just lashing out. We were trying to separate you from that guy, J.'

'Yeah, I was like a dog trying to protect my bone. What's worse is that that bone turned out not to be worth protecting. And anyway, Phoebe didn't deserve that. She's one of the best people I know.'

A small Nissan Hatchback pulled up outside the house across the road and a short, dark-haired, very harried-looking man jumped out.

'Gar-reeee! Why you make me wait?' The woman had stopped gardening and was now standing with her hands placed firmly on her hips.

'Sorry, Mamà,' the man said, as he ran around to the back of the car and pulled out some shopping bags. 'There was traffic.'

'You took the wrong road,' the woman admonished.

'There's only one road to take, Mamà.'

Suze and Monty exchanged looks. Garry didn't look that big or strong.

The woman drew Garry close and whispered something in his ear that made him turn back to stare at them.

'We should probably go before they call the police on us,' Suze said, standing up. 'I'll try knocking one more time.'

'Okay,' Monty said. He seemed glum.

Suze knocked on the door as loudly as she could. 'Phoebe,' she called out. 'I'm so sorry. I really wish you'd let me apologise to you.'

But she was only met with more silence.

'Maybe she really is out,' Monty said hopefully. 'We should leave a note.' He ran to grab a notebook and pen from his backpack in the car.

He started writing:

Dear Phoebe
    We came to see you but you weren't here. We will come back again.
    Monty and Suze

Monty added an awkward X.

'I'm not sure that will do it. Here, let me add something,' Suze said, taking the notebook and pen from him and adding:

    PS. We miss you.

She folded the note around the small pile of remaining postcards that J had given her and left it on the doorstep.

'Let's go,' she said. 'If we don't hear from her, we can try again next weekend.'

She really hoped it wouldn't come to that. She turned back at the gate to see Monty still lingering by the door. He slipped a cassette tape out of his pocket and left it with the other things.

He smiled a bit sheepishly. 'It's a mixtape.'

Suze's heart melted a little.

'Perfect,' she said. Maybe things would be okay after all.

Chapter 34

HIDING FROM SUZE and Monty had definitely been an all-time low point in Phoebe Cotton's short life. She hadn't hidden from anyone like that since she'd spilled an entire cup of Milo on Dorothy's Axminster carpet when she was six. Unless, of course, she counted the way she'd been hiding from Sandy for the last four years (which she tried not to).

While she hadn't felt brave enough to go out and talk with Suze and Monty, she was brave enough to return the phone to its cradle. Of course, she had thought it would start ringing immediately, but it remained silent for a few days, like it was sulking at ever being left off the hook for so long in the first place. And when it finally did ring, it wasn't Suze or Monty on the other end of the phone.

It was Libby Winston.

'I was wondering if you'd had any luck tracking down the remaining postcards,' Libby wanted to know.

'Actually, I have,' Phoebe said, her mind going to the shelf where the postcards had sat untouched since Suze and Monty's visit.

'I'll be in Melbourne this weekend and I was, um, wondering if it would be okay for me to drop by the house and collect them?'

'Sure. Any time is fine.' Phoebe knew for sure she wouldn't be doing anything.

'Great.' Libby sounded relieved. 'I'll see you at three on Sunday, then.'

'That's fine. The address is Number Six—'

'I know the address,' Libby interjected.

'Of course you do,' Phoebe replied.

After she hung up, Phoebe suddenly felt anxious all over again about the postcards. She'd been so focused on her own troubles that she'd managed to push all the speculation about her grandfather and his affairs to the side. She wondered how Dorothy would feel if she knew Phoebe was having her grandfather's mistress over for afternoon tea.

Moreover, she realised she couldn't go through with this alone. The trip to Ballarat Base Hospital had been scary enough, and she'd had *two* people with her and it had been in a public place. She needed someone else to be with her at Salmon Street, and she knew it couldn't be her parents. Even though her father had confirmed that Dorothy and Edward had had 'an understanding', she needed to be absolutely sure that Charlie's theory about Libby Winston was correct before she dragged them into it.

And it couldn't be Suze. She could still feel the sting of her words at the party.

It would have to be Monty.

Since he and Suze had tried to visit, she'd been listening to his mixtape nonstop, tying herself up in knots as she tried to read meaning into every song. 'To Be with You' by Mr Big seemed to be an invitation, but then Roxette's 'It Must Have Been Love' sounded like everything might be over before it had even really begun. And she had no idea what kind of message 'I Like to Move It' was trying to send. In the end, she forced herself to stop her endless dissection of the mixtape and just look at it as a whole: he had made it for her, he had delivered it to her. Even Phoebe had to admit to herself it was a good sign that he was still interested.

But she knew that it was only a matter of time before she would need to tell him her secret. How many more incidents with people crunching or chomping or slurping or smacking their lips or snapping their gum and Phoebe shutting down could there be before he came to his own conclusions about her?

I can do this, she told herself, looking at her reflection in the mirror.

Her heart was pounding as she dialled his number, and then, when Monty himself answered, it pounded even harder.

'Hi,' she said. 'It's me. Phoebe. I owe you an explanation.'

'Whatever it is, I don't care,' Monty blurted out. 'I just really like you, Phoebe Cotton.'

Phoebe paused for a moment, simultaneously buoyed and overwhelmed by his words.

Monty cleared his throat. 'Uh, which is to say, please continue.'

Phoebe swallowed hard. 'Well. Um. Other than my parents, only one other person knows what I'm about to tell you.'

She took a deep breath.

'I don't like eating noises.'

'Okay . . .'

'And when I say I don't *like* them, I mean they kind of hurt my brain. They make me feel irrationally angry or like running away.'

'Is that it?' He was sounding very confused.

For a split second, Phoebe thought that perhaps he was right. That there really wasn't much more to it than that. But deep down, she knew Monty needed to know what a terrible person she was. Anything else would be a lie.

'I don't think you understand,' she said. 'It's not a reasonable thing to want to smack someone in the head because they're crunching an apple. It's not reasonable to want to kick something because someone slurped their coffee, or want to scream if someone is chewing gum with their mouth open, or go home because someone behind you at the cinema is eating popcorn. I'm not a reasonable person.'

There was a long pause on the other end of the line. Phoebe began winding the telephone cord around her finger again and tried to keep breathing.

'So,' Monty said slowly. 'The popcorn I bought at the movies that time was a . . . mistake?'

'It wasn't a mistake if you were going to the movies with a normal, reasonable person. But again: I'm not a normal person. I'm not reasonable.'

They sat in silence for a moment. Phoebe's heart was pounding, like it was going to burst through her chest, and a thousand thoughts were racing through her head, none of them normal or reasonable.

'Well,' Monty eventually said. 'I stand by my original statement: I don't care what it is. I still like you, Phoebe Cotton.'

'Really?' she asked. She could hardly believe what she was hearing.

'Really.'

'Even though my brain doesn't work properly?'

'Whose does?'

Phoebe felt a huge sense of relief, as if a valve somewhere inside her had finally been opened. She felt like dancing or skipping or floating away on a cloud. After all these years of being a prisoner inside her own head, terrified that people would reject her if they knew the truth, it turned out her Year 5 Religious Education teacher had been right: the truth had actually set her free.

But then she remembered the other reason she had called him. 'Okay, so now we've got my deepest, darkest secret out of the way, there's another reason I'm calling.'

'Well, if that was as deep and dark as you go, I expect this conversation to be nothing but rainbows and lollipops from this point on.'

'Sadly, no. Libby Winston is coming over on Sunday.'

'She's what?'

'She's coming here. To my grandmother's house. In two days. To collect the postcards my grandfather wrote her. I think I need you to be here.'

'I think I need me to be there. What about Suze?'

A silence fell between them.

'She feels really bad about what happened, you know,' Monty offered.

Phoebe remained silent. She didn't want Monty to know she'd been listening to their conversation on the porch step, and already knew how bad Suze felt. But at the same time, she wasn't quite ready to face her.

'I might ring her later,' she eventually said, knowing that she probably wouldn't.

'Okay,' Monty backed down. 'For the record, I have loads

of odd quirks that I've been successfully hiding from you so far. For example, I hate feet. I never let anyone see me barefooted. And I'd never touch anyone else's feet, no matter how much they paid me. Feet are gross.'

Phoebe laughed. 'Really? I've never given feet that much thought.'

'And I've never given eating noises that much thought. You know, one of my cousins is a bit like you. He eats all his meals sitting up one end of the table, away from everyone else, with one of his fingers in his ear.'

'Maybe I should go out with him instead,' she said.

'He's only ten, so you might want to wait a while,' Monty replied. 'But hang on, does this mean we're going out?'

'Maybe,' Phoebe said. And for once, by 'maybe' she definitely meant 'yes'.

Chapter 35

Suze reached salmon Street only minutes before Libby Winston was due to arrive. She'd managed to read two paragraphs of the hardcover copy of *Anatomy of Criticism* that she'd brought with her, after which it had just become a weight-bearing exercise as she lugged it from the tram to the train and then to Phoebe's house.

Monty answered the door.

'How is she?' Suze whispered.

'She's good. Nervous but good,' Monty whispered back.

'Did you tell her that I was coming?'

'Not exactly.'

Suze felt her stomach drop away. When Monty had rung her about Libby Winston's offer, she'd agreed to come only if he told Phoebe first.

Phoebe emerged from the back of the house, bearing a tray with a jug of water and three glasses.

'Oh,' she said, her face going pale when she saw Suze. 'It's you.'

'Monty invited me,' Suze quickly said. 'I thought you knew I was coming.'

Monty looked sheepish. 'I knew if I told her, she would ask me to uninvite you. This was the only way I could think of to get you both in the same room.'

He took the tray away from Phoebe and quickly retreated to the lounge room, leaving the two of them alone in the hall.

Suze took a deep breath. She had broken this precious thing, this fledgling friendship, and now she needed to fix it. 'I'm so sorry, Phoebe. I really am. I was such a dick to you at the party, especially after you'd opened up and confided in me.'

'You were the first person I'd ever told, you know,' Phoebe said, looking at the floor. 'Other than my parents.'

'Not even Sandy?'

'Not even Sandy.'

Suze slapped herself on the forehead. 'I feel even worse now. I've let you down. I've let myself down. It's unforgivable.'

She went to leave, but Phoebe reached out to grab her arm. 'Don't go,' she said. 'I was very hurt and angry – and to be honest, I still am a little bit – but it actually forced me to tell Monty, something I might never have got around to otherwise.'

'So my shitty behaviour got you a boyfriend?' Suze asked hopefully.

'It kind of did,' Phoebe said with a smile, and the two friends hugged.

'I'm so sorry,' Suze said again.

Monty emerged from the lounge room. 'Okay. That's enough apologising and hugging for now. Libby Winston will be here any moment and we need to discuss our game plan.'

'I'll do the talking,' Phoebe said. 'After all, this is about my grandfather.'

'Are you sure?'

Suze noticed Monty putting his arm around Phoebe's shoulders and how fortified she seemed by it.

'Yes,' Phoebe replied. 'I'm sure. But if I completely freeze up, you two should step in.'

'Is there a safe word?' Suze asked.

'Pineapple,' Monty said.

'Pineapple? What kind of safe word is that?'

'The first one I could think of. I'm happy to go with other suggestions.'

'Pineapple is fine,' Phoebe said. 'I like pineapples.'

The doorbell rang and the three of them froze. Suze was reminded of the statues game she used to play in primary school, and she wondered who would be the first to break their pose.

It was Phoebe.

'She's here,' she said, and went to open the door.

'It's showtime,' Suze whispered to Monty, exchanging nervous glances as they quickly slipped into the lounge room.

'We should sit down,' Monty whispered back. 'If we're standing when she comes in, she might think it's an ambush.'

Suze chose one of the armchairs, whose cushions had been plumped up so much they looked like they were about to rise into the air and float away. As she sat down, there was a soft 'pfoot' sound. *The fart of an angel*, Suze thought. It was the kind of thing that Ky might turn into a (non)performance. The thought of Ky made her smile and shake her head, which was definitely an improvement on the tightening sensation in her stomach she used to feel.

'What's so funny?' Monty whispered.

'Life,' Suze whispered back.

'Oh my,' they heard Libby Winston say in the hallway. 'It's like walking back in time. This place is exactly the same.'

'Dorothy didn't take very much with her to the retirement village and my dad hasn't worked out what to do with all the stuff, so I'm the custodian for the time being,' Phoebe explained. 'Can I take your coat?'

Suze couldn't help but feel that Dorothy would be pleased with Phoebe's manners, even if they were directed at her dead husband's mistress.

'You remember Suze and Monty?' Phoebe asked as she entered the lounge room with Libby Winston. The last time they'd seen Libby, she had been in her hospital uniform at the end of a very long shift. Now, she almost looked like a completely different person in her black turtleneck jumper, which was tucked into high-waisted woollen trousers. Her short hair was slicked back and she was wearing lipstick and a single string of pearls that matched her earrings.

'I do,' she said with a smile that felt much more genuine than it had been in the hospital. 'But I don't think I caught your names when you door-stopped me in Ballarat.'

Suze stood up and reached over to shake Libby Winston's hand. 'I'm Suze. Nice to properly meet you.' Monty did the same.

'Can I offer you a cup of tea or a glass of water?' Phoebe asked Libby, but Libby was too busy looking around.

'Oh!' she exclaimed, delighted, going over to a display cabinet. 'The spoons are still there. Edward brought one home after every trip he took, and I used to help Dorothy polish them. The one with the map of Tasmania as its handle was always my favourite. It looks like it hasn't been polished for a while.'

Even though there was nothing accusatory in Libby Winston's observation, Suze saw Phoebe flinch and, not for the first time, she felt sorry for her friend having to be the custodian of this house. Suze imagined the responsibility was a bit like her Honours thesis, always hanging over her.

Suze sat back down in her armchair (the 'pfoot' factor was considerably reduced this time) and Phoebe settled next to Monty on the couch. Suze noticed how quickly Monty put his arm back around Phoebe and she felt glad for both of them. But her focus quickly joined Phoebe's and Monty's, and the three of them watched Libby as she continued to walk around the room. It was as if they were almost expecting her to start pocketing items or break something, Suze thought.

'I spent so much time in this room,' Libby said, as she examined the ornaments along the mantlepiece. 'Your grandparents were always so generous with their space. Nurses I knew boarding at other houses had to use the back entrance or were never allowed in the main house, like they were servants or second-class citizens. But Edward and Dorothy always made me feel at home.'

Eventually, Libby Winston settled on the empty armchair and focused on the postcards laid out on the coffee table in front of her.

'So, these are the remaining ones,' she said, picking them up one at a time to examine them. Phoebe noticed how carefully she was handling them, like they were precious artefacts in the museum. 'Thank you so much for getting them back.'

'It was quite the journey,' Suze piped up. 'We literally saved them from a fire.'

Libby looked over at her as if she'd only just remembered that she wasn't alone in the room and then went back to the postcards.

'They went to Venice,' she said, more to herself, as she stared at a postcard of the Bridge of Sighs. Suze knew the bridge from *A Little Romance,* one of her favourite movies when she was a kid. It had been one of her life's goals to kiss someone at sunset as she drifted under the bridge on a gondola. Perhaps she should save her money and do it, but by herself.

'All that water,' Libby Winston continued. 'Edward had been so against going there.'

She pressed her lips together, as if she'd just realised that she'd revealed more than she should have. Suze shot Phoebe a look and Phoebe nodded. She had this.

'It's okay,' Phoebe said. 'We know who wrote the postcards. We know about the affair.'

Libby's brow creased. 'You do? Who told you?'

'Nobody told us. Suze basically worked it out, and when my dad told me about my grandparents' understanding, it was an easy conclusion to make.'

Libby bit her lip. 'Do you think your grandmother will ever forgive me?' she asked in the same low voice she'd used when they'd first given her the postcards at the hospital.

'Well, she's not exactly the forgiving type,' Phoebe said, and from the little Suze knew about Dorothy, she had to agree. 'But it was so long ago, and Granddad is dead now, so really, I don't know what she could possibly be holding on to.'

'But I broke her heart,' Libby said, more to herself than to anyone in the room.

'No, it was Granddad who broke her heart,' Phoebe said. Suze felt deeply impressed by how wise her friend was being.

Libby Winston, however, just looked even more perplexed. 'What do you mean?'

'I mean it was Granddad who broke the rules of their marriage and had a relationship with someone so close to home. You weren't to know.'

Phoebe's face was the picture of gentle compassion. Suze wanted to applaud. In comparison, Libby Winston's frown had only deepened. She opened her mouth and then closed it again. And then opened it once more.

'It wasn't your grandfather I had the relationship with,' Libby said.

Monty gasped and Suze felt her jaw drop, like one of those cartoon characters on TV. Charlie had always said her gaydar was faulty.

Phoebe Cotton, however, was completely still, her face a blank slate.

'Pineapple,' Phoebe said.

Chapter 36

THE ROOM AND time and Phoebe's mind had stopped completely for one second, one minute, one year, and then, when she found herself uttering the safe word, Monty had gripped her shoulder and the world came rushing back in, like a jet of water through a pipe, powerful and ruthless and deafening.

'You had an affair with my *grandmother*?' she asked.

'Oh dear,' Libby Winston said, her face now devoid of all colour. 'I'm so sorry. I didn't mean to . . .'

Her voice trailed away and Phoebe leaned forward, as if to try and follow wherever the voice had gone, to find out more, to make sense of this madness.

'When? For how long? I mean, is my grandmother a *lesbian*?'

Phoebe remembered all the deeply homophobic statements

her grandmother had made over the years. 'Against nature,' she'd always said if they happened to pass a gay couple holding hands on the street. While Dorothy's comments had upset Phoebe because they were hateful, she had never thought for one moment that they might be a form of self-hatred.

But Libby Winston wouldn't answer her questions. She just stood up. 'Your grandmother's story is not mine to tell. You'll need to ask her those questions. And when – if – you do, please explain to her that I thought you already knew. I would never have . . . I'm sorry.'

Her hands were visibly shaking as she picked up the postcards and put them carefully in her bag.

'Thank you again for the postcards. All of them,' she said, looking first at Suze, then Monty, and finally Phoebe. 'I don't know if this helps or not, but you should know that your grandmother was the love of my life.'

And with that, she left.

After the final decisive click of the front door, there was a long silence. It felt like the handful of truth that Libby Winston had thrown into the air before she'd left the room needed to float down to the ground and settle before anyone could speak.

'Wow,' Monty eventually said.

'Yes, wow,' confirmed Suze. 'How are you feeling, Phoebe?'

She was looking at Phoebe with intensity, like she was trying to scan her very soul. Phoebe found she couldn't meet her gaze, not now, not before she had time to properly sit with this news.

'I'm just going to take a moment outside,' she said, removing herself from Monty's warm grasp and standing up. 'If you guys are hungry, there's some bread and stuff in the kitchen. You know, for sandwiches.'

She grabbed a coat and went out into the backyard to sit down on the wooden bench her grandfather had made. She looked up at the mulberry tree, its branches thin and spindly, like witches' hands pointing at the sky. Then she looked around at the garden her grandmother had planted and tended for most of her life. Phoebe had spent so many hours as a child here with Dorothy, being told off for being too rough or not rough enough with whatever minor task she had been assigned. She'd never pleased her grandmother. Not back then. Not now. But all this time, her grandmother had been carrying a secret that had hollowed her out, making her brittle and beyond being pleased by anyone or anything.

She wondered if her dad knew.

She wondered if her grandfather had known.

She wondered if she'd ever be brave enough to ask her grandmother about her side of this story, but then she thought of Dorothy's stern face and sharp tongue and realised probably not.

Behind her, in the kitchen, she could hear Monty and Suze speaking in low voices and opening and closing cupboards, as they made sandwiches.

She considered the word 'sandwiches' and took comfort in its certainty of meaning: two bits of bread and the stuff in between. Maybe, she thought, people were like sandwiches – everyone could see the bread, the outer layer, but the stuff in between wasn't always visible. Libby Winston's revelation was part of her grandmother's sandwich that Phoebe hadn't known was there, but maybe it was in fact a vital ingredient that held everything together, like mayonnaise or mustard.

But then, she thought, maybe people aren't at all like sandwiches and she needed to get her head together.

Suze and Monty came out, one holding a plate with a sandwich and the other a glass of milk, and she suddenly felt like a child again, sick in bed, being brought food by her parents.

'One half is peanut butter and the other half is honey,' Suze explained, handing her the plate. 'We weren't sure if you wanted a savoury sandwich or a dessert sandwich, so we mixed it up. Although, Monty tried to make a strong argument in support of peanut butter being a dessert topping, something which I outright reject.'

'It's sweeter than it is savoury,' Monty argued, and Phoebe had to laugh at how sweet and earnest the expression on his face was.

'It's true!' Monty exclaimed as he went to sit on the bench next to her, but then stopped. 'Suze, you should sit here. I'll go get another chair from inside.'

'I'm happy with the ground,' Suze said, plopping herself down at their feet. 'That was some pretty intense shit that Libby Winston just accidentally laid on us.'

'I should have guessed from the fact that T kept calling her Elizabeth when the rest of the world knew her as Libby. That's very much Dorothy's style,' Phoebe replied. 'But I don't understand why she signed her postcards with a T.'

'You'll have to ask her,' Suze offered.

'Are you kidding me? You've met her. You know how terrifying she is.'

'Okay, then don't ask her. But you'll need to accept that she's a puzzle you'll never be able to solve on your own. My grandfather changed his name halfway through the Second World War, but nobody ever asked him why and now he's been buried with that story and I'll never know why I ended up as Susan Cummings instead of Susan Comerford.'

'Susan Comerford? I think that sounds like a real estate agent,' Monty said and then quickly corrected himself. 'A very successful real estate agent with her face on billboards.'

Suze laughed, but Phoebe was too busy thinking about what

Suze had said. She bit into one half of the sandwich, the peanut butter half. It was definitely savoury.

MONTY LINGERED FOR a little while after Suze had left, but he must have been able to tell she needed some time alone. He kissed her on the cheek very gently and promised to ring her that night.

Once she was alone, Phoebe spent a few hours wandering through the house looking at the artefacts of her grandparents' life together. Or maybe not *together* together. What was that phrase she'd learned in Year 9 Italian? Soli insieme. Alone together.

She picked up the huge album that contained all the evidence of an ordinary life: photos of their wedding and her dad's christening and the bike they gave him for Christmas when he was about eight and the new car they'd bought in 1967, both of them posing awkwardly, her grandfather's face a weird blur because he had moved right as the photo was being taken. She stopped at another photo at the beach, with a large group of people posing, the women in stylish bathers and the men in shorts and open shirts. Her grandfather was beaming, ear to ear, the kind of smile that threatened to burst his face. Her grandmother's lips were pressed into a smile of sorts. Phoebe had always interpreted that smile as meaning Dorothy was having fun despite herself, but now she realised it looked like she was holding in a secret.

Phoebe examined the other people in the photo, the ones whose faces she'd always skated over, friends or acquaintances from long ago, who had never meant anything to her other than as extras in her grandparents' lives. And then she saw her: Libby Winston, young and smiling in a chequered bathing suit and holding a towel. She'd been there all along and Phoebe had just never noticed her.

She wondered if she should ring her father and tell him what she'd just been told. But then she thought of her grandmother and how much she would hate her secret becoming family gossip, even if only between her son and her granddaughter.

If Phoebe wanted to talk to her dad about this, she would need to talk to Dorothy first.

Chapter 37

SUZE SLOWLY MADE her way back to Fitzroy, weighed down by Libby Winston's revelation, her worry for Phoebe Cotton, her lingering embarrassment about her drunken behaviour and the copy of *Anatomy of Criticism* still untouched in her bag.

As she fumbled around for her key, she noticed that this week Emmy was dressed in a red-sequinned body suit and, for reasons unknown, had the words 'Chicken Tonight' written on her forehead with red lipstick. Suze guessed this was one outfit Charlie had thrown together while under the influence of something other than Chicken Tonight.

Inside the house, she found Matt sitting on the couch, waiting for Sacha to get ready.

'We're looking at a two-bedroom worker's cottage in

North Carlton. The listing says it has wall murals,' Matt said. 'I'm hoping it's something urban and edgy, maybe by a graffiti artist.'

'And I'm hoping for mountains at sunset,' Sacha added, as she descended the stairs.

Suze secretly hoped it was neither and that they'd be so crushed they would decide to stay in the Moor Street house after all.

'Where's Charlie?' Sacha asked. 'I thought he was coming with us.'

Charlie loved a house inspection. Suze couldn't count the number of times he'd dragged her along to openings and auctions, rushing from room to room and planning aloud where he'd put imaginary furniture. ('It's like playing grown-up doll house,' he'd say.)

'He changed his mind. He got a phone call while you were in the shower and then he said he was going to the Standard to see a boy band, but he told me not to tell you.'

Suze made a mental note never to trust Matt with any of her secrets.

'A boy band at the Standard?' Sacha asked, aghast. 'No wonder he didn't want us to know.'

But Suze had quickly surmised what was going on. 'Was the boy band called "The Carlosses"?'

'That's the one,' said Matt.

'Sweet baby Jesus,' said Sacha.

'What?' Matt looked confused.

'Do you think we should conduct a search and rescue?' Suze asked.

'We should at least do a welfare check,' Sacha replied.

'What about the inspection?' Matt interjected.

'Fuck the inspection,' Sacha said. 'There will be other houses.'

'But not one with murals.'

'You don't even like art,' Sacha said. 'Anyway, this is more important.'

They raced around the corner to the Standard. Charlie wouldn't be in the front bar ('The front bar is no place for gays,' he'd always said), so they went around the back, where they found Charlie sitting by himself at a small table in the corner.

'Sprung bad,' said Sacha.

'Et tu, Brute?' Charlie said to Matt, who was hanging back a little sheepishly, Suze thought.

'I thought you were seeing a boy band,' Matt tried to explain. 'I didn't know that they would march over here.'

'My boyfriend doesn't keep secrets from me,' Sacha said with great pride. 'So where is he?'

Her head had started turning around like *The Exorcist*, trying to locate The Carlosses.

'He's running late.'

'But he's the one who invited you, like, twenty minutes ago, right?'

'He might have had a slight mishap on the way.'

'A slight *mishap*? Where's he coming from? 1942?' Sacha wanted to know.

'He'll be here soon.'

'Well then, we'll wait with you,' Suze said, sitting down next to Charlie.

Matt rubbed his hands together. 'Right,' he said. 'I'll get some drinks in. What do people want?'

As Charlie and Sacha placed their orders, Suze felt the usual panic when people might have started doing rounds. She could afford one drink (maybe) but not a whole round.

'I'm okay,' she said.

'Are you sure? I'm happy to get you a drink with zero expectation that you'll get me a drink back.'

'Matt doesn't believe in rounds,' Sacha reassured her, and Suze felt herself relax.

'A vodka and orange, please,' she said.

While Matt was at the bar, Sacha pulled Charlie and Suze in tight. 'Okay, this is an extra-emergency convening of the Order. What the hell are you doing, Charles?'

'Meeting a friend for a drink.'

'I'll repeat: what the hell are you doing, Charles?' Sacha said again, this time with slightly more force.

'I'm meeting a friend for a drink,' Charles repeated, this time jutting out his chin in defiance.

Sacha glared at him with the intensity of the Death Star destroying a planet.

'Okay, okay,' Charlie relented. 'I'm hoping to get back together with him.'

He hung his head in shame. Suze put her arm around his shoulders.

'And why is that a bad idea?' she asked.

'Because I can't change him. I can only change myself,' Charlie recited, his head still down.

'Is everything alright?' Matt asked, as he returned to the table with a tray of drinks.

'Yes,' Sacha said, patting Charlie on the hand. 'I think the fever has broken.'

'But it hasn't,' Charlie said to the table. 'The thing is . . . I *am* already back with him. Well, I think I am.'

'You what?' Suze and Sacha said in unison.

At that very moment, The Carlosses arrived and quickly charmed everyone into submission with a flurry of air kisses and compliments.

'Suze, I love your hair. It's the perfect you. Sacha, your man is even more handsome that Charles described.'

He pronounced Charlie's name *Sharlessss*, and even Suze got butterflies when he said it, so she could only imagine the power it had over Charlie.

As the group talked, Suze sat back and took note of every time The Carlosses touched Charlie's arm and how it made Charlie beam with happiness, but she also couldn't help but notice how The Carlosses still looked around the room as if he were expecting to find someone better at any moment.

Suddenly, she wanted to stop the conversation and tell The Carlosses that there wasn't anyone better than Charlie. But she couldn't make The Carlosses see that. And nor could she make her friend see his own worth. He had to discover it himself, kind of like she had finally discovered hers in J's granny flat.

'Hey,' said Charlie, interrupting her memory of J's Dire Straits CD. 'Isn't that your supervisor over there?'

Suze glanced over at a tall thin woman in a floral dress sitting at a table in the far corner.

'I don't think so,' she said, turning back to the group. 'That dress is a bit too Laura Ashley for Claire.'

'Um, I do think so,' said Charlie. 'She's looking right this way.'

'Suze?' the woman seemed to be mouthing.

'Claire!' Suze jumped up and made her way over to the table in the corner. Up close, she was surprised to see that her supervisor's hair had been curled, and she was even wearing make-up.

'I told you we would see one of my students if we came to a pub,' Claire said to the rakish-looking man in black sitting with her. 'This is Suze, one of my brightest sparks.'

Suze blushed.

'And this,' Claire continued. 'This is Nathan Harman, my, er, friend.'

'I prefer the term "gentleman caller",' Nathan said. Suze could have sworn that Claire giggled.

Nathan reached out his hand to shake Suze's. 'Nice to meet you. We were just getting some drinks – would you like one?'

Suze thought of the half-finished drink back at the table and the study she'd promised herself she'd do tonight, but she said 'Yes' anyway. If Claire Portelle could dress in floral and wear make-up, then she, Susan Cummings, could accept two drinks. It was obviously that kind of night.

After Nathan went to the bar, Claire patted a vacant chair for Suze to sit and said in a low voice, 'He's from Computer Science. We met at an academic misconduct meeting. This is our first date.'

'He's very dashing,' Suze said, sitting down.

'He is, isn't he?' Claire was smiling and Suze couldn't help but wish she'd smile like that when she was talking to Suze about her latest chapter. It would make all the difference.

As if sensing Suze's thoughts about her thesis, Claire's smile disappeared. 'How's the writing going? Have you reframed that Irigaray quote?'

Suze wished she hadn't left her copy of *Anatomy of Criticism* back at home. It could have been proof that she was at least *thinking* of doing some work on her next chapter, even if she wasn't actually doing it yet.

'It's going okay. Just not right now. It's Saturday night.'

'Yes, it's Saturday night!' Nathan had arrived with the drinks and Claire's smile instantly reappeared. Maybe Nathan could sit in on all future supervision meetings to ensure the smile came along too.

'Thanks for the drink,' Suze said to Nathan.

'You're most welcome.'

As the three of them sipped their drinks and made awkward

small talk, Suze became acutely aware of the fact she was the third wheel on their date. But she also didn't want to just take the drink and go. It would seem ungrateful.

Luckily, a loud outburst from her original table saved her. Charlie was howling in pain.

Suze quickly finished the last of her drink. 'I should probably return to my friends before they start killing each other.'

Back at the table, Charlie reached for her like a drowning man. 'Suze! You've got to save me from these people! Matthew here said he didn't mind Molly Ringwald's prom dress in *Pretty in Pink*, and then Carlos said he had never even seen it.'

Suze gasped dramatically. 'We should organise a screening somewhere,' she said, sitting back down at the table. 'Attendance will be mandatory.'

Despite the inverted triangle dress, *Pretty in Pink* was one of Charlie's favourite films. Charlie had said a few times that he and Suze modelled their friendship on Andie and Duckie. Charlie, of course, was Andie, and Suze was Duckie.

'We can host it at our house,' Matt said. 'When we have a house, that is.'

'Sacha's going to let you have a *television*?' Suze said. This time her gasp was 100 per cent real. Sacha had always been the most vocal about not letting a television darken their lounge room.

'We haven't talked about it yet,' Sacha said.

'What's there to talk about?' Matt asked.

'Oh my.' Charlie's hand clutched at imaginary pearls. 'I think we should get in a round of drinks, Carlos.'

As Sacha started to explain to Matt exactly how much there was to talk about when it came to the subject of televisions, Charlie and The Carlosses escaped to the bar. Suze took shelter under the table, pretending that she had to do up the shoelaces on her Doc Martens. She really felt like staying under there for the rest of the evening: first there was the shock of Charlie being kind-of-sort-of-maybe back with The Carlosses, then there was the trauma of seeing Claire Portelle on a date, and now there was this argument. Relationships were hard work, whatever way you cut them.

But by the time she resurfaced, the argument seemed to be over. Sacha and Matt were holding hands and Charlie and The Carlosses were returning with drinks, both laughing at a private and clearly super-hilarious joke. Over in the corner, Claire Portelle and Nathan Harman were leaving the pub, Nathan with his arm around Claire's shoulders.

Greg had been right: change really was the one thing she could rely on.

Chapter 38

PHOEBE WAS GRATEFUL when her father insisted on driving her to the Western Retreat to see Dorothy. It was one way of ensuring she actually went through with the visit and didn't just stay on the tram, change her name and start a new life at the end of the line.

Monty, too, insisted on coming for emotional support. Phoebe was grateful about that, but also nervous. Not only did she now have to worry about talking to Dorothy, but also about Dorothy meeting Monty. He'd already won over her parents earlier in the week at the weekly Tuesday dinner, but that hadn't been hard. Monty was the first person she'd brought home since Sandy. She could have brought Charles Manson for dinner and Ellen would have been thrilled she had made a friend. But meeting Dorothy was like the Olympic Games of winning someone over.

Monty had bought a bunch of flowers from Sims Supermarket, which he handed to Dorothy the moment they were introduced. Dorothy made some remark about flower farms, but Phoebe could tell she was pleased.

Dorothy was less pleased with Phil's offering of apples from his tree.

'For an apple pie,' Phil said.

'Oh Philip. I'm far too busy to do any baking these days,' Dorothy replied, in lieu of any actual thanks. 'And in any case, these are riddled with brown spots.'

'Which is why they're perfect for pies.'

Dorothy's eyebrows made a rapid upward journey. She pointed to a piece of paper on the kitchen counter. 'There's the list for Buggings.'

'Bunnings,' Phil gently corrected her. He had offered to pick up some equipment and potting mix for the communal garden Dorothy was setting up at the retirement village.

'Do you need some help?' Monty offered. He'd promised Phoebe he would go with Phil to Bunnings so that she could be left alone with Dorothy.

'Sure,' Phil said, clearly chuffed. He turned to Phoebe. 'Would you like to come, too?'

'No, I'll stay and keep Dorothy company,' Phoebe replied, although every cell in her body wanted to graft itself to both of them and get the hell out of there.

'You will, will you?' Dorothy eyed her somewhat suspiciously.

'Yes, I will.'

Monty reached out to squeeze Phoebe's hand before they left, and Phoebe took whatever strength she could from that small act. Her heart was pounding so hard now she could barely hear anything over the sound of its thrum.

'I'll make us some tea,' Dorothy said, once the men had left.

As Dorothy busied herself in the kitchen, Phoebe quickly scanned the bookshelf, looking for evidence to support the question she was about to ask her grandmother. She was instantly fortified by a copy of Gloria Steinem's *The Beach Book* tucked in between *The Reader's Digest New Illustrated Guide to Gardening* and *The Thorn Birds*.

'We went to visit Libby Winston,' she called out. 'In Ballarat.'

The tea-making noises in the kitchen paused for a second or two and then continued.

'How was she?' Dorothy asked from the kitchen. Her voice sounded like her throat was trying to strangle itself.

'She asked after you.' Phoebe's heart was pounding so hard inside her tight chest, as if it was about to stage some kind of jailbreak. But she kept going. 'She wanted to know why you never sent the postcards.'

It wasn't exactly the truth, but it was the only way Phoebe could think to begin the conversation.

But Dorothy quickly shut it down. 'I have no idea what she's talking about.'

Phoebe forced herself to walk over to her grandmother in the kitchen and face her. 'Libby said she thought you would never forgive her. She thought she broke your heart and she was so, so sorry.' Phoebe paused and took a breath. She'd delivered the penny, now it was time for the pound. 'She said you were the love of her life.'

Dorothy stared back at her for the longest moment, wide-eyed and slightly slack-jawed, almost like she'd been hypnotised. She swallowed and then spoke slowly and carefully in a voice carried in from a billion miles away. 'She's mistaken me for someone else. I'm not that person. I was never that person.'

'But . . .'

At that moment, the door was flung open and Phil reappeared.

'I forgot the list,' he said cheerily, grabbing it off the counter. 'I'd forget my own head if it wasn't screwed on. Did you know that the average human head weighs five kilograms?'

When Phoebe didn't respond with her usual 'Well, now I've heard everything', he stopped and looked at her and then at his mother, who was scooping tea into the pot with shaking hands.

'There are also one hundred thousand hairs on the average human head,' he continued, with some trepidation. 'But only three on mine.'

Phoebe averted her eyes while Dorothy made a point of banging some crockery.

'What's going on?' Phil asked.

'I have a headache,' Dorothy replied at the very same time that Phoebe said, 'I'm not feeling well.'

'Okay,' Phil said. He held up the list for Bunnings. 'Do you still want these things?'

Phoebe turned to look at her grandmother, who seemed to snap back into herself, like an elastic band that had been stretched and then released.

'For goodness' sake, Philip. My headache shouldn't be a barrier to the success of the community garden,' she said sternly. 'You can deliver the goods straight to the storage shed.'

'Are *you* well enough to come?' Philip asked Phoebe. She gave him a small nod that hid her desperation to get out of there. 'Okay then. Let's go.'

AFTER THE BUNNINGS shop, they stacked everything carefully in the garden shed at the Western Retreat, as per Dorothy's very strict instructions. Phil dropped Monty off at the nearest station so he could head on to the Lost Suitcase cousin's engagement party. Phoebe had originally planned to go with him, but now she had to keep up the ruse that she was feeling sick. And in any case, she wasn't in the mood for a party.

As Monty got out of the car, she could tell he was bursting to ask her what had happened, but he would have to wait.

'He's a nice lad,' Phil remarked as he pulled back out onto the road.

'He is,' Phoebe replied, and she thought of how good it had felt to be hugged by him after that ordeal at Dorothy's unit.

And what an ordeal it had been. Dorothy's denial felt impenetrable, like the Great Wall of China. Phoebe wished she'd photocopied the postcards before they'd given them to Libby, so she could find some incontrovertible proof that Dorothy was or wasn't 'T'.

'You're not feeling sick, are you?' Phil asked, after a while.

Phoebe shook her head.

'What happened?'

'Everything. But also nothing.'

'The story of my life,' Phil sighed dramatically, but then quickly realised that Phoebe wasn't smiling at his joke. 'Are you okay?'

'I'm more worried about Dorothy. I asked her a question about the past and she completely shut down. It was like that time the garage door broke.'

Some mechanism in the garage door had broken when Phoebe was a kid, causing it to fall suddenly, crushing her bicycle. She could still remember the sound of metal crushing metal.

Phil sighed again, this time without the drama. 'The thing is . . . your grandmother doesn't ever look back. She never has. Even after she's cut you down with one of her famous remarks, she doesn't pause to consider what she's done or how you might feel – she just keeps going. It's terrible, but it's also a little admirable.'

Phoebe thought about how much time she spent caught up in her own head, thinking about the past and what she did and didn't do, and she was only twenty-five. By the time she got to Dorothy's age, there'd be so much past to get tangled up in, she might effectively truss and gag herself permanently.

'Being grown up is turning out to be much more complicated than I thought it was,' she said.

'Really? I always think it's much easier. I never thought I'd have a job and drive a car and be married and become a father, because it all seemed so hard. But look at me now.'

Phoebe smiled. 'Look at you now,' she repeated.

'Here's a fun fact. Studies have shown that the older people get and the more adult they become, the happier they are.'

'So what you're saying is that you're happier than me, and Dorothy is happier than you?' Based on her conversation with her grandmother just then, that would mean none of them were happy.

'Not exactly. I'm happier now than I was at your age, and Dorothy is happier now than she was at my age.'

Phoebe looked out the car window at the lampposts whizzing by. 'When I was in high school, Sandy and I used to wish we could just skip ahead ten years so we would know who we would become and not have to suffer the uncertainty in between.'

'But how could you be certain you'd become who you were supposed to be if you hadn't gone through all that uncertainty?'

Phil had raised a good point. Phoebe sighed and continued to stare out the window, but then they stopped at the lights next to a car where the driver was eating gum with her mouth open. Phoebe turned back to her father, only to find him already looking at her.

'You never rang Sandy back, did you?' he said.

Phoebe had been caught out in another lie, but she saw no point in denying it.

'No. I used to think we were close, but now I realise that we'd really held each other at a distance. And now it feels like that distance has grown so much it feels overwhelming.'

'No distance is too great,' Phil replied.

'Don't tell Mum.'

'I won't tell her, if you promise me you'll actually ring Sandy. Ah, who am I kidding? I won't tell her whatever you do. But I do think you should ring her.'

Phoebe silently agreed.

BACK IN SALMON Street, Phoebe headed straight to the fridge to get Sandy's number.

'Three,' she said when Sandy answered her phone. It was an old game they'd played where they counted how many rings passed before the other picked up the phone. The goal was to pick up without a full ring, which meant pretty much sitting on top of the phone twenty-four hours a day. It used to drive her mother mad.

'It would have been two if I wasn't wearing such ridiculous heels,' Sandy replied.

'Sure, sure,' Phoebe said, suddenly relieved that Sandy hadn't just hung up on her. 'Anyway, I'm ringing to say I'm sorry for being such a . . .'

She couldn't think of a word that could sum up her behaviour over the last few months.

Sandy saved her.

'It's okay,' she said. 'I know I've been a bit pushy, but I thought that's what it would take to bring you out of your shell. But all I did was push you further in. Like that wine cork.'

'Oh yeah, the wine cork . . .' Phoebe repeated, remembering how they'd stolen a bottle of wine from Sandy's parents the night before Sandy moved to Canberra, but they didn't have a corkscrew and had tried to open it with a butter knife.

As they started to exchange small talk about jobs and relationships and travel plans, Phoebe felt herself easing back into the friendship, like sinking into a warm bath. But when Sandy talked about her new psychologist and the dialectical behaviour therapy she'd been undertaking, Phoebe checked herself. There was still work to be done.

'Sandy,' she began. 'There's something that I have never told you about myself. I have my own food issues.'

'Ah,' said Sandy. 'I always wondered if you did. I just couldn't work out what they were.'

'I can't stand the sound of eating. It hurts my brain and makes me feel tense and angry.'

The words came out easily this time.

'You can't?' Sandy sounded surprised.

'I can't. That's why I was always keen to do stuff that didn't involve food when we were at school.'

There was a long silence on the other end of the phone. 'I wish you'd been able to tell me that,' Sandy eventually said. 'But then again, I didn't really tell you about my stuff either. And by the time I was able to, you never returned my calls.'

'I was scared to hear what your big breakthrough was,' she admitted.

'What big breakthrough?'

'Remember how you called my parents' house and you said you'd just had some breakthrough with your therapist that you wanted to share with me and . . .' She paused and looked down at her feet. 'I knew your breakthrough was that our friendship had contributed to your illness.'

'What?'

Phoebe blushed. It sounded really silly now that she'd said it out loud.

'My breakthrough was probably about not internalising things so much and making more effort to share what was going on for me. Most likely, I just wanted to tell you that. You didn't cause my illness. That's bonkers.'

Phoebe felt deeply ashamed. By assuming Sandy's illness was all her fault, she had managed to make it all about herself, rather than thinking about Sandy. 'I'm so sorry that I've been such a shit friend.'

'I wouldn't say that. We've both just been caught up in webs of our own making.'

'Still, I wish we could go back in time and be more honest with each other. We could have helped each other more.'

'It's never too late to start again,' Sandy replied. 'So let's do it. Let's start again.' She cleared her throat dramatically. 'Hello, I'm Sandy. I'm a recovering anorexic.'

Phoebe smiled. 'Hello, I'm Phoebe. I hate the sound of eating.'

Chapter 39

Suze woke up early on Saturday morning, feeling lighter than she had for months, maybe years. Without the time-suck of hanging around waiting for J to drop by or call, she'd submitted another two chapters to Claire Portelle and was forging ahead with two more. Claire had said that she might make an academic of her yet.

She found Matt making breakfast in the kitchen, humming as he flipped pancakes.

'You're in a good mood,' she observed.

'It's a Saturday. The sun is shining. I don't have to go into the office today. Sacha's not working. The fridge is full of beer.'

'And we've found a new place,' Sacha said, emerging from the bathroom.

'You have?' Suze's good mood instantly evaporated.

'In Abbotsford. We're getting the key next week, but Matt's offered to pay my rent here until the end of the month so I don't have to move out right away.' Sacha kissed Matt and then glanced at the fry pan. 'You're burning that pancake.'

'The bin likes its pancakes well done,' Matt replied, sliding the burnt pancake directly into the bin.

'Next week? Have you told Charlie?'

'Yes.' Sacha's mouth had formed into a thin line.

'And . . .?'

'He should probably tell you himself.'

'Is it as bad as I think?'

'He should probably tell you himself,' Sacha repeated.

Suze sighed, releasing all the motivation and optimism she'd woken with. *Business as usual*, she thought.

AFTER SACHA AND Matt disappeared back upstairs, Suze loitered on the couch with intent. When she heard Charlie's door open, she sat upright.

'What's going on? Sacha said you had something to tell me.'

'Oh yeah, that,' Charlie said, sinking down onto the couch next to her. 'I'm moving in with The Carlosses.'

'You're what?'

'He just signed the lease on this amazing two-bedroom worker's cottage on Westgarth Street, but the rent's pretty high and . . .'

Suze sensed more (or less) to this story than Charlie was letting on. 'So you're not actually moving *in* together?'

'Yeah, we're moving in together.'

'But will you share a room?'

'We'll have our own personal spaces,' Charlie replied breezily.

'So you're going to be his housemate.'

'Don't be so pedantic, Susan.'

'Oh, Charlie.' Suze couldn't hide her worry for her friend.

'I'll be fine. I always am,' Charlie said. 'But what will you do?'

'I don't know. I'll work something out.'

'Remember my floor will always be available to you.'

'Or maybe I could move into The Carlosses' bedroom.'

'Keep your filthy paws off his silky drawers, Susan,' Charlie laughed. Suze put her arm around him.

'You promise me you won't get your heart *too* broken?' she said.

'Just a little bit broken.' Charlie lay his head on her shoulder. 'To be honest, there's really not that much left to break.'

EVEN THOUGH SHE was uncharacteristically on time, Suze found Phoebe already sitting at their usual table at the Black Cat, nursing a hot chocolate. She looked even more pensive than usual.

'Are you okay?' Suze wanted to know.

'Not really.'

Phoebe told Suze all about her encounter with her grandmother.

'What will you do now?'

'I think I'll leave it alone. Maybe this is one mystery that will never be solved.'

'Like those girls at Hanging Rock,' Suze said. 'When I was nine, I prayed to God that when I die, I'll find out what happened to Miranda. I thought she was a real person.'

'Ants,' Phoebe Cotton said.

'What?'

'She got eaten by ants.'

Suze laughed. 'You're pretty funny, Phoebe Cotton.'

Phoebe looked quietly pleased with the compliment. Suze found herself thinking about the first time she'd met Phoebe and how stiff and quiet she'd seemed. She'd have never imagined they would become friends like this.

'What's happening with you, Suze? Did Claire like your chapters?'

'She loved them. She actually smiled when she gave them back to me. I thought her face was going to crack into a million pieces.'

'You don't seem very excited about it.'

'It's kind of been overshadowed by my impending homelessness.'

Now it was Phoebe's turn to exclaim 'What?'

Suze explained the situation, ending with the news about Charlie and The Carlosses.

'That handsome guy from the party?'

'That's the one.'

'So where will you and Groovy Joe go?'

Suze felt terrible. She hadn't even thought of Groovy Joe. She couldn't imagine The Carlosses would like cats. And Sacha had never really warmed to Groovy Joe like Charlie and Suze had, adding 'doesn't really like animals' to the list of surprising facts about someone who was apparently 'of the earth'.

'I'm not sure. I was going to look at the ads at Readings this afternoon. I'll probably end up being the mother hen in a share house full of first-year Arts students all wanting to major in Post-Soviet Women's Folk Art.'

Suze could already picture the house, so far north it was practically Brunswick, the long queue to use the single bathroom, the fridge empty of anything save a lone tub of low-fat cottage cheese. She let out a long sigh.

'You can move in with me,' Phoebe blurted. 'I mean, not forever, but for as long as you need. You wouldn't have to pay rent, just utilities, and hard labour in the garden.'

'Really?' Suze was overwhelmed by Phoebe's generosity. 'That's . . . very kind of you, Phoebe Cotton.'

'I mean, you would have to live on the wrong side of the Maribyrnong . . .'

'Don't care. I'll even learn how to spell Maribyrnong!' Suze exclaimed.

'You'll be the first.'

As they discussed which room she could take ('You can have my dad's old room. The box room out the back is more of a closet than anything,' said Phoebe), Suze began to imagine her new life, walking down to West Footscray Station to catch the train – to some job in the city. She'd buy a briefcase or a grown-up lady's handbag and wear a pencil skirt and court shoes with sheer stockings. Or not. And then she'd come home at the end of each day, and she and Phoebe could cook together and talk about their workday, and she could spend the evening without her thesis hanging over her or the possibility of her latest Fitzroy lothario dropping by, but instead cuddled up on the couch with Groovy Joe and a romance novel.

'Will your grandmother really be okay with Groovy Joe coming too?'

'I'm not sure my grandmother is ever going to talk to me again anyway, so it probably doesn't matter.'

Phoebe looked sad when she said that.

'Hey,' said Suze. 'I'm sure she'll get over it. She strikes me as a tough old bird . . . who probably wouldn't appreciate being called a "tough old bird".'

'Amen to that.'

'You're religious now?'

'You're the one making pacts with God.'

The two of them laughed, and as they started to plan how to get her stuff to Salmon Street, Suze felt the sunshine of the morning return.

Chapter 40

A T THE WEEKLY staff meeting, Glenda's announcement that she was retiring was met with the murmur of many softly spoken people speaking even more softly than they normally did, like a slow-moving river on a winter's day.

There would be a reshuffle to cover her responsibilities at the library, she said, with several new permanent positions opening up. The slow-moving river quickly turned into white water rapids.

'I'm hoping you will consider applying for one of the new positions, Phoebe,' Glenda told her later, when she caught her alone in the workroom. 'It would make my old heart glad knowing that the library is left in good hands.'

Phoebe was gobsmacked. She never thought in a million years that Glenda would see her hands as anything less than mildly mediocre.

'I am definitely considering it,' she told Glenda, and for once it was actually true. Minglu was back from maternity leave in just a matter of weeks and Phoebe's job would go back to being Minglu's job. In the normal cycle of short-term employment, Phoebe would have already lined up her next temporary contract by this stage, but she hadn't quite got around to it, perhaps out of some small hope she might not need to.

'Good. I hate to be leaving, but it's time. I can't keep up with these new computer systems. They keep changing. At least with the cards, we pretty much just had variations of the one system for decades, maybe centuries.'

Phoebe blinked. She'd always assumed that Glenda knew everything and the reason she always got Phoebe to do data entry was because she was being punished. She'd never guessed it was because Glenda, herself, couldn't do it.

Also, this was the chattiest Glenda had ever been in the whole nine months Phoebe had been working there. And that might have been the most surprising thing about the day if she hadn't returned to Salmon Street to find her father's car parked outside and Dorothy waiting for her on the verandah, leaning on a walking cane.

'Is something wrong? What happened to your leg? Where's Dad?'

'And a good day to you,' Dorothy replied. 'No, there's nothing wrong. Also, it's not my leg, it's my knee – I overdid it at the garden working bee the other day. As for your father, Philip is helping Dimitra with a small matter.' Dorothy gestured across the road at Mrs Pap's house. 'Apparently, Garry hasn't visited for a while. He really needs to step up.'

Phoebe knew for a fact that Garry had visited just a few days ago. If he stepped up any further, his head would be in the clouds.

'Well, aren't you going to invite me in?' Dorothy's tone wasn't exactly conducive to an invitation, but it was a whole lot friendlier than their last encounter.

'It's your home,' Phoebe said, although she couldn't remember the last time her grandmother had actually visited the house.

'No, Phoebe. It's yours now.'

Phoebe fumbled with the keys as she opened the door. When she'd first moved in, she'd lived like there could be a spot inspection at any moment, but she'd recently relaxed a little. Maybe a little too much. She couldn't remember if she'd cleared away the dishes from dinner the night before or if there would be evidence that she'd had her feet on the lounge.

Luckily, there were no dishes lying around or foot imprints on the furniture. She set Dorothy up in her favourite chair in the lounge room and quickly scurried off to the kitchen. It wasn't until she was alone that the nerves really kicked in. Why was Dorothy really here? Why had there been no warning, not even from her dad? Were they supposed to pretend that their conversation about Libby Winston had never happened?

'You need to stay on top of the dusting,' Dorothy said, as Phoebe carried the tray of tea things into the room.

'Yes, Dorothy,' she said, as she laid the tray on the coffee table. Her hands were shaking so much by now that the cups were clinking around on their saucers, like tiny warning bells.

'You've used the Dorchester set,' Dorothy said, with an approving nod, evidently choosing to ignore Phoebe's nerves. 'It would have been nice to have some flowers from the garden, though. I always kept a cutting or two in a small vase. I think I read about it in a book my mother gave me on how to be the perfect wife.'

'I can still do that,' Phoebe said. Anything to delay actual conversation.

'Then do it,' Dorothy said.

Phoebe rushed out to the front yard and pulled up some nasturtiums because they were the first thing she saw that she could easily pluck with her hands. As she was about to go back inside, she saw Phil trying to escape from Mrs Pap's clutches. He was halfway out of the gate, but she was still talking to him. He turned and caught Phoebe's eye. They exchanged the smile of prisoners in different cells.

'Nasturtiums will have to do,' Dorothy said, with a small sigh, as Phoebe returned. As it was only a small sigh, Phoebe decided to take this as praise.

'Well, aren't you going to serve me?'

'I thought, well, last time . . .' Phoebe stuttered, remembering how severely she'd been rebuked the last time she'd tried to serve her grandmother tea.

'We're in your house now,' Dorothy explained. 'You should be the hostess. Honestly, whatever did they teach you at college?'

'There's not a lot of tea parties in the library,' Phoebe said, and then regretted it.

'Touché,' Dorothy said.

Phil arrived as Phoebe was carefully pouring the tea. He looked like a man who had just made a lucky escape.

'What took you so long?' Dorothy snipped.

'I would have thought the question would be, what took me so short? I had the usual delicate negotiations around the liquorice rocket fuel and kourabiedes and managed to evade both.'

As Phoebe poured Phil some tea, she made a mental note to get some pointers from him for future visits across the road.

'So,' said Dorothy, once Phil had settled himself in his chair with his cup of tea. 'Now that we're all here, I thought I should clear up the misunderstanding Phoebe and I had the other day.'

Dorothy paused to take a small sip from her cup, her little finger raised in a silent salute.

Here we go, Phoebe thought, her heart now filling her throat, making it impossible for her to drink her tea. Phil shot her a panicked look as if he'd realised he'd jumped from the fat into the flames.

'Twenty-five years ago, I fell utterly and completely in love.' Dorothy's voice was calm, but her mouth looked smaller and tighter than usual, and one corner of it was twitching ever so slightly. Was it possible that she was nervous too?

Dorothy turned to look at Phil. 'I'd always been very fond of your father, despite his ways. But this was different. This was with a woman.'

She busied herself with taking another sip of tea while Phil and Phoebe swallowed this news. The look of complete and utter shock on Phil's face left Phoebe wishing she'd told her father about the trip to Ballarat so he would've been better prepared for this moment.

'I fell in love and then I had to climb my way out. I was a married woman, a mother, and the treasurer for the gardening club. I wasn't an adulterer. I wasn't a *lesbian*.'

Phoebe sensed Phil sitting up straighter at the mention of the L word.

'It started as a friendship with a depth I hadn't really known since I was a girl. Elizabeth wasn't like the other boarders we had. She didn't stay in her room. She wanted to talk to me about her day. She wanted to know about *my* day. Nobody ever wanted to know about *my* day. As a mother and a wife, you're just there as a supporting actor in other people's lives.'

Phoebe couldn't imagine her grandmother ever settling for a supporting role. She'd always loomed large in Phoebe's life.

'Over time, we grew very close. I began to open up to her

in a way I'd never been able to before with anyone – she said I was her evening primrose flower, blooming late at night. And rather than scaring me, it excited me. I could see that I could become a better version of myself, one that I actually liked, with Elizabeth by my side.'

'What happened? Why did she leave?' Phil asked.

'After Elizabeth had lived with us for eighteen months, Edward and I went to Europe for six weeks. I wanted to stay with Elizabeth and tried to encourage Edward to go by himself. I even went so far as to suggest he take one of his "special friends" instead, but he was insistent. He wanted to make a grand gesture for our twentieth wedding anniversary.'

'I remember driving you both to the airport,' Phil interjected. 'Dad was excited – he kept calling it "the trip of a lifetime" – but you . . . you were . . .'

'I was what?' Dorothy said in the kind of tone that could take an eye out.

Phoebe guessed that if Dorothy herself had not been around, he'd say that she had been very 'Dorothy' about it. But he didn't say that. He just bowed his head.

'It's fair to say, I was *not* excited,' Dorothy continued, her voice returning to its previous calmness. 'But Edward was right: it *was* the trip of a lifetime – just not in the way he wanted it to be. That trip had the biggest effect on the rest of our lives. To be honest, the trip itself was exhausting. Edward had over-planned it and we were in a new city almost every day. I bought and wrote postcards to Elizabeth at every destination but didn't end up sending them because I was worried they wouldn't arrive until after we got home.' Dorothy paused and turned to Phoebe. 'The post was much slower back then.'

Phoebe nodded as if she was already very much aware of international postal transit times in the late '60s.

'So I kept them all hidden in the lining of my suitcase, hoping to give them to her when I got home.'

Dorothy took the last sip of her tea and placed the empty cup on the table. The three of them looked at the empty cup. Phoebe wondered if she should offer Dorothy more tea. But before she could, Dorothy continued.

'I remember the plane ride home. I remember thinking that I felt strong enough to make a change. To leave Edward and to find a way to have a life with Elizabeth. All around us, women were burning their bras and protesting on the streets, and there was this sense that the world was opening up, and that the impossible might actually be possible and two women could love each other and live together. But when we got back home, the garden was overrun with weeds and Elizabeth was gone. I'll never forget how dead the air felt when I walked back into this house.'

Phoebe imagined it would have felt like when she had walked through the front door and found no messages on the answering machine, but maybe multiplied by a million.

'I remember those weeds,' Phil said suddenly. 'It was like *The Day of the Triffids* out there. Did you know that John Wyndham was almost fifty when he published that book? It was his first work of science fiction. Before that, he mostly wrote detective novels.'

'So why did she leave?' Phoebe asked, not wanting her father's nerves to derail the conversation.

'I never knew.'

'You didn't ask?'

'She didn't leave a note, and yet her message was clear. Our relationship was over. And so I put that version of myself aside.'

'What do you mean?'

'Do you remember when you were in high school and into

all those attic flower books with the dreadful covers?' Phoebe nodded. 'Are you that person now?'

Phoebe shook her head, although truth be told, she did still like to read the *Flowers in the Attic* series when she was sick.

'There's my point. There are going to be many more Phoebe Cottons over the years ahead. Just as there have been many Dorothy Cottons, and many Dorothy Wallaces before that. And many Philip Cottons, too.'

Phoebe quickly glanced at her father. She couldn't imagine that there had been that many versions of him, but then, maybe she was wrong. She'd been wrong about a lot of things lately.

'But don't you think there is some constant thread between all the different versions of ourselves,' Phil ventured. 'Or perhaps even one version of ourselves that is a little more authentic or closer to our true self?'

'Perhaps,' Dorothy said. 'But I choose not to look back. There's no point in dwelling in the past or digging it up. Once a suitcase has been misplaced by the airline, for example, I no longer think of it as *my* suitcase, even when it's found twenty-five years later.'

'Did Dad know?'

'Possibly,' Dorothy said, and then, after thinking about it for a few more seconds, she added, 'Probably. But he wasn't someone to hold a grudge, even if I had broken the very rules I'd set for him.'

Dorothy began to ease herself out of her chair. It was obvious her knee was giving her trouble. Phil rushed over to assist her, but she waved him off. 'Don't fuss. It's an inflamed bursa, not a terminal disease.'

Phil stepped to the side, like a footman. 'Now,' Dorothy said, once she was standing. 'I'd like to see the backyard. Philip, can you please get my gloves from the car?'

While her father fulfilled his footmanly duties, Phoebe followed her grandmother into the kitchen. Dorothy paused in front of the fridge to look at Libby Winston's number, pinned there next to Sandy's and Monty's numbers.

She turned to Phoebe, her eyes like blue paint left out in the rain. 'I've had a good life. A full life. But I'm not going to be one of those old ladies who sits around, holding their memories like precious objects, wishing that they could change the past. There are far better ways to spend my time. I have the latest version of Dorothy Cotton to get on with. I have my friends, my pottery and my weekly aqua aerobics class. You should come to a class one Saturday,' she added. 'Bring your friend, the construction worker.'

Phoebe's face must have revealed that she had no idea who her grandmother was talking about because she then clarified, 'The one in the boots. Susan or Suzanne, I believe.'

'Ah yes, Suze. I'll ask her.'

Dorothy went to open the back door but then turned and touched Phoebe's arm.

'Thea,' she said, looking down at the back of her own hand.

'What?' Phoebe asked.

Dorothy raised her eyes to look squarely at Phoebe.

'Elizabeth called me Thea, short for Dorothea. And so you are aware, she was the love of *my* life. Also, please don't say "What?" in that manner. It makes you sound uncouth.'

And with that, she stepped out into the backyard and launched into an extended and rather harsh review of Phoebe's gardening.

And much later, long after Dorothy and Phil had left, Phoebe noticed that Libby Winston's number was no longer on the fridge.

And she didn't know what to think.

Chapter 41

THE NIGHT BEFORE Suze moved to Salmon Street, Charlie convinced her to go to one last Fitzroy party.

'Shall we?' Charlie dragged the Case of Wonders from underneath his bed. The Carlosses had gone to Sydney for the weekend and Charlie was in the mood to party.

Suze looked at the open case for a moment and then shook her head. 'Not for me,' she said. 'Tonight, I plan to go as myself.'

'Suit yourself,' Charlie shrugged.

As she watched Charlie pull out costume bits, like a magician pulling scarves out of a hat, she felt a wave of sadness.

'I can't believe I'm moving out tomorrow,' she said.

'She's leaving home, bye bye,' Charlie sang, as he started applying some fake silver eyelashes. He then stopped and turned around to look at her seriously. 'I will miss you, Susan.'

'And I will miss *you*, Charles.'

'Luckily we're, like, each other's best friend in the whole world and we'll, like, talk every day on the telephone and stuff,' Charlie said in his best Valley Girl accent.

'We'd better,' Suze said. 'But maybe not every day. You're actually quite dull company.'

'As if!' Charlie exclaimed, as he stepped away from the mirror. He'd opted for a silver jacket to match the eyelashes. According to him, he was being 'low key in a Vegas kind of way'.

In the lounge room, Matt and Sacha were sitting on the couch with a pile of documents. Sacha appeared to have been marking things off on a checklist attached to a clipboard, and Matt, in his 'Whassup?' T-shirt, had the air of a man who would prefer to be at the pub.

'Are you sure neither of you want to come?' Suze asked. Matt immediately perked up.

'No, we don't,' Sacha quickly said, before he had a chance to answer.

'Suit yourself,' Charlie said. 'But mark this: once you've shacked up, then you'll be married and pregnant and you won't get invited to parties anymore. You'll just have boring dinner parties with other married couples and their babies, and all you'll talk about is home renovations, investment properties and tax liabilities.' And with that, he sashayed out the door.

'Is that true, Sash?' Suze heard Matt ask as she left the house. He sounded worried.

'Only if you want it to be,' Sacha reassured him.

CHARLIE AND SUZE walked up Nicholson Street.

'Whose party is this again?' Suze asked, as they stopped

in front of a house heaving with music and people dressed in black.

'No idea,' Charlie said. 'The Carlosses heard about it from a guy who's going out with one of the girls who used to live here.'

'So we got a personal invitation then,' Suze joked.

'It's called a *Fitzroy* invitation,' Charlie corrected her. 'Now if you don't mind, I need to find the bar.'

Suze stood on the footpath for a little while longer. How many of these parties had she gone to? How many had she actually enjoyed? How many had she returned home from, drunk and in tears? There was something about moving to West Footscray that felt like growing up.

'Is this Macca's party?' A tall handsome guy asked her. He was maybe mid-twenties, wearing a collarless shirt, tweed trousers and Docs.

'I think so,' Suze responded. 'I don't really know who lives here. We're here on a Fitzroy invitation.'

'What's that? I've only just moved to Melbourne, so I don't speak the language yet.'

'It doesn't matter. I don't think it's a real thing. Where have you moved from?'

'From Newcastle. I literally got here yesterday.'

'And you're already going to your first party? You work fast.'

'Macca's my cousin and the only person I know in Melbourne. It's just a happy coincidence,' he shrugged. He extended his hand. 'I'm Freddy.'

'I'm Suze.'

They shook hands.

'Now you're the second.'

'The second what?'

'The second person I know in Melbourne.'

'Well, let's go find you some more friends, shall we?' Suze

offered her arm to Freddy, who took it gratefully. She felt like she was entering the party with a really expensive handbag on her arm that was the envy of all the girls.

The first person they met was the now legendary 'Macca', who was dancing in the lounge room under a disco ball tied to a light fitting. At the sight of him, Freddy's arm unlinked itself from Suze's, and he took her hand instead and pulled her forward. Suze was surprised by how nice his hand felt in hers.

'You made it!' Macca roared, pulling Freddy into a huge bear hug. Suze was sad that this meant Freddy dropped her hand.

'This is my new friend Suze,' Freddy shouted over the music, once he'd been released from Macca's hold.

'Welcome to the party!' Macca shouted back, saving Suze from having to explain the seventeen degrees of separation between her and the people who were *actually* invited to the party. 'Go get yourselves a drink and I'll find you later.'

They left Macca dancing beneath the disco ball and continued to push through the crowd until they ended up in the backyard, where J and Ky, painted silver head to toe, were at opposite ends of the patchy lawn, waving semaphore flags at each other. Suze waved cheerfully to them both.

'You know them?' Freddy asked, as he linked his arm back through hers.

'Yeah. I would introduce you, but I don't think they should be your third and fourth.'

'There you are,' Charlie said, appearing from nowhere like a magical genie. He was holding two cups. 'I thought you'd changed your mind and gone home. They've got a frozen margarita machine and vodka jelly shots! Whoever these people are, they know how to throw a party.'

As he thrust the cup into her free hand, he saw that her other arm was attached to Freddy, and he stopped dead still.

'Oh,' he said. 'You have a new friend.'

'And so do you,' Suze explained. 'This is Freddy. He's new in town and he only knows Macca, whose party this is. Freddy, this is Charlie, my housemate. Or rather, my soon-to-be former housemate.'

As Suze explained the dissolution of their share house, she noticed Charlie regarding Freddy with an odd expression on his face.

'What do you do for a living?' Charlie asked.

'I'm a musician. I've moved here to be in the Victorian Opera orchestra.'

'Really?' Suze asked. 'What do you play?'

'The cello.'

Suze almost swooned, like a nineteenth-century lady. 'I love the cello,' she blurted. 'I've always wanted to play it ever since I watched that TV show *Fame*.'

'And what do you think of the movie *A Room with a View*?' Charlie interjected.

Freddy seemed surprised by the question, but he answered it graciously. 'It made me want to go to Florence.'

Charlie gave Suze a significant look and she rolled her eyes at him. She took a sip of her drink. It was sickly sweet and very alcoholic. Then she realised she was being rude.

'Sorry, you don't have a drink yet,' she said to Freddy. 'Let's get you one.'

'I can get my own drink,' Freddy said. 'I'll be right back.'

As he made his way over to the makeshift bar in the corner of the yard, Charlie gave a low whistle.

'Dear god. He's just your type.'

Suze was busy examining a green thing in her cup, maybe a bit of mint, maybe something else. 'He seems nice.'

'Are you kidding me? I couldn't have designed a better guy

for you, even if I had the same set-up as those guys in *Weird Science*.'

Suze fished the green thing out of her cup and flicked it to the side. 'If you say so. I'm not really looking for someone right now.'

'What the hell are you talking about? You're always looking for someone. That's who you are. You're like me – you're a seeking person.'

'I am a seeking person, you're right. But I just feel like seeking things other than a relationship right now.'

As she said those words, she found that she really meant it.

Charlie looked at her with admiration. 'Whatever you've taken, I want some too.'

Suze laughed. Freddy was coming back, carefully carrying three drinks. She noticed some girls watching him and whispering, and the expensive handbag feeling came back briefly but then died away.

'I thought you'd find some more friends at the bar and we wouldn't see you again,' she said.

'Nah, two is enough for one night.' Freddy handed them their drinks. 'I thought I'd save you the trip.'

Charlie had already drained his first cup, so he took the new one happily. Suze was now left holding two drinks she didn't really want.

'I'm just going to find the bathroom,' she said, handing one cup to Charlie and one cup to Freddy.

The party had reached critical mass and she had to literally push her way through the crowd, cutting into conversations as she did. ('You're much better looking than that mole.' 'He did a shit on our kitchen floor.' 'So it turns out my boss is a Scientologist.') The queue for the only bathroom was intolerably long, but at least she got to listen to a couple behind her have an argument about who was the designated driver. If she had to put money on it, she guessed it would end up being the guy.

As she made her way back to Charlie and Freddy in the yard, she found J and Ky having a break from their important semaphore work. J's silver make-up was smudged with sweat, giving him the look of a waxwork robot starting to melt.

'Hey, Suze,' J said.

Ky just nodded solemnly at her.

'I heard you were moving out of Moor Street. Where you headed?'

'West Footscray.'

'Wow,' J shook his head. 'Ky and I are moving to Port Melbourne and we thought that was remote.'

'You're moving in together?'

'My new place didn't work out,' Ky said.

'And I'm a bit sick of my housemates and all their house rules.'

J said 'housemates' without a hint of irony, even though he knew that Suze knew they were in fact his parents.

'Well, good for you both,' Suze said. As she watched Ky pull out her make-up bag from somewhere beneath her silver robes and start fixing J's face, she wondered if Ky would end up doing J's laundry, or if J would end up doing Ky's. She concluded that they'd probably do no laundry at all and have a sacrificial burning of the dirty clothing every full moon.

'I'll leave you to it,' she said and made her way back to the yard.

'There you are,' Freddy said, handing over her drink. Charlie didn't hand anything back. He'd clearly drunk hers already. She hoped it was the one that'd had the green thing in it.

'Thanks,' she said. 'What's been going on here?'

'Freddy here was just saying that rugby union was the best of all the sportsballs,' Charlie offered, miming a yawn.

'Charlie!' Suze said, with a laugh.

'So you're not into sport?' Freddy asked him. 'Why did you let me go on about it?'

'Because you obviously felt very deeply about it. I hate to tread on anyone's hopes and dreams.'

At that moment, Macca interrupted the conversation, dragging Freddy off to meet someone.

'Okay, so he's not perfect for you,' Charlie confessed. 'Seriously, for an arty type, he is surprisingly passionate about sportsballs. You're going to spend every weekend either freezing your arse off on uncomfortable stadium seating or watching *Wide World of Sports* on television.'

'People like what they like,' Suze said.

Charlie gripped her arm with a sudden realisation. 'But in not being perfect for you, that will probably make you want him more. Here we go again . . .'

'We're not going anywhere, except maybe home. I think you've had a little too much to drink too quickly.'

Just then, 'Groove Is in the Heart' came on over the speakers by the dance floor.

'I LOVE THIS SONG!' Charlie shouted. 'One dance and then I'll definitely be ready to go home.'

OF COURSE, ONE song turned into ten songs. But when she and Charlie finally started the walk home, Suze wasn't too drunk and she wasn't in tears, making this the most successful party outcome of recent months.

At Charlie's insistence, they walked through Carlton Gardens, stopping at every single flowerbed to admire pretty much every single flower. ('Spring has sprung!' Charlie said, at least seventeen times.) Eventually, Suze persuaded him to sit on a bench and look up at the stars instead.

'Quick, make a wish,' Charlie said, pointing excitedly at something moving in the sky.

'That's a plane, not a shooting star,' Suze replied.

'You should make a wish anyway.'

'Okay,' she said. And she closed her eyes.

When she opened them, Charlie was looking at her intently. 'Did you make a wish?'

'Yes, I did. I wished something for the both of us.'

Charlie feigned outrage. 'Why, Susan, I have no intention of turning straight, if that's what you wished for.'

Suze laughed. 'No, I wished that we both find happiness in these next chapters of our lives.'

'That's nice,' Charlie said, turning his attention back to the sky. 'Of course, it won't come true now that you've told me.'

'It wasn't a falling star, so I don't think the normal rules apply.'

Charlie reached out and took her hand. 'You're so good to me.'

'I am,' she replied. 'Now you just need to be good to yourself.'

'If that's not the pot turning on the black kettle.'

'It's actually the kettle calling the . . . never mind,' she replied. She squeezed Charlie's hand and looked back up at the stars. She thought of Freddy's phone number in her back pocket and how she wasn't in a great rush to ring him any time soon and she knew in her heart that she was actually following her own advice.

She was finally being good to herself.

Chapter 42

Seven weeks later

PHOEBE AND SUZE gladly accepted Phil's offer to drive them to the aquatic centre near the Western Retreat Retirement Village. He had promised Dorothy he would get some more mulch from 'Buggings' now that the weather was warmer and the weeds were making a bid to overtake the otherwise thriving community garden, and Phoebe had promised her that she would finally bring her 'construction worker friend' to an aqua aerobics class.

'As long as we can also bring the policeman, the cowboy, the biker and the GI,' Suze had said, when Phoebe had extended her grandmother's invitation.

'What?'

'The Village People. Didn't you see that film?'

'No, I didn't, because . . .' Phoebe had paused for a second and then decided to tell the embarrassing truth. 'I knew it had a song about milkshakes and I was worried there would be a lot of slurping noises in it.'

Suze had laughed at that and then Phoebe had laughed too. 'We'll need to fix that at our next trip to the video store,' Suze had said.

Now, as they drove in the car towards the Western Retreat, Suze leaned forward from the back seat to ask Phil if he'd ever seen *Can't Stop the Music*.

'No. But did you know that the concept for the Village People was invented by two French men?'

'Well, now I've heard everything,' Phoebe and Suze said in unison.

'How's the thesis going?' Phil asked Suze.

'Good,' Suze replied. 'I've almost finished. In fact, I'm heading to the Baillieu after this.'

'On a Saturday?' Phoebe was surprised. Suze had been travelling to the library every day, like she was going to a job in the city, but going on a Saturday was taking it to another level.

'I'll be home for dinner.'

'Good,' Phoebe said. 'Charlie says he and Monty are going to make a roast. Also, a crumble now that there are mulberries on the tree.'

'Have they ever made a roast before?' her father asked. Phil, himself, was an expert roast maker. 'Or a crumble, for that matter?'

'No. But Charlie says the Salmon Street kitchen has inspired him. He even found a floral apron in his Case of Wonders.'

'Is there anything that case doesn't have?' Suze said in wonder. Phoebe shook her head. She'd never seen such a magnificent collection of dress-ups.

Charlie had moved into the box room at Salmon Street a

couple of weeks ago, declaring that he was literally 'going back into the closet'. Things hadn't worked out with The Carlosses. It had become very clear very quickly that The Carlosses had just wanted someone to do his laundry and the dishes and pay full rent – 'All without anywhere near enough hanky-panky,' according to Charlie, who pretended he wasn't heartbroken, but who was heartbroken nonetheless. Suze had been apologetic about him lobbing up on their doorstep, but Phoebe hadn't minded. She was no longer terrified of him, not now that she knew him better.

If she were perfectly honest with herself, Phoebe knew she wanted them to stay forever. Being open about her hatred of eating noises made life so much easier than it'd been at the Share House of Cereal in her uni days. Nobody ever tried to have an important conversation with her while shovelling chips from a packet into their mouth. Instead, everybody took care not to slurp their hot drinks in front of her, and the three of them had even adopted the 'Hallelujah Chorus' strategy when they had shared meals, after Suze had been introduced to it at Phoebe's parents' house. (That Tuesday night, as Suze had witnessed the lengths Phil and Ellen went to in order to accommodate Phoebe's sound sensitivities, her eyebrows had broken any record ever set by anyone in her family with the heights they'd reached, but she'd understood.)

That was the best thing. Feeling understood. And accepted.

Phil pulled up in front of the aquatic centre. Across the road, Phoebe could see Dorothy, dressed in a bright floral cotton dress (without even the slightest hint of beige), walking arm in arm with another woman, both of them laughing. Phoebe recognised the woman instantly.

'Far out,' Suze said under her breath. 'Is that . . .?'

'It is,' Phil said, nonchalantly. Phoebe looked at her father in surprise as he unbuckled his seatbelt and climbed out of the car. She and Suze followed suit.

'Hello Philip, hello girls,' Dorothy said, the laughter still in her voice. 'You all know Elizabeth.'

Libby Winston smiled at the three of them. She seemed younger than she had at their previous two meetings, like the years had loosened their grip on her. Meanwhile, Dorothy looked like a woman who had just freed herself from a tight and very uncomfortable bra and could finally breathe properly again.

While Phoebe and Suze continued to flounder about in their shock, Phil stepped forward to kiss Libby Winston on the cheek.

'Great to see you again,' he said. 'And thanks again for the other night. Ellen said they were the best meatballs she's ever eaten.'

'They were marvellous,' Dorothy concurred.

Phoebe felt gobsmacked. *Her parents* had eaten *meatballs* with *Libby Winston* and *Dorothy* and Dorothy thought the meatballs were *marvellous*? She wondered if the secret life of grown-ups would ever cease to be this surprising.

'You're most welcome,' Libby Winston said, beaming at the compliment. 'The secret is to bake them and not fry them.'

'Oh, so do you bake them in the sauce?'

As Libby went into great detail about her meatball-making methods, Phoebe glanced at her watch.

'Um, aren't we going to be late for the class?' she asked, suddenly anxious about her grandmother running late for something. Laughing with Libby, eating baked meatballs, and now running late. It was almost too much.

'Chill,' said Dorothy in the most un-Dorothy moment ever recorded in history.

'Chill?' Phoebe said, her eyes wide.

'Elizabeth's been teaching me some youth talk,' Dorothy explained, placing her hand affectionately on Libby's arm.

'Which I've picked up from my niece,' Libby offered, placing her own hand on top of Dorothy's.

'I'll pick you up in an hour,' Phil said to Phoebe and Suze, before giving quick hugs to both Dorothy and Libby. 'See you, Mum. And hope to see you again soon, Libby.'

'No need to hope,' Dorothy said. 'I've told Ellen we're coming to dinner on Tuesday. You should come too, Susan.'

Suze looked over at Phil.

'Yes, you should,' he called as he started to climb back into the car. 'And Monty and Charlie, too. The whole family.'

Phoebe had to smile at Phil's use of the word 'family'. It was as if that uncertain boy growing up in the shadows of Salmon Street had finally found his tribe.

Inside the aquatic centre, Dorothy and Libby headed straight to the pool, while Phoebe and Suze went to the change rooms. There, they quickly tried to get into their bathers underneath their clothes, like they were getting changed for PE class at school. Meanwhile, the women around them were in various states of undress, many completely and unashamedly naked, their lumps and bumps and curves and sags all on proud display.

'What about that Libby Winston?' Phoebe asked, as she pulled her bra out through her shirt sleeve.

'I told you your grandmother would call her,' Suze replied from inside her own shirt.

Phoebe shook her head, still grappling with this plot twist. She had been pretty certain Dorothy had taken the telephone number from the fridge with the intention of destroying it. But when she'd told Suze about the surprise visit and the missing number, Suze had felt differently. 'I think we're going to see another version of Dorothy Cotton very soon,' she'd said.

By the time they got in the pool, the aqua aerobics class had begun, and 1950s music was blasting from a small boombox. Dorothy and Libby were already in the water, singing along to 'Splish Splash' at the top of their voices as they pushed their arms through the water. The class was full of women in ruched bathing suits and swimming caps, some with a full face of make-up, others with their hair standing on end. Phoebe and Suze were the only people under fifty.

'Everyone, make sure you've grabbed a noodle,' the instructor said, waving at the large pile of pool noodles on the side. The women immediately formed a human chain, passing the noodles along so that soon every person in the class had one.

The instructor turned to the two young women. 'Is this your first time with a noodle? Some of these women have had loads of experience with noodles. I'm sure they can show you how to handle one.'

Phoebe and Suze exchanged looks and then Suze started giggling and Phoebe wondered if she had picked up a double entendre where there wasn't one, but then she realised all the women in the class were laughing too.

'Forgive me,' the instructor said. 'It's these women. They bring out the worst in me.'

'But we bring the best out in our noodles,' one woman called out and some of the women hooted.

The rest of the class continued in that vein ('Carry On Aqua Aerobics' Suze later called it) but Phoebe hadn't laughed that much in ages, nor had she ever seen her grandmother laugh like that either. In the water, Dorothy had lost any remainder of her stern stiffness, and she was more relaxed and happier than Phoebe had ever seen her, even more so than at the birthday party with the cabaret-style seating.

As she watched Dorothy playfully splashing Libby with

water, she found herself feeling sad that so much of Dorothy's life had been weighed down by the expectations to be the perfect daughter and wife and mother – the supporting actor – all at the cost of being the perfect version of herself.

'Now ladies, get your leg over the noodle,' the instructor shouted. The women all laughed, and Phoebe realised with a jolt how, up until then, she had never really thought of old people as having bodies. Sure, they had ailments – many, *many* ailments – but they also had bodies and sexuality and passions of their own.

Phoebe thought of Sandy and how good it would be to show her these women, so at ease in their own skin. Maybe the next time Sandy came down to Melbourne, she could get her to come along to a class.

A young boy sat on the edge of the pool, watching the women doing their class. He was eating gum with his mouth wide open.

But for once, the mixing desk in Phoebe's head didn't separate out that track, and, instead, the sound of the boy's chewing was absorbed by the roar of the aquatic centre. Family to the right of her, friendship to the left, she felt held by the water and the sound.

She felt happy.

Acknowledgements

T<small>HANK YOU TO ...</small>
  The Wurundjeri Woi Wurrung and Bunurong peoples
of the Kulin nation, the traditional owners of the land upon
which this book was set and written. It is a privilege to live,
work, write and dream on this land. *Always was. Always will be.*

My wonderful publisher, Meredith Curnow, and fabulous
editor, Shané Oosthuizen, and the rest of the team at Penguin
Random House Australia, including (but not restricted to)
Tessa Robinson, Tanaya Lowden and Bronwyn Sweeney: for all
your care, hard work and support to bring Phoebe Cotton and
her friends to readers. Thanks also to Alex Ross Creative for
another magnificent cover.

My agent, Jane Novak: for believing I could do it. Turns out
I could.

My fellow amateur surgeon, Dr Matthew Thompson: for inspiring the idea of the (un)art movement back in 1996. I was not the same person after that operation we performed in the abandoned cannery.

Jenny Green and Mike Paterson: for generously sharing your experiences as librarians. I'm so sorry I continue to arrange my books by colour.

Olympia Panagiotopoulos: for helping me breathe life into Mrs Pap and for sharing your mother's garden with me.

My colleagues and friends at the University of Melbourne: for being such great cheerleaders (especially Laura Juliff, my work wife and fellow misophonic).

My friends and family: for endlessly putting up with me and my quirks of personality.

My writerly friends: for acknowledging that writing is fucking hard and doing it anyway.

My trusted beta readers Silvia Ercole, Rachelle Walsh, Heather Brown, Katie Houghton and Julie Hudspeth: for reading my work before it was fully cooked. This would not be a book without your generosity and insights.

Katherine Collette, Paul Dalgarno and Kate Mildenhall: for reading and endorsing this book. As I'd once declared that blurbing other books was even harder than writing a synopsis, I was humbled by your enthusiasm.

Emilie Collyer: for our weekly accountability emails that keep me afloat.

Jacquie: because I told you I would put you in the acknowledgements.

The young adults in and out of my life: I love you with all my heart.

Derek: for patiently waiting until there is other sound playing in the room before you eat. You are my person.

About the Author

IMBI NEEME IS a recovering blogger, ardent novelist and spreadsheet enthusiast. Her manuscript *The Spill* was awarded the 2019 Penguin Literary Prize and published by Penguin Random House Australia in 2020. She blogged for many years at *Not Drowning, Mothering*, which won the 2010 Bloggies Award for best ANZ Weblog. She lives in Footscray, Melbourne, on the right side of the Maribyrnong.

IMBI
NEEME

the spill

The Spill

Winner of the 2019 Penguin Literary Prize

In 1982, a car overturns on a remote West Australian road.
Nobody is hurt, but the impact is felt for decades.

Nicole and Samantha Cooper both remember the summer
day when their mother, Tina, lost control of their car – but
not in quite the same way. It is only after Tina's death, almost
four decades later, that the sisters are forced to reckon with
the repercussions of the crash. Nicole, after years of aimless
drifting, has finally found love, and yet can't quite commit.
And Samantha is hiding something that might just tear apart
the life she's worked so hard to build for herself.

The Spill explores the cycles of love, loss and regret that can
follow a family through the years – moments of joy, things left
unsaid, and things misremembered. Above all, it is a deeply
moving portrait of two sisters falling apart and finding a way
to fit back together.

Praise for *The Spill*

'Skilfully constructed, deeply affecting and all the more enjoyable for its measure of sadness and regret, *The Spill* marks a dazzling debut for author, Imbi Neeme . . . Told with the sympathy and skill of a natural storyteller, *The Spill* seeps below the surface of fractured families to fathom deep seated resentments but the book has the heart to search for healing and the making of amends.'

— Richard Cotter, *Sydney Arts Guide*

'Imbi Neeme's prose thrums, and her characters are so deep and richly imagined that it's astounding to think *The Spill* is her first novel . . . I was hooked at first by the writing, but I soon found myself so invested in the characters that I didn't come up for air until I'd finished.'

— J. P. Pomare

'In *The Spill*, Imbi Neeme evokes through Samantha and Nicole how easily one's memories, histories, and perceptions are malleable – yet how we can't escape them. Each of Neeme's characters are authentic in their foibles, and the tribulations of this imperfect family will draw you in. This is a debut that aims to articulate the tangled mess that is family, and it succeeds. An engaging story from an author who is only just getting started.'

— Jack Callil, *The Age*

'Well formed, courageous and very enjoyable . . . Perfect for those who love the domestic dramas of Liane Moriarty or Alice Munro.'

— Chris Gordon, *Readings*

'Imbi Neeme has crafted a clear-eyed, compassionate novel with crackling dialogue and endearing characters struggling to put together the fragments of a misremembered past.'

– Roanna Gonsalves, *The Saturday Paper*

'Intriguing, subtle and brimful of subterranean sadness, *The Spill* sucked me in from the first page. A thoughtful, sensitive look at the lies we tell ourselves and the stories we tell each other, and the ways we help piece together the people closest to us.'

– Jane Rawson

'Brilliantly comic and tender, this is a sharp and intimate portrayal of that most mystifying of things: family. Neeme gives us a real world; of chaotic fragments drawn with charm and compassion. These are people, like us, making lives of their messes.'

– Robert Lukins

'This compelling, beautifully crafted story introduces us to a pair of sisters, and then peels back the layers of their history to reveal the complexities and contradictions at the heart of love. Reading *The Spill* feels like being welcomed into a new family and gradually making sense of their complicated dynamics. The sisters and their troubled mother are flawed, frustrating, and at times infuriating, yet relatable and deeply endearing. Imbi Neeme is a hugely talented writer with an eye for the nuances that inform relationships. The family and their history will linger on in your mind long after you've finished the book.'

– Kerri Sackville

'*The Spill* explores the dangers of silence, secrets, and loneliness. Each significant moment in the sisters' lives is traced back to a decision, and each decision traced back to a past, often seemingly insignificant, trauma. By deftly dissecting the sisters' recollections, Neeme examines the fickleness of memory and illustrates how the intense fear of past mistakes can actually lead you down the path to repeating them.'

– Chloe Cooper, *Kill Your Darlings*

'*The Spill* is the gorgeous debut novel from Imbi Neeme which tackles life's painful moments with poise and love. I absolutely adored this book to the very last page, where hope nestled itself into the pages despite heartbreak and regret.'

– Ashleigh Berry, *The Booktopian*

'Imbi Neeme's accomplished and coherent sister-gate, exposes the bond and the cause of friction between the siblings as these flawed, troubled and likeable women track their "missing pieces". The book's engaging cast sing convincingly on the page. The intriguing characters are engaging as they wrestle with the past, find acceptance and forge new beginnings.'

– Gillian Wills, *Arts Hub*

'*The Spill* is a feat of clever handiwork, like a series of magical sleights of hand. Sometimes there appears to be not much going on the surface. The dialogue, in everyday Australian vernacular, sometimes veers into the banal. But it's all deliberate and, subsequently, darkly funny. "I'll have the Atlantic Salmon," one of the characters says, at a restaurant, overcoming her issues with another character's money and ordering the most expensive thing on the menu. Dark humour aside, Neeme investigates issues that are not trivial at all. Her characters, traversing their contemporary lives, are barely hanging on. Satisfying and well-wrought.'

– Michalia Arathimos, Overland

'It is extremely snappily written. There is some obvious talent here as a writer. It takes you by the hands, sit back, you're gonna be told a story and it's going to entertain you. And there are going to be waymarks that you'll feel comfortable having reached. And I also think there's probably been a brilliant editor working on it, because as a debut novel, I mean, it's pretty flawless in what it wants to be and knowing what it wants to be.

– Cassie McCullagh, Radio National, The Book Show

'This is a story of tumultuous family relationships, especially that of the two sisters. The snapshots we see of their lives, always under the shadow of the crash, are poignant and illuminating. I absolutely devoured this book and enjoyed every page of it!'

– Anna, Constant Reader

'A warm, deftly observed multi-narrative about the inherent messiness of life and relationships.'

– Thuy On, The Big Issue

'A thoughtful, touching read.'

– New Idea

Discover a
new favourite